LOVE, MARRIAGE, DIVORCE, BABY

Here's how the fantasy goes: I look ravishing, stunning, really. As I put Jack's dinner on the table, he says something lovely about my cooking, the effort I made, and how much he loves me. I pour a glass of wine for him and tell him that I know we've had a tough road of it over the last few years, but that I want to get our marriage back on track. My eyes well with tears of joy and I tell him I have some exciting news. He asks why I'm not drinking any wine—then, in an instant, he knows

Here's how the reality went: I looked pretty good. Not bad. I was bloated but relieved that it was because I was pregnant and not just a cow, as I'd originally suspected. I didn't have quite as much time to primp as I'd planned because I kept repeating the home pregnancy test and calling the people at Planned Parenthood, asking them to please check my test results again to be sure they hadn't accidentally switched my results with someone younger and more fertile than me. Anyway, just as I was about to tell Jack the news, he blurted out that our marriage had run its course and he wanted a divorce. "I love you as a person, but I'm not in love with you and honestly, I don't think you're in love with me either."

At the moment, I want you dead.

"So what did you want to tell *me*?" he asked.

It was a home pregnancy commercial gone terribly, terribly wrong.

Books by Jennifer Coburn

THE WIFE OF REILLY

REINVENTING MONA

TALES FROM THE CRIB

THE QUEEN GENE

Published by Kensington Publishing Corporation

Tales
from the
Crib

JENNIFER COBURN

KENSINGTON BOOKS
KENSINGTON PUBLISHING CORP.
http://www.kensingtonbooks.com

KENSINGTON BOOKS are published by

Kensington Publishing Corp.
850 Third Avenue
New York, NY 10022

ISBN-13: 978-0-7582-0983-2
ISBN-10: 0-7582-0983-5

First Trade Paperback Printing: January 2006
First Mass Market Paperback Printing: February 2008
10 9 8 7 6 5 4 3 2 1

Printed in the United States of America

*For the late Rita Ellenson
and her ebullient sister, Bernice Coslow—
they are more important to me
than they could ever know.*

Acknowledgments

Thanks to my fabulous editor, John Scognamiglio, and hilarious agent, Christopher Schelling, for their huge part in turning this idea into an actual novel.

I am forever grateful to the women who read early drafts and gave me their feedback (and tireless support). Many thanks to Rachel Biermann, Evelyn Waldman, Joan Isaacson, Audrey Jacobs, Belen Poltorak, Deborah Shaul, Marg Stark, Deborah Rappaport-Rosen, Edit Zelkind, Nancy O'Nell and Kathy Krickett-Irizarry.

Vince Hall, Robert Mackey, Jim McElroy, Mike Poltorak, Kory Smith and Bob Slavik are the guys who make everything run smoothly behind the scenes at book parties without ever asking for anything in return. I immensely appreciate all you do.

Thanks to my mother, Carol Coburn, for a lifetime of laughing at my jokes and for all of her love. And to my father, Shelly Coburn, who I wish could be here to share in this wonderful experience.

Most of all, I acknowledge William for going above and beyond the call of duty in every part of our marriage. Nothing is possible without him.

Chapter 1

I wasn't entirely surprised when Jack said he wanted a divorce. Our marriage had been rocky for the last few years. On another day, it could've been me asking to end the relationship. But on this day, Jack's timing could not have been worse. I knew we had serious problems, but this was not the ideal moment to call it quits.

We'd been to marriage counseling, taken several unsuccessful weekend getaways, and even, embarrassed as I am to admit, enrolled in a Tantra Yoga class together. Each was more of a disaster than the other.

Our therapist actually dumped us after six months. I never knew they could do that, but one day we showed up at Dr. Lee's office and he wasn't there. There was no note, no apologetic phone call, no explanation whatsoever. I called three times to try to reschedule, but Dr. Lee never returned any of my calls. I knew he wasn't dead because a few months later I saw him at the movie theatre with two young boys I assumed were his sons. I know he saw me because he self-consciously snapped his head in the opposite direction and sped away. Jack didn't seem at all bothered by Dr. Lee's disappearing act. He said he was probably just busy, and he'd get to us when he had time. Why do men think this modus operandi is acceptable in every context? I needed a real patient-therapist breakup. Who was Dr. Lee so busy with anyway? Other couples with more interesting problems than ours? Couples he thought had a fighting chance at marital success? Loath as I am to confess this, I once drove by Dr. Lee's office and tried to peek in the window to see another couple he was counseling. My near miss of a parked car scared me away from future stalking of my unfaithful ex-therapist.

The weekend getaways were so full of promise, I still wonder how they went wrong. Actually, that's not true. I can plainly recall the points when our romantic weekends soured. Every trip has a few glitches, and depending on the state of the relationship, these snafus can either bring a couple together or drive them to each other's throats. I know a couple who was kidnapped on their honeymoon in Mexico. Ten years later, they still admiringly recount how cool the other was under pressure. "Karl is fluent in Spanish, so he was able to negotiate with the kidnappers," Audrey sighs. "Oh no," Karl always protests. "If it weren't for your suggestion that they take your grandmother's ring, we would have never gotten out of there alive." They've recalled this nightmare a dozen times and still tell it as though it's a great love story. I'm happy for them, really. It's just a depressingly stark contrast to Jack's and my lemon-oil incident during our last romantic weekend together. I'll get to that in a moment.

My friend Zoe recommended a Tantra Yoga class for Jack and me. She said that she and her boyfriend took the workshop and suddenly became amazingly in synch with each other. "Mind-blowing doesn't even begin to describe the sex I had with Paul this weekend," Zoe said as she rested her exhausted head blissfully in her hands. "Everyone I know who has taken this class says it has completely and totally transformed their relationship," Zoe promised. Since Jack and my fourteen-year marriage had disintegrated to a veritable piece of shit, a complete transformation sounded like just what we needed.

During our first day of the Tantra Yoga workshop, we were told to gaze into the eyes of our partner and try to see his soul. I actually saw a Knicks game. Instead of focusing on my husband, I started looking at the other couples and, I don't know, maybe I was jealous, but they looked silly to me. When I say I started laughing, I don't mean a dainty little giggle escaped. I burst into hysterical, uncontrollable laughter where tears rolled from my eyes. "What's so damn funny?" Jack asked.

"I'm sorry," I tried to stop laughing. "Let me catch my breath." But the more I tried to stop, the more I laughed. It took a full three minutes to stop laughing, and while the teacher seemed sympathetic if not amused, she suggested that Jack and I take a class together called Orgasmic Laughter. We declined that offer, but picked up a brochure for a lovely looking resort in the Berkshires. We rented a cabin with a cozy hot tub, fireplace, and king-size bed with a comforter so thick a couple could get lost in it. The full-wall-of-glass window overlooked an overgrown forest of lush trees and giant-leafed plants. It was like Jurassic Park without the dinosaurs. The landscape was carpeted with dark moss, rocks, and a stream. In the cabin, a small CD player offered Jack and me classical and jazz music, as well as one selection called *Nature's Soundtrack.* There was a luxurious calm and a rustic sensuality about the place, which was accentuated by the scent of freshly burnt firewood and clean, pure rain.

Jack's and my cabin at the inn was probably the most romantic place on earth. Until we arrived, that is. On our first night, I suggested we run a warm bath and set a few dozen candles around the rim of the tub. That always seemed to work in the movies. My girlfriends and I just about died during the bathtub scene in *The Bridges of Madison County,* when Clint Eastwood and Meryl Streep slid out of their real lives and into unforgettable, eternal love. I had twice as many candles as they did, and my secret weapon—lemon oil.

When I was in Longevity Natural Foods a week earlier, I stared at the hundreds of tiny black bottles of aromatherapy oils that lined the wall. A nice woman who worked there approached me and asked if I had any questions. I told her my husband and I were taking a trip together, and confided that our marriage had been rather stressful for some time. "Do you have anything that will help us, you know, slide out of our real lives and into unforgettable, eternal love?" I asked.

"Why don't you try this?" the woman suggested, handing me a small bottle of lemon oil. "Put two drops of this in your tub and you'll bliss out together."

I figured if two drops was good, twenty would be excellent. She had no idea how much more stressed we were than the average, overworked couple. It might have been thirty drops of lemon oil I put into the tub. I don't know. It was dark and I just turned the small bottle upside down and shook most of the contents into the water.

At first, Jack's and my bath together seemed idyllic. "This is nice," he said, reaching for my shoulders, pulling my back against his chest. I settled into Jack's body like an old, comfortable chair. Enveloped by warm water, Jack's embrace was heaven. His arms reached around to the front of my body and he began to sweep my hair behind my back. As Jack's firm, calloused hands moved across my stomach and toward my hips, I took a deep breath and tried to release my feelings of physical inadequacy. I had gained twenty pounds since Jack and I met in grad school. My stomach and thighs now looked as if they'd been spackled with dough. But chunky women could still be beautiful these days. All the magazines were saying so, as they trotted out articles about how my size twelve was the same as Marilyn Monroe's. Besides, I wanted to let go of my body angst because I knew Jack would sense it. Zoe says that, like animals can smell fear, men can smell confidence, and that there is nothing in the world sexier than a woman who feels gorgeous. Silently, I repeated the mantra I learned from a Goddess Body workshop I took with my mother and cousin Kimmy last month. *I am a goddess and my body is to be worshipped.* Easy for those two to say, but it took several repetitions before I stopped repeating *Yeah, right* after my positive affirmation. My attention snapped back to the present as Jack abruptly stopped touching my hips.

"Lucy, do you feel something tingling?"

"Honey, remember it takes me a little longer to get warmed up than—"

"I'm not talking about being turned on, Lucy," he snapped. "I meant does your skin feel funny?"

"Funny like—"

More frantic, he shouted, "It's getting worse. The stinging! Doesn't your skin feel like it's burning?!"

As soon as he mentioned it, a thousand tiny pinpricks attacked my body. Then they spread to create an all-out burning on every part of my body that was submerged in water.

"Oh shit!" I said, standing up naked in the tub. "It must be the lemon oil."

"The what?" Jack demanded, now also standing and scratching his arms frenetically.

"The lemon oil, the lemon oil," I repeated, as if that would explain everything. "I put lemon aromatherapy oil in the tub to help relax us."

"Well done," he snapped and moved on to scratching his legs.

"I don't think you should scratch it, Jack. You'll just irritate your skin."

"Irritate my skin?! Whatever the hell New Age snake oil you put in this tub is irritating my skin!" And with that, things got worse. Jack slipped and fell back into the tub and a tidal wave of unholy water splashed into his eyes and all over his face.

Like Audrey during her honeymoon kidnapping, I would be grace under pressure. Jack and I would one day tell the story of our lemon bath together and how Cool Hand Lucy saved the day. I grabbed his arm and took charge. "Jack, you're going to be fine. Let's get you out of this tub and rinse your eyes with fresh water." As I led my blinded husband out of the tub, his foot knocked over one of the candles and set the bathroom rug on fire. It was a small fire, but big enough to burn part of Jack's left foot. I didn't know if the lemon oil was flammable, so I filled a small bathroom glass and dumped fresh water on the burning rug. Twice. Then a third time before it was fully extinguished and the smell of firewood and rain was overpowered by burnt wool and lemon.

After a few minutes, Jack's vision returned, and I ran clear water through the shower for us to rinse our stinging bodies. "God, Lucy, that was awful," he said, sounding much softer. "For a few minutes there, I thought I could be blind for the rest of my life. And all I kept thinking was I might never see my family. I might never see my gallery. Blind, Lucy! Do you know how bad that would suck?"

Jack picked up the bottle of lemon aromatherapy oil

and read the back of the label. "May irritate skin," he said. Subtext: You might not have nearly blinded me if you'd simply read the label, you idiot. Sub-subtext: Can't you do anything right?

That night, I stupidly asked Jack if he wanted to light a fire and snuggle under the cloud of a comforter. "Lucy, my dick has no top layer of skin. I'm not exactly in the mood right now," he said rolling over.

Believe it or not, the next night we had amazingly passionate sex. It wasn't making love. It was sex compliments of an excellent bottle of red wine our waiter insisted we try. Our night was release-stress, really, but I wasn't about to complain. I was so grateful for the contact that I just played the hand I was given and hoped it would grow into something better eventually.

I think that's the night I got pregnant. In fact, I'm sure it is because it was the only time we'd been together in months.

Nearly five months later, I prepared Jack's favorite meal—prime rib and garlic mashed potatoes with Caesar salad—and planned to tell him about the baby over a glass of red wine. Here's how the fantasy goes: I look ravishing, stunning, really. As I put Jack's dinner on the table, he says something lovely about my cooking, the effort I made, and how much he loves me. I pour a glass of wine for him and tell him that I know we've had a tough road of it over the last few years, but that I want to get our marriage back on track. My eyes well with tears of joy and I tell him I have some exciting news. He asks why I'm not drinking any wine—then, in an instant, he knows. He jumps from his chair, this time knocking nothing over and starting no fires, lifts me in his embrace, and tells me he's overjoyed.

Here's how the reality went: I looked pretty good. Not bad. I was bloated but relieved that it was because I was pregnant and not just a cow, as I'd originally suspected. I didn't have quite as much time to primp as I'd planned because I kept repeating the home pregnancy test and calling the people at Planned Parenthood, asking them to please check my test results again to be sure they hadn't accidentally switched my results with someone younger and more fertile than me. The clinician assured me that since I'd peed directly onto the stick that we both watched turn pink, a lab mix-up was impossible. Anyway, just as I was about to tell Jack the news, he blurted out that our marriage had run its course and he wanted a divorce. "I love you as a person, but I'm not in love with you, and honestly I don't think you're in love with me either."

At the moment, I want you dead.

"So what did you want to tell *me?*" he asked. It was a home pregnancy test commercial gone terribly, terribly wrong.

Chapter 2

"**H**ow could you not know you were pregnant for four months?" Jack demanded.

"I thought I was starting menopause."

"At thirty-nine?!"

"It happens!" I defended.

"What about the weight of an entire first trimester of pregnancy?!" he asked, as though he was talking to an utter moron.

I started to feel more righteously indignant than apologetic, which is a great feeling to take into an argument. "Look, Jack, I just said I thought I was starting menopause. Women gain a little weight. Our periods stop. It's not like I'm a twenty-two-year-old fertility goddess, now is it?"

He sighed in surrender because he knew I got him with that one. "You know the doctor said I'd probably never be able to conceive again. You know we never use birth control anymore. I'm just as surprised by this as you are. You're not the victim here. No one tricked you into anything. You can still have your stinking divorce. You know I'd never do anything to stand in the way of you and your child. I know how you feel about being a dad. Don't act like I've wronged you by getting pregnant, Jack. This didn't happen to me alone."

Jack sank into his chair, pursed his lips, and nodded his head. I knew this gesture too well. It meant I was probably right, but he needed a few minutes of quiet to digest it all. I've made the mistake before of interrupting Jack's precious silence by interjecting a thought or two, and was always quickly met with a crossing-guard hand signal to stop. He'd then remind me he needed time to think. This time, I just cleared his plate and waited for him to respond.

"Okay, I assume that given everything, you're going to keep the baby?" Jack asked. I nodded.

Given everything. Everything. What an amazingly nonspecific blanket statement for what we'd been through over the past few years. When I was thirty-three, I got pregnant for the first time and miscarried in the first trimester. I soon learned why people don't tell their friends and family until after the three-month mark. It's incredibly taxing to have to keep answering the same questions to beaming faces who want to know what names we're considering, when the baby is due, and whether I'm planning to take time off. The next miscarriage happened a year later after fourteen more failed attempts to get pregnant. This one was a bit earlier in the first trimester, so no one knew except Jack and me. That was enough, though. I could already tell he thought the miscarriages were my fault. He would never say such a thing, but blame emanated from him like stink from a garbage dump. It wasn't as though I drank or smoked, or went bungee jumping while pregnant, but coldly, silently, Jack wondered why I couldn't do a simple thing like keep a baby growing inside me. All of his friends' wives did so without much problem. The third miscarriage was also in the first trimester, and this time Jack was so detached, I told just about everyone about it in a desperate need to connect and mourn the way I should have been able to with my husband.

I was one of those people who always thought miscarrying in the first trimester was no big deal because there wasn't enough time to get attached. What I hadn't realized was that I'd been attached to the idea of having a baby since I was a child myself. I was in love with the possibility long before I saw the thin pink line. I realized that in the first trimester, pregnancies were more about hopes than babies, but I still missed the baby that would never be born. I missed the hope that died.

The fourth miscarriage was technically an abortion, but I have a hard time thinking of it as one. I have no problem with a woman who decides she's not ready to become a mother and terminates an unintended pregnancy. It's just that this was not the case for me. A little over three years ago, I was seven months pregnant with Jackson Jr. We were going to call him JJ. His room was dusty blue with Dr. Seuss characters that Jack painted on the walls of our new home in Caldwell. In the corner of JJ's room was a white glider where I would nurse him, and boxes of stuffed animals, outfits, and toys we'd received at the baby shower a week before the miscarriage. It wasn't a miscarriage like the others because it wasn't spontaneous. This one was a thousand times worse than the others because I was so far along, and because I had to schedule it. I wasn't hit with the piercing pain that prompted Jack to sweep me off to the hospital. The last time, I was in my doctor's office for a regular prenatal checkup. All thoughts of losing the baby had long since passed, so my heart didn't even speed the slightest bit when the nurse applied gel to my robust tummy and began scanning it with the sonogram. When she knit her brows and said, "Hmmm" quizzically, I didn't give it a second thought. She shot a series of questions at me so intensely, I began to lose that mother-to-be calmness I had been settling into so well over the last month. Then, the nurse called the doctor, who made a disturbing series of sounds and began ordering tests with names so long I couldn't even pronounce them. At the end of the day, the only phrase that stuck with me was "severe fetal anomalies incompatible with life." Apparently JJ's heart was forming outside of his body and his lungs were so malformed they could never function outside the womb. The doctor rattled off numerous body parts I'd never heard of, all of which were also not developing properly. The doctor recommended I have a dilation-and-extraction abortion immediately. He recommended a physician in New York who was one of a handful of doctors who could perform the procedure, and within a couple of days I was scheduled for the late-term abortion.

There was no surgery that could be performed in utero. JJ would most likely die in my womb within the next two weeks, they said. There was no chance of a healthy delivery and no surgery that could ever bring JJ back to the healthy baby I assumed he was.

"What if I take my chances and see what happens?" I asked the doctor.

"It would be extremely dangerous, perhaps even fatal for you, Mrs. Klein," he said.

Three years later, in our kitchen, I told Jack that I desperately wanted to have this baby. He nodded furtively and agreed that it was probably my last chance to have a child. *If the pregnancy even makes it to term*, neither of us said aloud, but could not help thinking.

"That makes sense," Jack nodded. "I respect that decision." Funny, the qualities I once found so attractive about Jack were the very ones that now infuriated me.

When we first met, his pragmatism was so incredibly sexy. Because I was raised by a family ruled by passion and contradiction, Jack's measured demeanor was like a rare delicacy for me. I found it intriguing that a man who was in a Master of Fine Arts program for visual arts could be the polar opposite of what I expected an artist to be. He reminded me more of my mother's boyfriend, a businessman, which is what Jack wound up to be, so I guess I wasn't too far off.

After the second miscarriage, I asked Jack if he blamed me for losing the babies. "Don't be ridiculous," he said, half listening as he ate a sandwich. I know what he meant. I did nothing to cause the miscarriages. Of course, they weren't my fault. Intellectually we could both understand that. But deep down, on a purely emotional level, wasn't there part of him that was angry with me? "No way," he dismissed. I thought perhaps he was just trying to spare my feelings by shielding me from the truth. I definitely got the sense that Jack harbored some resentment toward me, but he felt guilty about feeling this way because it was so illogical and patently unfair. So, I thought I would open the door and reveal a deeply vulnerable truth to him.

"I do," I barely was able to utter.

"You do what?" Jack asked, genuinely concerned by the tone of my voice.

"I am so angry, and so incredibly disappointed, and sometimes I do wonder what's wrong with me that I can't make it past the first trimester of pregnancy. So, I guess what I'm trying to say is that if you have anything you need to talk to me about, I'm listening. I mean, about your feelings about the miscarriages, you can tell me because they're probably some of the same thoughts that have crossed my mind too. Maybe it'll help us get through this together. So, Jack, let me just put it out there: sometimes I wonder what's wrong with me. I wonder if I'm being punished. I wonder if this is God's way of telling me that I'd be a really shitty mother."

"That's silly, Lucy," Jack said kindly. "Don't feel that way."

Don't feel that way. That was Jack's advice. I shouldn't feel that way. But I already did. And the only thing worse than feeling this way was telling him about it, reaching out for some sort of emotional connection, and discovering that I was alone.

Chapter 3

Jack and I were both enrolled in the same MFA program at the University of Michigan when we met. He was a painter, but also did disturbingly insightful charcoal sketches of the grittiest side of street life. I remember one sketch he did of police officers taunting a hooker that just brilliantly captured a moment of cruelty and humiliation. Jack was never a happy-go-lucky kind of guy, least of all in his art. He did a sculpture of Jesus on the cross made entirely of two-inch nails bent and twisted every which way. That won a prize at the Ann Arbor Art Festival the town put on every summer. His art always had a similar theme—death, pain, and isolation. Not exactly the most commercial stuff. I mean, who wants to decorate the family room with Jack's painting of a nude street urchin held captive in a church basement?

I was in for creative writing, and had planned to write women's fiction, short stories, and eventually a novel. Jack's and my first date lasted two days. I don't think we stopped talking for a single waking moment. The deal clincher for both of us was when we both shared the same fantasy—to start an artist colony where musicians, painters, sculptors, and writers would stay with us anywhere from six months to two years. We would provide food and housing, and artists would be free to focus on their art. People from all over the world would stay with us, creating a rich cultural Mecca. I pictured myself wandering the property in a white gauze dress, popping into studios and watching painters capture on canvas every wonderfully insane image they'd ever conjured up. I'd hear music as it was being composed, watch glass being blown, and run my hands through raw, wet clay that would soon become sculpture. Of course, I imagined my children being beneficiaries of this explosively creative environment as they learned about social studies by living it instead of reading about foreign lands in textbooks. Jack and I planned to homeschool our three children. He would paint. I would write. Other than the occasional anxiety over our eldest daughter being seduced by the visiting French poet, it seemed like our own personal Valhalla.

We used to spend hours drinking sangria on the upper balcony of Dominic's, a woodsy-looking pizza place popular among University of Michigan students. When we agreed with each other, we completely agreed. I'd squeal, "I have always thought that!" It was like Jack had flown to Manhattan one weekend and read ten years' worth of my journal entries. When we disagreed, it was always with great passion. We seemed to be the only two people on the planet who hated the *Breakfast Club* and *Breakfast at Tiffany's* even more. And yet our favorite meal was breakfast. At every meal, we always agreed on the best two entrees on the menu, so we could always share. Food was as important to Jack as it was to me, so we never wasted a meal on drive-through or bad take-out. Meals were our foreplay. Neither of us needed poetry or slow caressing. The better the food, the more likely we were to sweep our dishes off to the side of the table and make love right there next to a casserole.

That was life in our early twenties. In our late thirties, Jack was no longer painting, but owned a gallery and represented a handful of enormously talented artists. I had spent the last ten years writing incredibly important literary works. Perhaps you've heard of my best-known work: Peanut Butter Cheerios; you've never tried nut, nut, nuthin' like 'em! Or maybe you've seen my television work where two gaggles of blond 'tweens face off at a skateboard park because they each want the last of the Sunny Delight. The script that nearly sank me into a job-related depression was one where an overly amped-up man with a mop of red hair completely lost his mind over how sticky Doubly-Sticky brand adhesive tape is. He was thrilled because it solved his huge problem of tape insufficiently adhering to surfaces. (Doesn't that just happen to you all the time?) Thank the good Lord for Doubly-Sticky! No wonder Red was willing to risk head injury running around crashing into walls with excitement. A combination of severe budget cuts and an obvious repulsion for my job put me at the top of the list for layoffs at the advertising agency where I worked. For the last year, I've been writing freelance for second-rate magazines and drafting newsletters and annual reports for small businesses.

As I mentioned, we live in Caldwell, New Jersey. Suburbs, that is. Not an arts community where our precocious children wander freely and critique the painters for being overly influenced by Goya and inhibiting the development of their own style. Jack hasn't painted in years. My novel has yet to be outlined.

We bought this house in the second trimester of my last pregnancy, the one we were sure would last. The suburbs are the last place on earth I ever imagined myself, but Jack insisted that we move from the city to raise our kids. His adamancy was a tad insulting. It was as if he thought being raised in Manhattan was the worst thing you could do to a child. I spent my early years on West Eleventh Street in a brownstone building in Greenwich Village that my mother bought when she divorced my father. The building had four apartments, one in which we lived. She rented the other three.

My mother took the nicest apartment, which was a triplex six-bedroom with a common area that rose through all three stories. My bedroom was on the top floor and I used to love peering from the wooden rail and looking down forty feet into our living room. In the center of the living room was an enormous brick fireplace surrounded by a leather sectional and chairs so comfy they could absorb you. Some walls were brick, while the others were a light wood that continued up the rails and on to the upper floors. On the brick wall, my mother hung a dark-blue neon light outline of the Manhattan skyline. The rest of the space was covered with posters of shows she produced.

My mother owns the Drama Queen bookstore in the theatre district and has the Midas touch when it comes to producing off-Broadway gay theatre. Her most recent success was with the all-male musical *Oklahomo!* The entire cast was clad in tight leather overalls or fringed chaps.

Jack and I rented an apartment in my mother's building for the first eleven years of our marriage, but then he insisted that we make a "real" home for JJ. My mother hardly comes to see us because she claims she's allergic to the suburbs. She also is lactose intolerant, and sneezes uncontrollably in the presence of flowers that aren't for her. We visit her every month or so, enjoy a slice of Ray's Pizza from the corner, then drive back to the house in the suburbs we bought for our ghost baby.

The night I announced this pregnancy, Jack offered what he called a radical idea. I called it insanity. "It's not like we hate each other, Lucy. Look, the marriage has ended, but we get along well enough to be around each other."

For the most part, I didn't say.

"Let's stay married, live together as friends, you know, do our own thing, and raise the baby together."

"Do what?"

"Look, I said it was a radical idea," he shot back. "Didn't you see the article in the *Times* a few months ago about how couples couldn't afford to divorce anymore because running two households was cost-prohibitive? Plus they had children they didn't want to upset, so they hung out together till the kids went to college. Co parenting, they called it. Everyone seemed pretty happy with the deal."

"Jack, have you lost your mind?!"

"Lucy, I don't want to be a Sunday father." I knew his father left Jack's family when he was eight, visited every other Sunday for three years, then remarried and disappeared into his new life. Jack hears from his father once every few years when something major happens, like a wedding or a funeral. I knew Jack's greatest fear in becoming a father was becoming his father, too busy with other things to care about his children's lives.

"Jack, you can visit the baby any time you want. We can share custody."

"I don't want to share custody. I want to be there every day. Seriously, Lucy, be practical. Where are you going to live? Anjoli has three-year leases on all those apartments. What about health insurance?"

This pissed me off! Where was I supposed to live when I wasn't carrying his child? Didn't he care about my dependence on his health insurance when it was just me?

"Come on, Lucy! It's the perfect solution and you know it. We each have a built-in babysitter for when we go out. We've got a friend in the house to help. You'll do the child care. I'll pay three-quarters of the bills. Hey, you can finally write your novel with all your spare time."

"Jack, you can't bribe me like this!"

"How can I bribe you, then?"

"You said you wanted a divorce. Now you suddenly want to be my husband again?!"

"No," he answered too quickly. "I don't want to be your husband. I want to be a full-time father to our baby, and want to make you an offer that will suit your needs as well as mine. I think it's a fair deal."

Why couldn't he see that being asked for a divorce is an unsteadying event? I needed time to absorb the rejection I felt. All he wanted to do was close the deal.

"I don't want a divorce," he said.

"You did ten minutes ago."

"Things are different now."

"Because of the baby?"

"Well, yes, because of the baby. If everything . . . " he trailed off.

"Go ahead, you can say it."

"Say what?"

"Jack, you were about to say that if everything goes well this time."

"No, I wasn't. Come on, Luce, let's stay married as friends," Jack said.

"Could I date other people?" I asked.

"Absolutely!" he answered, again too quickly.

"I'm not sure."

"Lucy, let me run this article off the Internet for you. We aren't entering uncharted territory. Other couples are living separately ever after, and it's working well for them. Ask any single parent whether they'd like an extra set of hands around the house and they'd take it."

They'd take it if it wasn't the set of hands belonging to the rat bastard who asked for a divorce the same day the pregnancy test read positive.

"I'm not sure," I said.

"What do you need to make you sure?"

"Time to think about it."

"How much time?" Jack pushed.

"I will need exactly as much time as I need, Jack. That's my answer. If you don't like it, I can help you pack a bag, call a realtor tomorrow to sell the house, move back into Anjoli's apartment, and apply for public prenatal care. Back off and I'll have an answer for you in a reasonable amount of time, okay?"

"Okay," he said, upbeat. "Great meal, by the way. Absolutely superb!"

Shut the fuck up.

After a month of lobbying, Jack convinced me to try this new arrangement for one year. I would have a friend and co-parent in the house, medical coverage, and complete freedom. Plus, we'd get to keep our house and not sell it in a down real estate market. Jack put together a graph that showed our separation of duties and responsibilities, and even drafted a mission statement for our family. It wasn't exactly how I'd envisioned bringing a baby into the world with this co-parenting arrangement, but it seemed more practical than going it alone. And Jack was a good guy. I understood his motives were pure. He wanted to be a part of our baby's daily life. How could I begrudge him that? It was just for a year.

Chapter 4

In my seventh month of pregnancy, my friend Zoe insisted she throw a baby shower, and I reluctantly agreed. Given my history, everyone had an opinion as to whether or not this was a wise move. My two aunts, my father's sisters, reminded me that in the Jewish faith we weren't supposed to accept gifts until after the baby was born. My mother was born Catholic and is currently a convenient practitioner of New Age philosophy. That means whenever her minister advises her to do something she doesn't want to, Anjoli notes that it is merely a suggestion. When it is something she agrees with, she insists everyone follow the advice religiously. She said that having a baby shower was a positive affirmation to my baby that I believed he would be born. "Act as if," Anjoli said, "and so it shall be." Kimmy said whatever I decided she would completely support me.

Kimberly Fawn is my cousin who's one year younger than me, six inches taller, twenty pounds lighter, and three shades blonder. There is no measure that can really capture the difference in our overall appearance. I'm not altogether horrible-looking. In fact, when I put on makeup and do a little something with my hair, I can look quite attractive. But mere mortals like me can't compete with Kimmy, a former model who currently sells corporate jets. When Kimmy and I were thirteen and fourteen, we sneaked into Studio 54 with fake identification that we probably didn't even need since they gave out free passes to the club in front of our prep school. It was fabulous getting out of the taxi and watching the velvet rope drop, along with the jaws of every guy in the snaking line for admission. We were in the ladies' room when Kimmy was discovered. "Do you have an agent?" an anorexic flapper asked Kimmy, then handed her a business card.

"Do you need a towel?" an overweight bathroom attendant asked me, then handed me a square of Bounty.

About the baby shower, Kimmy said she would "support" my decision, which is pretty much her standard answer when she's asked to weigh in on an issue. She's a recovering alcoholic and cocaine addict who's been clean for twenty years but still attends meetings every night. She and Anjoli get along famously because there are so many similarities between the language of recovery and New Age. Kind of like Spanish and Portuguese. They take healing workshops together; they chant for inner peace together; they even get French manicures at the same salon.

Between my mother, a platinum blond, pale version of Sophia Loren, and Kimmy, I've always felt a bit like a garnish.

Zoe wanted to have a baby shower for me I think partially to redeem herself for the last one. Again, it's one of those things that doesn't make any sense, but was clearly the case. "Let me throw you a proper shower this time," she said. Her last shower was quite proper. It's the pregnancy that wasn't.

Her parties at college were far beyond the standard kegger. We had a Super Bowl party where Zoe went all out to create the ultimate football party. She put white tape all over our kelly-green carpet to mark the yard lines. We served Denver fans Bronco Brew, a mixture of Everclear and orange Kool-Aid. Redskins fans drank Bronco Blood, which was the same drink in red. She wanted to give our guests a party favor, so she designed a pigskin purse that was the size and shape of an actual football. As luck would have it, our pal, Dan Alcott's girlfriend, went mad for the purse and showed it to her father who happened to sit on the board of directors at a trendy clothing manufacturer. So, if you ever wonder who designed those adorable leather purses in football, bowling ball, soccer ball, and basketball shapes, it's my friend Zoe.

Zoe wanted to throw a baby shower because she loves me. I have no doubt about it. My mother wanted me to affirm that the baby would make it because she believed that would bring me good fortune. I am certain of her pure intentions. My aunts, Bernice and Rita, cared about me and didn't want me to piss off God by being presumptuous. And Kimmy supported whatever decision I made because she is a kind, decent, and genuinely supportive person. But everyone had her own baggage around my baby shower.

Everyone, that is, except Jack, who had moved into my old home office. He said he didn't have an opinion about whether or not I had a baby shower. Whatever I decided, he said, was cool with him. The difference between Jack's response and Kimmy's was that my sort-of-husband was emotionally checked out. It's not that he'd support whatever decision I made. He just didn't care.

The shower was at my mother's apartment in Greenwich Village because, as she put it, "No one's going to New Jersey." She had a point. I didn't know any of the women in my neighborhood because they were all mothers, so we never connected through playgroups, preschool, or at the playground. Even without friends who had children, I always knew exactly how old JJ would have been. Going to birthday parties for other kids would've been too much. Plus, it wouldn't be fair to the birthday child to have some psycho grab the piñata stick and beat the rainbow-colored donkey because she was enraged at the injustice of her infertility. Who needs the childhood memory of me swinging a bat, screaming through tears about how any crack whore living in an alley can give birth, but I couldn't?

Zoe tried to find a no-carbohydrate dessert, and quickly found that there's no such thing. Oh sure, some diabetes boutiques try to pass off their asparagus torte as a delectable treat, but no one in their right mind would consider it a dessert. I kept telling Zoe that she should cater the party for the guests and not concern herself with the fact that I couldn't eat anything sweet or with more than a teaspoon of flour.

Gestational diabetes. I got that diagnosis about a week after the sciatica became so severe I needed a cane to walk. I remember the call came through on my cell phone just as the Wendy's near my house was mounting a thirty-foot inflated chocolate frosty cone on its roof. No cookies or cake. No rice or pasta. No bread. A bite of fruit and maybe three beans were acceptable. The nurse assured me there was food I was able to eat—cheese, meat, and all the leafy vegetables I could pile on my plate. Oh joy. It was basically the Atkins Diet with the added bonus of needling my finger and analyzing blood three times a day. And let's not forget that fabulous way of waking up every morning by peeing on a matchstick-sized strip of alkaline paper. I'm not a morning person and the strip was quite small. 'Nuff said.

At the baby shower three women from the agency where I used to work filled me in on all the post-layoff gossip. Kimmy wore a winter-white leather jumpsuit that looked as if it were tailor-made for her, which it very well may have been. Sometimes I look at her and try silently brokering body swapping deals. Some may call this prayer. First, I ask if I can look like her, then counter my own proposal by offering to settle for a week with her body. Then I compromise again, and say I could be happy with her legs and face, and pretty soon I'm chopping my lovely cousin into parts and taking the leanest, loveliest cuts for myself. Her arms are quite well defined too, but I'm not greedy. I just want the legs and face. Maybe the ass and tummy too, if I may.

My aunts Rita and Bernice drove in from Long Island for the shower. They are a portrait in opposites. Bernice sees the good in every situation. When her husband died, she said that while she'd miss him very much, she was happy to get a break from his heart-healthy diet. Rita, on the other hand, is in the habit of pretending to spit after any of her negative comments. In other words, every time she speaks, there's cause to pretend she's spitting on the ground beside her. Once I was trying to shave off a few pounds and declined her offer for ice cream. "Why no ice cream, big shot?" Rita snapped. "You think you're too good for ice cream?" I have no idea where this came from, or if, for that matter, there were people who felt too good to eat ice cream. Was there a moral position on ice cream?

Zoe told the group about a new reality television show she was producing called *Real Confessions*. Basically the show would consist of pixelated faces confessing their sins to a hidden camera. At the end of the confession, an Alan Funt-like character would ask through the screen if the congregant had ever heard of *Real Confessions*. In theory, the person would have a knee-slapping great sense of humor about this and exclaim, "Well Jesus, Mary, and Joseph, am I on TV?!"

"Zoe, I was raised Catholic," my mother chimed in. "No one wants their confessions aired on national television. Why would anyone agree to this?"

"Complete absolution," Zoe said. "No contrition. No Hail Mary. No rosaries, no nothing. Let us air your confession and you get off with no penance."

"A 'get out of hell free' card?" I asked.

"Exactly!"

"How do you get the Church to go along with it?" Kimmy asked.

Zoe explained. "Plenty of churches have turned us down, believe me," she rolled her eyes as if to suggest they were being ridiculous. "The show offers a $15,000 donation to the parish for every confession we're able to air."

"So if the person gets mad that her sins have been recorded by a hidden camera, the priest has an economic interest in smoothing things over?" I asked.

"Cash money, baby. Father O'Neil on Staten Island is one smooth operator, let me tell you," Zoe laughed. She put on her best Irish accent. "No one made you do the sinning, my boy. You and the devil did that on your own. Now make good with the Church and let these fine people air your confession. No one but God, you, me, and the fine people at FOX Television will ever know it's you. Think about it, Tommy boy. We're looking at lots of rosaries for adultery. Aren't there other things you'd rather be doing?"

My guests laughed at Zoe's story. "There's a church in Schenectady that plans to replace their stained glass with their proceeds from the show."

Kara from the agency asked if congregants might shy away from confession if they fear they'll be recorded.

"Maybe people will behave better so they won't have to confess and risk being caught on hidden camera," Zoe said.

"I'm not religious, but it seems more than a bit tacky to turn a spiritual ritual into entertainment for others," Anjoli said.

"This is why Jews don't have confession," Aunt Bernice chimed in. "Who needs the whole world knowing your dirty laundry? Better to just feel guilty for a bit, promise to nevah do your bad deeds again, and go about your business."

"That's *not* why we don't have confession," Rita snapped. "You think Talmudic scholahs were thinking about reality TV when they voted against confessionals?"

"I don't think they voted, Rita." Bernice pursed her lips with victory.

"I've got to tell you, I don't think people are going to watch a bunch of faces they can't see," I added.

"Sure they will," Zoe agreed. I didn't love everything Zoe did professionally, but I adored her, and therefore accepted some of her harebrained schemes. I proudly mention her cute sports ball bags, but typically don't let people know about her failed endeavors, like the handbag designed to look like human testicles—hair and everything. Truly gross.

The discussion of confessions was a segue for Anjoli to tell one of her favorite stories about herself—the time she was banned from Ceausescu's Romania for illegal trading of Kent cigarettes for crystal. Apparently Kent refused to export to Romania after some falling out over taxes. The people, however, were hooked and loyal to Kent brand smokes. There was also some scuttlebutt about Anjoli's affair with the goalkeeper for the Romanian national soccer team. "So I told the guard that simply carrying forty pairs of men's Levi's did not make me a smuggler," she regaled. The story went on for twenty minutes before my friends from the agency declared that Anjoli was hilariously outrageous and they wished their mothers were more like her.

"Thshe was defnnnntly a trwipp," I spat.

"Jesus, Lucy, what happened to your face?!" Zoe cried.

"A chaleyre!" Rita pretended to spit on my mother's hardwood floor.

"There's no evil curse on our Lucy," Bernice said.

"Whath?" I noticed spit shooting out of the right side of my mouth. I picked up my cane and hobbled to the mirror as fast as I could. One eye was open too wide and the right side of my face looked frozen.

"She's having a stroke," Zoe panicked. "Get a cab. We need to get Lucy to the hospital."

"I am?!"

"Let's go," Anjoli grabbed her purse and headed toward the door. "The hospital's across the street."

As I used my cane to hobble across the street to the hospital, I wondered if something was wrong with the baby. "If I'm having a stroke, will the baby be okay?" I asked my mother.

"All is well. Your body is in perfect harmony. You are a vibrant, healthy soul encountering a momentary health challenge. You are releasing disease and embracing health," she said in a hysterically calm voice.

Zoe chimed in. "A stroke won't affect your baby," she said so assuredly I believed it. Then I caught a glance of myself in the reflection of a window.

"Holy schlit!" I looked like Mary Jo Buttafuoco after Amy Fisher shot her in the head.

Chapter 5

As it turned out, I was not having a stroke, but rather was mysteriously stricken with Bell's palsy. No one knows for sure whether it's a virus or a hex or what, but this wretched thing paralyzed half of my face. I'd never really appreciated how much I move the muscles in my face until half of them quit working. In the hospital emergency room, Anjoli brought me a bottle of mineral water from the cafeteria. After the first swig, I felt the cool water rolling down my chin and onto the right side of my crushed silk emerald top. "Holy schlit! My mouth won't close," I cried.

"Let me get a straw for you, darling," Anjoli offered. She returned moments later with a white plastic straw and the suggestion that I seal my lips closed with my fingers. "I dunt fink vat will be neshassary," I rolled my one good eye. But it was. As soon as I sucked on the straw, I felt water shoot out of the right side of my mouth.

"This is going to make eating rather challenging," Anjoli said sympathetically.

I slurred, "Eating became difficult when cookies went off the menu."

"*Challenging*, darling," Anjoli corrected. "Release the struggle consciousness. Challenges can be overcome. One can rise to a challenge. Difficulty sounds so hopeless. Words are affirmations. Affirmations are manifestations. Manifestations—"

"All right already! Eating will be *challenging*, are you happy?"

"In general or at the moment?"

"Good God, Mother!"

Anjoli was right. Trying to eat without the use of the right side of my face was extremely challenging. I used my hand to push my jaw up and down to help chew food. But my greatest obstacle to surmount was the fact that my right eye would not fully close. When one considers that we blink every few seconds, it's easy to see how after only an hour my eye became a stinging, irritated dust trap.

"Mom," I said, on the brink of tears. "My eye is challenging me."

"Darling!" Anjoli hugged. "Where is that doctor?! First they leave you in a waiting room, then they keep you waiting in an exam room. This is what's wrong with Western medicine."

Before she could start the inevitable tirade about the arrogance of doctors, I asked if she could find a patch to protect my right eye. "Of course, Lucy. You let Anjoli take care of everything."

I must say, our day in the hospital was Anjoli at her most nurturing. When I say she doesn't have a maternal instinct in her body, I don't mean to sound harsh. And I don't mean to sound as though I don't love her deeply. My mother is a vivacious woman who's had more adventures than anyone I've ever known. She has friends in every corner of the world, and has been banned from three countries for harmless yet illegal shenanigans. Yet mothering wasn't really her thing. She was her thing. The upside of having a self-absorbed mother was that I became self-sufficient at a young age. It certainly wasn't as though I was left completely on my own. I knew that if I ever really needed help, my mother would be happy to outsource it to the most qualified consultants. As a child, sometimes I wondered why Anjoli wasn't more involved in the day-to-day aspects of parenting. As an adult, I realize that she simply could not give what she didn't have.

In fifth grade, I remember my best friend, Vicki DeMattia, opening her lunch box and finding a note from her mother. *I love you, Vicki!* Sometimes Mrs. DeMattia included more, like what they would do together after school or how many kisses Vicki owed her from their Monopoly game the previous night. I got notes from Anjoli, too. They were typed and left on the dining room table. They went something like this: *Lucy: I'm at the theatre tonight and won't be home till after you're asleep. On the table, please find ten dollars for dinner. Be sure to include a vegetable and a green salad. Rinse lettuce thoroughly. Pesticides can kill you. Anjoli.*

By seventh grade, the notes stopped and it was assumed that I'd know how to fend for myself for dinner if there was a ten dollar bill on the table. There were three dinner options at my house. In reverse order of preference: Number three—broiled chicken dusted with paprika. Number two—ten on the table. And number one—dinner with Mom and her boyfriend, David, at a five-star restaurant. For ten-on-the-table nights, I memorized the take-out menus of every restaurant within a ten-block radius of West Eleventh Street, which was no small task. The family of my old pal from PS 41 owned a Chinese restaurant on West Eighth Street. There was always Ray's Pizza down at the corner. And sushi bars were just starting to sprout up all over Manhattan. Some nights my friends would call and ask if it was a ten-on-the-table night. If it was, I'd eat at their house for dinner, cut them in for three bucks, and pocket the rest. This is how I got the money for my first stock purchase. That, and undercutting the Quad cinema's popcorn prices and selling it to moviegoers who were waiting in line.

When I was a kid I asked my mother if there was a Santa Claus. She asked if I wanted the truth or the bourgeois lie.

"Truth!" I insisted.

"Santa's a character, not a real man," she told me.

"What about robbers?" I asked.

"Real," she answered.

"Monsters?"

"An illusion."

"How 'bout witches?" I asked.

"Debatable. It depends on what type of witch you mean."

I didn't understand what she meant. The only type of witches I knew wore pointy black hats and flew around on broomsticks. "Oh, Lucy, they're fake too," Anjoli said. She noticed I seemed a little overwhelmed by the avalanche of information. "Look, darling, I could feed you some pedestrian bullshit about the tooth fairy and Santa and the Easter bunny, but I think more of you than that. You're a child, not an imbecile, and I refuse to patronize you. How will I have any credibility with you later in life if our first years together are based on lies?"

"There's no tooth fairy?" My worm-sized lips quivered.

"I'm the tooth fairy," Anjoli told me.

"Oh."

"How do you feel about what I just told you, Lucy?"

"Sad."

"For that I am genuinely sorry, darling. Two good things have come from our chat, though. One, you now know that Anjoli would never lie to her little girl. And two, you have expressed your feelings beautifully. I'm sorry that you're sad, but identifying and articulating your feelings is a real breakthrough in a child's development. Now that that's settled, I need a favor from you. You know I'm mad about you and you're the most fabulous daughter a mother could want. When you call me Mommy, it pushes my buttons and makes me feel older than I really am. Plus, you're a precocious child. Why don't you call me Anjoli?"

We weren't like mother and daughter. It was more like two single women sharing an apartment in Greenwich Village in the seventies. Except I was five.

Nearly thirty-five years later, we were in the same hospital where I was born. Anjoli had just found an eye patch, which I was securing to my head as I walked to the bathroom. The doctor on staff popped his head in the door. "Whoa, an eye patch *and* a cane! All you need now is a parrot on your shoulder and you could be a pirate." He laughed alone. "Err, um, okay, what have we got here today?" He grabbed my chart and read, "Mrs. Klein?"

"A wannabe comedian in a white coat," Anjoli shot back. I glared, hoping she would cease her attack on the doctor. My mother absolutely hated doctors. If they were a racial group, my mother would be considered a bigot. They were all arrogant jerks as far as she was concerned. She didn't need to know anything more about them except that they were doctors. I had tired of her anti-doctor tirades years ago, but it was disconcerting to think that she was about to anger the doctor who was ready to treat me.

"When are you due?" the doctor asked.

"Her due date is February second," Anjoli answered for me.

"Groundhog Day," Dr. Michaels added. "My favorite movie."

"One of mine too!" Anjoli sounded excited, and far less hostile toward the doctor. "A light comedy with a profound spiritual message about repeating mistakes until we evolve with foresight and wisdom." Oh God, she sounded like a movie reviewer for *Flakey Times*. "What about you, doctor? What drew you to the film?"

"Oh, well I think Bill Murray's hysterical," he said. I knew this answer would undoubtedly disappoint Anjoli. He put on his best Bill Murray slur and said, "I'm going to blast those darned gophers!"

"I think that was actually *Caddyshack*," I said.

"Whoa! What happened to your face?"

My mother let out an audible sigh of disgust. "We were so very hopeful that you might be able to tell us that, *doctor*."

I don't know exactly why my mother despises doctors, but her skepticism for their ability to heal people is palpable. When Anjoli has a cold, which is pretty much all the time, she takes herbs, chants, and listens to her *Sacred Place of Health* CD. She drinks sixty-four ounces of distilled water and three ounces of wheat grass juice every day. (Her mouth isn't the only orifice that consumes the wheat grass juice, if you catch what I'm saying.) She looks about my age, but feels as old as her grandmother most of the time because her immune system has been weakened by all of the pure foods she puts into it. I remember learning about how one generation of bugs could be wiped out by a dusting of pesticides that would have no effect on the next generation. The phenomenon was called resistance and resurgence. My mother desperately needed to have a cheeseburger, fries, and a Coke to build up her resistance to the impurities in the world, New York City in particular.

Every weekend Anjoli attends workshops on energy healing, Qi Gong, chakra spinning, past life regression, future life karmic reparations, and skin care. A few years ago she got Lyme disease at a "total health" retreat in the Pennsylvania mountains. The weekend courses included Chanting for Total Health, White Light for Total Health, and Lymphatic Drainage for Total Health. Never a word about tick repellant. Though Anjoli was weak from the Lyme disease and the much-protested antibiotics, I'd never seen her happier than when she had so much healing to do. Last year, she got into radionics, which is where you give a healer $500 to look at a photograph of you, and they do some behind-the-scenes hocus-pocus till you're good as new. Shockingly, it didn't work. This past summer, Anjoli went to an "exclusive" Brazilian healing center located at a "very powerful place on the globe." Apparently the longitudinal and latitudinal bearings made it a perfect spot for healing. To apply for admission, she had to place her hand on a sheet of white paper for a half hour while she remained silent and as motionless as possible. She then mailed the blank paper to Brazil where a team of monks determined whether or not she needed healing. Guess what? She did. She was about as excited as when I was accepted at the University of Michigan. Anjoli made her airline reservation within ten minutes of receiving her call from the admissions office in the Amazon jungle.

Dr. Michaels looked at my face and scrunched with discomfort. "Does that hurt?"

"Only when I look in the mirror," I said, still garbled. "Listen, can you give me the Bell's palsy shot and make my face go back to normal? Please?"

"Gosh, I'm real sorry, but that's not the way it works. These things take some time."

"What do you mean?" I panicked.

"Most Bell's palsy takes a few months to—"

"A few months?! A few months?! I'm having a baby in a few months. I can't spit all over him when I sing lullabies. Think about it, doctor. Is *this* the first face you'd want to see coming out of the womb?!"

"Newborns can't see," he answered.

"Not my point! Isn't there anything you can do?" I pleaded.

"I hate to bring this up right now, but as your attending physician, I do need to let you know that some Bell's palsy never goes away."

"Oh my God!" I shouted in a bloodcurdling scream that surely alarmed the entire emergency room. Lowering my voice, I went into desperate insanity. "Doctor, please, please, I'm begging you. My face cannot stay like this. There's got to be something you can do."

"Lucy, calm down!" Anjoli shouted. "You'll frighten the baby."

Alarmed by my intensity, Dr. Michaels asked if I wanted him to call a neurologist who could better explain Bell's palsy to me. "A neurologist?! There's something wrong with my brain? What about the baby? Is the baby's brain okay? Is his face going to be disfigured too? Oh my God, oh my God," I kept repeating as Dr. Michaels left the room. A few minutes later, he returned with an Indian woman in a white coat.

"You're in luck, Mrs. Klein," Dr. Michaels exclaimed. "I found Dr. Gupta upstairs. She can tell you a lot more about Bell's palsy than I'm able." As happy as I was to see a new doctor, one who was purported to be knowledgeable about Bell's palsy, I didn't feel as though I was "in luck." I think you're permanently disqualified from the lucky category after four miscarriages, a virtual divorce, and a face that could scare small children.

"Are you a neurologist?" I asked. She nodded. "Is my baby okay?"

"That you will need to ask your obstetrician, but the Bell's palsy should have no effect on your baby," she said annoyingly calmly.

"Should?"

"It would be exceptionally rare," she said.

I heard a voice from the past—a male voice without the accent. *I'm afraid your baby has exceptionally rare fetal anomalies incompatible with life.*

"How can we find out for sure?" I asked. "My baby isn't due for another two months."

"There is nothing that we know with entire certainty," she said. This sparked a deep philosophical conversation with my mother. I grabbed my cane and hobbled toward the hospital exit so I could use my cell phone to call Jack.

As it turned out, Jack, being knowledgeable about most everything, had heard of Bell's palsy. He disclaimed that he was not an expert on the condition. More important, after fourteen years of marriage, he was an expert on me. Jack assured me that the baby would be fine. "The baby is fine. I guarantee it." For all of our troubles, I still loved him. He knew exactly what I needed—guarantees. I heard him tapping on the keyboard of his computer, researching Bell's palsy. He read numerous excerpts from articles, all of which were exactly what I wanted to hear. The baby was fine. My face would go back to normal.

"Are you staying at Anjoli's for a few days?" Jack asked.

"I can still get around just fine," I said. "It's just my face that's paralyzed, not my legs." Then I reconsidered. "It is late, and I don't feel like driving back right now, especially with the eye patch. I think I will stay in the city for a few days."

"That's wise," he said. "I'm printing out facial exercises you can do to help rehabilitate your muscles. I'll swing by your mother's apartment tomorrow before I head to the gallery."

"Thank you."

"Lucy, the baby is fine. Your face will go back to normal in no time, I promise. What does Anjoli always say, 'Conceive it and believe it, and so it is.'" We laughed. "Hang in there, kiddo. You're going to come out of this fine."

Kiddo? Did he just call me kiddo? When the hell did I become kiddo?

Chapter 6

The next morning, I heard the doorbell ring and Anjoli twitter that she was on her way to answer it. It was Jack with a brown bag of bagels, cream cheese, and lox, and a spelt bagel for Anjoli. He'd long since given up the idea that a whole wheat bagel was in the realm of things Anjoli would touch. "Where on earth did you find spelt bagels, darling?" Anjoli giggled from downstairs.

When I agreed to live together as friends and co-parents with Jack, one of my conditions was that we not disclose our new status to friends or family. I found the new deal more than a tad humiliating. It isn't too often that you hear about couples where the wife announces she is pregnant and the husband replies, "Great, let's be friends, shall we?" I know Anjoli would be accepting. God knows I had to deal with an unconventional home with her and David, her part-time live-in boyfriend, who also happened to have a wife and kids in Westchester.

My mother and David were together for five years before I found out their relationship was actually an illicit affair. I was always told that David was only with us three nights a week because he traveled a lot for business. At eight years old, I didn't question this. At thirteen, I began to suspect there was another woman in David's life. Never did I imagine it was his wife. He also had two teenage daughters, which I learned about at the worst possible time in my life. It was less than a week after my father's funeral when we ran into one of David's colleagues lunching at Maxwell's Plum. The guy was wearing an Armani suit and a tremendous smile when he approached David's and my table. "Leslie!" the man approached me excitedly. "I haven't seen you in years. You look terrific!"

David's horrified expression filled me in on five years of deception. I'd never seen this man in the suit before, but smiled and said hello as if I knew exactly who he was. David looked relieved that I seemed willing to play along.

"You remember Mr. Anderson, don't you, Leslie? Without his company, Alloretics would have practically no distribution."

"*Practically* no distribution?!" Mr. Anderson said jovially. "Y'ain't runnin' around with no other distributors behind my back, now are ya, y'old dog?"

Oh you have no idea what a tangled web we weave, Mr. Anderson.

"Of course, I do," I smiled. "It's a pleasure to see you again, Mr. Anderson."

"Y'lost weight, haven't ya, Leslie?"

No, Mr. Anderson, I haven't. You've unwittingly notified me that my mother's boyfriend has another family, including a fat daughter named Leslie. Ten days ago my father overdosed on heroin, and within thirty seconds of your leaving this table, David is going to apologize by offering me an afternoon at Bloomingdale's. I haven't lost any weight. I've lost my childhood.

"Jeez, Lucy," David said after Mr. Anderson left the table. "I'm sorry about that. What do you have planned for the rest of the afternoon? Want to do a little shopping?"

When Jack saw me enter Anjoli's kitchen, he asked what my plans for the day were. "Going to do a little shopping in the Village?"

"I don't think so," I told him. "I was thinking maybe I'd do a little writing. Maybe I'll start an outline for my book. I'm not sure yet. I definitely need a nap."

Jack's gallery didn't open until ten and the Drama Queen opened at noon, so both my mother and faux husband were night owls. But I won the grand prize last night by staying up until 4:00 A.M. researching Bell's palsy on the Internet. I was convinced that there really was a shot or pill I could take that would make my face go back to normal. Then, of course, I was in heavy contract negotiations with God, promising that I'd never complain about my appearance if he would just let me wake up the next morning with a face that functioned properly on both sides.

"Terrific, kiddo!" Jack said, self-consciously trying not to stare at my face.

"Jack, aren't you going to say anything about my face?" I asked.

"Must dress, darlings. Do excuse me," Anjoli said, as she and her sky-blue silk night ensemble dramatically ascended the stairs. Mother always wore something that looked like it was bought at the Norma Desmond House of Garb. She lifted her wide sheer sleeve to bid us farewell as though she were departing for a year in Europe rather than a trip to the loo.

"How are you hanging in there, kiddo?"

"How does it look like I'm hanging in there?"

"You seem tired," Jack said.

"Jack! What about my face? Aren't you going to say anything about this monstrosity of a mug I'm wearing?!"

"You look fine," he said. "It's hardly noticeable."

"Hardly noticeable?! Jack, please don't lie to me. I know it's very noticeable. You don't *notice* that half of my face is drooping? You don't notice that I'm wearing an eye patch? You don't notice that every time I speak, spit flies out of my mouth?!"

"I'm sorry," he shouted, not sounding at all sorry. "I don't want you to feel bad, that's all."

"Ahhhhh!" I screamed. "Jack, I already feel bad! Quite bad, in fact. Half of my face won't move. I look like something out of a horror movie. The emergency room doctor was taken aback by the sight of me, Jack! I shocked the emergency room doctor. Do you have any idea how hard that is to do? The man sees gunshot wounds, dismembered limbs, shit oozing out of people's brains, and my face, my ugly face was shocking to him."

"Okay," Jack said. "I'm not really sure what you want from me."

"I want you to stop trying to deny every feeling I ever have, Jack. I want you to stop telling me not to feel bad when I already do. I want you to stop telling me I look fine when it's so patently obvious that I don't. I want you to stop being so uncomfortable when things aren't perfect that you immediately start trying to pretend they are." Even as the words were coming out of my mouth, I realized how unfair I was being. Yes, I wanted him to accept my emotional reality. But only when it suited me. I also wanted him to tell me that the baby would be fine when it was what I needed to hear. At least Jack was consistent. I was a nut job.

"Jack, I think I need a nap," I said. "I'm sorry, but

the last twenty-four hours have been a little over-
whelming, and I can't even eat a cupcake to cheer me
up."

With that, he laughed. "Come here, kiddo." He
opened his arms. "It's been a rough pregnancy for you,
I know. Soon as you deliver this baby, I'm going to
make you the ultimate carbohydrate dinner: risotto,
baked potato, Italian bread, and rice pudding." I laughed
as my tears were absorbed into Jack's shirt. "Your face
has seen better days, but it'll get better. I downloaded a
few articles I found on Bell's palsy and a list of facial
exercises that lots of people are saying speed up the recovery." This is all he ever needed to say. Other than the
"kiddo" part, Jack said exactly what I needed to hear.
"I'll bet if you do these religiously, your face will be
back to normal by Kimmy's wedding."

Kimmy's wedding! Those two words jarred me from
the comfort of the moment. I'd completely forgotten
about perfect cousin Kimmy's perfect wedding to the
perfect guy on the perfect date. Kimmy would be
married on St. Valentine's Day in the world famous
St. Patrick's Cathedral on Fifth Avenue. Each year, three
million people from all over the globe visit the Gothic
church with its solid bronze baldachin, Tiffany-designed
altars, and a spire that reaches higher than 300 feet.
(Surely this majestic three-organ church would never
allow Zoe's *Real Confessions* to turn their confessionals
into television recording studios.) I was scheduled to
meet Kimmy there next week to go over some details
with her wedding planner. With my distorted face and
cane, I'd look like the Hunchbelly of St. Pat's.

I absolutely had to get my face back to normal by
Kimmy's wedding. Her engagement party was like
Fashion Week, with stunning women all wearing next
season's size two fabulousness. Even the men were better groomed than I was. Kimmy's queer brigade wears

purposefully sloppy hair and uses special shavers that leave rugged day-old stubble. I've seen real day-old stubble on Jack on Sunday mornings. It's kind of sexy, but it covers the entire face, not just parts specially selected to accentuate exquisite bone structure. Kimmy's friends were warm and engaging. They all had the gift of making you feel as though you were absolutely fascinating, and that there was nowhere they'd rather be than talking to you. Charming and beautiful people were hard enough on the ego in the best of times. I imagined the manufactured smiles of Kimmy's friends as they stared at my freakish face.

At Kimmy's engagement party this past summer, Geoff, her fiancé, seemed like the kind of guy who was the president of the student body association in high school. His brown hair was combed neatly and he wore a jacket that matched those of several of the straight guys in the room. I later learned it bore the crest of a fraternal business organization to which they all belonged. He will make a great father, I thought. They'll move to Connecticut and have a hunting dog named Raider who sits at Geoff's feet as he reads *Fortune*. They'll undoubtedly wallpaper the family room in the Burberry Nova pattern. When Geoff toasted "his Kimmy," I thought it sounded a little possessive. Now that my pseudo-husband had taken to calling me "kiddo," it sounded pretty good.

"Thank you for coming by with the facial exercises, Jack," I said. "Your visit has cheered me up." I silently vowed that whatever the facial workout program suggested, I would triple it. I was going to have the quickest Bell's palsy recovery the doctors had ever seen.

"Lucy, I know how you get when you're down. Promise me that you'll get out of the house today. Take a walk around the neighborhood. Check out the holiday lights. I know you can't get too far with the cane, but don't stay cooped up inside all day. Take advantage of the warm winter we're having, okay?"

"Maybe you could come back after the gallery closes and we could walk down to St. Mark's? Grab a bite to eat at Dojo's?"

"Another time I'd love to, kiddo, but I've got plans tonight."

"Big date?" I asked, half kidding, half hoping he'd be appalled at the very thought.

"Yep," he nodded.

"That's great! Good for you," I forced. "Have fun."

Who is she? What's her name? Is she prettier than me? Without my handicap of the facial paralysis is she prettier than me? Is she skinny? What does she do for a living? Oh God, please don't tell me she's already written her novel! Please don't tell me she's a supermodel who just so happens to have won a Pulitzer for her eighth novel the critics all call "brilliant!"

"Anyone special?" I couldn't help from slipping out.

"Not sure yet," he said. "Remember, Lucy, no hermitage. Even if you just walk down to Ray's for a slice, make sure to get out today."

I can't eat pizza, or these fucking bagels for that matter, you insensitive jerk!

"You don't think you could've waited till I gave birth to start dating?" I snapped.

"Why?" Jack asked.

"It's not that I'm upset you're getting a head start or anything, but don't you want to be helpful with the pregnancy? I mean, if you're so gung ho about fatherhood, how 'bout being accessible to me in my time of need?"

"I think I'm very accessible." Jack gestured at himself as if to say, *I'm here, aren't I?*

"What if I need you while you're on your big date with Miss Could Be Special?"

"You've got my cell number," Jack said, shrugging.

As I heard the front door shut, I fought down a lump in my throat. "Good-bye," I said as a tear escaped.

We borrowed David from another family until he eventually had to return to Westchester for good or face the wrath of his wife's lawyer. Daddy partied himself into an early grave. JJ never made it out of the womb. And now Jack was gone too. It seemed every man in my life was a loaner.

Chapter 7

Anjoli walked into my bedroom as I was doing my "smile-ups." My bedroom was in the same state as when I left for college. The walls were pale blue with champagne floorboards and window frames. A Victorian oak headboard supported the bed, which was covered by a floral spread. There was a vanity with pictures stuffed in the frame of the mirror and a wall lined with ribbons from horse shows I'd won or placed in. Never having too much of an eye for detail, Anjoli left a 1984 calendar hanging on the wall. The month was still August, according to my time warp of a bedroom. My clock radio was still set to WPLJ. On my bed rested a floppy-eared stuffed dog given to me by my high school prom date.

I'd just tried to start writing the opening pages of my novel and almost finished the first sentence when I got distracted by my reflection in the mirror. The problem with this book I wanted to write was that I wasn't exactly sure what I wanted the book to be about. I figured if Jerry Seinfeld could make a television show about nothing, why couldn't I write a book about nothing?

Unfortunately, the Seinfeld writers came up with witty observations about everyday life. All I came up with was a dark, rainy night and some chick named Desdemona wandering a cobblestone alley.

"Oh, are you doing the nonsurgical face-lift?" Anjoli asked, sounding overjoyed that we might be able to share our thoughts on the program.

"It's for the Bell's palsy," I said. "Thirty-four, thirty-five, thirty-six."

"Of course it is, darling. I simply wondered if it was adapted from the nonsurgical face-lift program."

"No," I sighed impatiently. "I'm hoping to regain movement on the right side of my face. I'm not trying to give myself a face-lift."

Her own face was shining from the base of oils and creams she applied after her shower. "Don't turn your nose up at it, darling. Kimmy and I took the class and it was wonderful," she said, exaggerating the final word. "I purchased the DVD if you'd like to watch it with me. Five minutes a day and you'd be amazed at how the facial muscles tone up. Plus, forcing all of that oxygenated blood to your face helps smooth wrinkles so you won't ever have to have a face-lift."

"Mother! My face is paralyzed. In another week, I'm going to be further along in a pregnancy than I've ever made it. I kind of have more important things to deal with right now. Plus no one *has* to get a face-lift."

She inhaled through her nose and straightened her back. "Point well taken. What do you need from me, darling?"

"I don't know if you can help me with this. I need to relax. I feel like I'm constantly on the brink of tears. I want to know for sure that the baby is okay, and I know this sounds so vain, but I need to know my face will look normal again." *Oh my God! My "important issues" are the same as hers.*

She smiled. "I have an idea for this evening," Anjoli said. "Why don't you finish your exercises, then we'll take a short walk? I'm going to make a quick phone call and have Alfie open the shop today. Think about staying with me for a few more days, darling. It will be like old times. We can light a fire, sit by the tree, and gab for hours."

"We never did that."

"So, we'll do it now!" Anjoli beamed. Staying in the city for a few days didn't sound like a bad idea. I couldn't walk for more than four blocks, which in Caldwell would place me right in front of someone else's suburban home. In Greenwich Village, the same distance would take me by Jefferson Market gourmet foods, the Joffrey Ballet, street vendors, restaurants, and the public library.

Anjoli's home was always extraordinarily decorated for Christmas. Because her living room ceiling extended to the top of our three-story apartment, she could easily fit a twenty-foot tree. Each year she had a tree-trimming party where nearly a hundred guests brought ornaments, from drag Santa to hand-painted glass snowflakes. Since Anjoli knows mostly theatre people, nearly half of her guests could play piano and do wildly entertaining numbers where they'd play holiday songs, then engage the guests with a five-minute comedic commentary about the party—set to music. Anjoli's best friend Alfie's specialty was replacing lyrics of holiday classics with his own. Guests shouted famous tunes and Alfie reportedly made up new ones on the spot. He claimed they were improvised, but I knew he secretly wrote and rehearsed them beforehand.

Never one to miss the chance to throw a dinner party, Anjoli also hosted a Seder at Passover for her Jewish friends. In New York, even the Roman Catholics were Jewish friends. They set out a cup of wine, not for the spirit of Elijah, but for Liza. Minelli, that is. Every year they sent her agent an invitation to the Seder and pretended they were completely shocked when she didn't show up. "Some alcoholic she turned out to be!" Alfie gasped.

I picked up a book at the library and bought a furry black beret from one of the guys on Sixth Avenue. "No problem is so big that a new hat can't fix it," Anjoli claimed as she handed the vendor ten dollars. When we returned home, she insisted that I take a nap because sleep was the best medicine. Other times she said it was water. Often it was echinacea. But today the remedy was rest and I couldn't have agreed more.

The doorbell rang. "Perfect timing!" She fluttered to the door. Anjoli is birdlike in her stature and movements. Painfully thin, she has the body of a ballerina, which she, in fact, once was. After having spent a lifetime of extending her neck, it is unusually long and slender. It supports a dainty head with porcelain skin and a sharp nose. She has a European sexiness about her as opposed to Kimmy's milk-fed Ivory-girl look. "Entrez-vous, Henri." In entered a gorgeous, tan twenty-something Frenchman with a shock of wavy brown hair and a smirk that said "I'm so sexy, I'd blush if it weren't so uncool." Unaware that I was standing at the rail of the third floor looking down, Anjoli shouted to me. "Lucy, I have a little surprise for you. Someone is here to help you relax!" she sang. My mother is never one to overlook the healing properties of a sexy man's company.

My mother is the best! I was such a lousy ingrate to ever say that my mother is not nurturing. She is undoubtedly the coolest mother on the planet to bring home this fantastic man for me. This is soooo going to relax me! I absolutely love her to—huh? What the hell is that? What is that thing he's schlepping in the front door? What does he need a harp for? Oh man! He's not here for therapeutic sex? He's going to play music for me? Sweet thought, but I'm not going to be able to fall asleep with Henri in my room. I haven't had sex in seven months. That's two full seasons without the feeling of a man's firm body pressed against my flesh. My God, just the mention of sex—even in the context of not having it—is driving me wild with desire. I am supposed to take this delicious creature upstairs to my bedroom and lie in bed while he plays harp for me? And I'm supposed to fall asleep during it? Ha! I'll be lucky if I can refrain from humping my stuffed dog's paw while Henri plucks and caresses the goddamn harp strings.

"Yes, Anjoli?" I descended the staircase with a dramatic flare usually reserved for her entrances. "Oh, hello," I said as if I'd just noticed that yet another gorgeous Frenchman was in our living room.

"Mademoiselle," Henri said, kissing my hand.

You think you could use a little tongue?

"I read an article in *Healings and Feelings* that harp music is very therapeutic, darling. Even alpha wolves are completely docile when they listen to harp music. The vibration of the harp music is deeply relaxing."

Deep? Vibrations? This evil woman is simply toying with me!

"Zees eez true," Henri concurred.

"Henri's harp will really take the edge off, Lucy," Anjoli said.

Not as much as a long passionate night of exhilarating, glorious, and ultimately exhausting sex.

"You haven't heard music until you've experienced what this man can do with his instrument," Anjoli smiled.

Oh now she's just being cruel.

"Okay, off to the bedroom, you two! And don't you come out until Lucy's off in dreamland."

Bitch!

As we walked up two flights of stairs, Henri asked if it was "deefeecult" to climb stairs with my cane.

"Make yourself comfortable in zee bed and tell me when I am to begin," Henri said. This guy would be so excellent in bed. Jack never asked when I was ready to begin. No guy ever told me to make myself comfortable in zee bed before. "Can I bring you some water?" Henri offered. He is so accommodating. I wonder how he would react if I matter-of-factly asked him to lick my inner thighs and lightly bite the skin on my legs. I mean, if I just said it like it was the most normal request in the world, he might think it's an American bedtime ritual and just do it. "Should I close zee curtains to keep zee sunshine outside?" Henri asked, reminding me that it was two in the afternoon. When there's a Frenchman in your bedroom, it always seems like one in the morning.

Pull me in by my ample waist and kiss me as if you've been waiting a lifetime to have me. Rip my blouse off right now. Run your extremely heterosexual razor stubble across my burgeoning, rotund breasts immediately. Hold my hands down with your strong grip and thrust into me so hard that I will feel you inside me weeks later.

"Yeah, great idea, Henri," I said. I closed my eyes and tried to focus on the soothing wave of music coming from his harp. I felt my head sink into my old pillow as the smell of home began to unwind my nerves. The clean Egyptian cotton sheets rose to meet my skin, beckoning them to meld with it. I felt fatigue leave my body and sink into the mattress. The left side of my face grew as placid as the right as my breathing slowed and steadied into a meditative state. I instinctively knew that everything was going to be all right. I wasn't sure what everything was, but I knew that all would turn out exactly as it should. I felt more of a sense of peace than I ever remember experiencing.

"Relax, ma chère. Let yourself have sleep, beautiful girl."

My eyes shot open and my body stiffened. *Was he talking to me?! Beautiful girl? Ma chère? There's no way I'm sleeping through this. Just talk to me, Henri. Just look at me with those French eyes and keep telling this seven-months-pregnant fat chick with facial paralysis that she's a beautiful girl. There's no way I'm sleeping through this!*

Chapter 8

After I spent three weeks, including the holidays, at my mother's apartment in the city, Anjoli grew suspicious that all was not well on the suburban frontier. After all, Jack drove to the gallery every day and could have easily taken me home with him at night. I loved being back in the Village, walking past my old elementary school yard, checking out the dynamic graffiti art, and remembering simpler times with my father as I walked to Washington Square Park. I missed Jack, and probably would have returned home if he protested my absence. But he didn't so I stayed. He was dating someone, and I didn't have the energy for a fight. What would I have done anyway, clubbed her knee with my cane like Tanya Harding's thug boy-friend? I preferred to lay low and keep my twisted face out of sight.

I had no articles or company newsletters due and my doctor said it was best if I just took it easy for the last month of pregnancy. I used this as an excuse to not return to the keyboard to continue with the tragic tale of Desdemona in the rain, or even think about what she was doing wandering that dark cobblestone road anyway. I was, however, exceptionally motivated to do my facial exercises, which were amazingly effective. In just under a week, some of the movement had returned to my face. Still, I hadn't returned home.

"I'm thrilled to have you, darling, but isn't Jack missing you at home?" Anjoli asked one day after she placed our dinner delivery order from the Zen Palate. Normally they didn't deliver, but for Anjoli they made an exception. Everyone did. Even her auditor from the IRS had a little crush on her and helped her fix her many careless errors on her tax returns. Most of the time, she cheated herself out of money, so there was no question that Anjoli was simply scatterbrained.

"Thank you for letting me stay here," I said. "I really appreciate it." I sat in front of the Christmas tree and inhaled the evergreen scent and eucalyptus candles burning on the mantel. I sank into a chair and pulled a silver chenille lap blanket over myself. She brought a cup of Fortune Delight tea for herself and sat next to me.

"That's what mothers are for. I am rather concerned, though, that you seem to be in no hurry to return to New Jersey. God knows I can't blame you for avoiding suburbia, darling, but seeing how you and Jack chose to make your home there, I'm curious why you're not there with your husband."

Now would be a good time to mention that, in addition to being a Manhattan snob, Anjoli was raised in New Jersey. So while she never has a kind word to say about the "other" boroughs, Westchester County, or Long Island, she has a special place in her arsenal for New Jersey. She says she never fit in to the Newark Catholic social scene, but the breaking point was when she was disqualified from a beauty contest for a talent entry of a performance art piece far too radical for the 1950s. "They are all such small-minded bigots in New

Jersey," she says, missing the irony of the fact that she's made a sweeping generalization about an entire state. "Twenty years later, Yoko Ono did the same damn thing and everyone said she was a genius. That's why I ran away to the Village. Why bother putting a state so close to New York if everyone's going to act as though they're in Iowa?" Mother's a bit snooty about the Midwest as well. I attended several writing conferences at the University of Iowa and fell in love with the area. Anjoli once looked out from her airplane window and concluded that there was "nothing" in the Midwest. I reminded her that she was above the clouds at 30,000 feet, but she was convinced that it was snow. Two more things. Anjoli loves to talk about her "running away" to Greenwich Village, but she didn't exactly tie a hobo bag to a stick and hitchhike through the tunnel. She left New Jersey at nineteen to attend NYU and lived in a very cozy apartment paid for by her parents. Anjoli was actually born Margaret Mary DeFelice. When she was thirty-three, she went to a weekend workshop on "finding your true name." A guru looked deep into her eyes and saw that she really and truly could bring home the bacon, fry it up in a pan, and never, ever, ever let you forget you're a man.

"I still can't believe you decided to move there," Anjoli shook her head.

"We live in an excellent school district," I reminded her for the zillionth time. "It's a great place for kids, which I'm thrilled to say is exactly what we need right now."

"Then why aren't you there?"

"The baby isn't here yet," I said.

"The husband is, though. Tell me, darling. You can tell Mommy what's wrong."

"Nothing's wrong."

"Darling, I know what a troubled marriage looks

like," she said, reaching over to brush my hair from my eyes. Except there was no hair in my eyes. I think she saw the gesture in a script note once and thought it seemed like a maternal thing to do, so she adopted the move.

I had a dozen bitchy comebacks about how she was familiar with unhappy marriages because she'd caused so many of them, but I refrained. I knew it would be too cruel a lob. I knew she hadn't really caused any troubled marriages as much as she'd capitalized on them. But most of all I knew I was just being harsh because she was coming so close to finding out that Jack pretty much regarded me as a friend and incubator. Another part of me wanted to tell someone—anyone—what was going on with Jack. Since she was right there, Anjoli was my choice.

"You're right," I admitted. I knew if I laid these two words at her feet, she would go easy on me. "Jack's and my relationship has changed. We're sort of married in name only. We'll raise the baby together, but have separate lives."

"That sounds like a divorce."

"No, we'll still live together. We'll just be friends—and co-parents."

"There was an article in the *Times* about this!" she said excitedly. Then she gave a moment of thought with knit brows. She rarely knit her brows because of the wrinkle it caused. In fact, every night she's walked around the house with a piece of Scotch tape between her eyebrows so she would not create a "concentration line." So when she knit her brows, I knew she was in serious contemplation. "Jack is gay, isn't he?" Anjoli said.

"No, he's straight as ever."

"Are you sure? I could see him being gay."

"Mother, Jack is *not* gay. He's already dating—women!"

"He may still be in denial."

"Jack is not gay, Anjoli! Stop saying that."

"Please don't tell me they've turned you into a homophobe out there in *New Jersey!*"

"Mother, stop it! Look, if Jack were gay, I'd say he was gay, but he's not."

She seemed disappointed. "Oh. He seems so gay."

"Mother! What is your problem?!"

"I have no problem, darling. It's just I know someone I think Jack would really hit it off with, but if you say he's not gay then it won't work." Anjoli continued, "It would be so much easier if he were gay."

"Why is that? Do you think I'm hoping for a reconciliation?" I accused.

"No, darling. It seems such better PR to have him gay, though. If he's gay, no one will say the breakup was because you were difficult, or because of another woman. Oh come now, Lucy, be sensible. Let's tell people he's gay. I have a friend, Marlies, in California who lives with her gay husband and she came out of the whole thing beautifully. Who could blame the wife if it turned out the husband was just gay?"

"Mother, is that what you think?! That unless my husband is gay, the breakup is my fault?"

"Of course not, darling, but you know what imbeciles people can be."

"I certainly do," I shot. "Might I remind you that you and Daddy divorced when I was six months old? Did anyone say it was your fault? Or did you just tell everyone he was gay?"

"Lucy," she said with overdone sympathy. "Your father was a drug addict."

"Mother, frankly, I can see why."

I hated when my mother called my father a "drug addict." Yes, he smoked pot daily, and did more than his fair share of LSD, cocaine, and heroin, but he did other things too. Admittedly, they were not necessarily performed as coherently as they may have otherwise been, but to call Sammy a drug addict seemed to detract from all his other qualities. Drug addicts were useless losers who pissed on themselves in alleyways. Guys who simply did drugs on a daily basis were something different. They were musicians. He never missed a visiting Sunday, a school play, a horse show, or a parent-teacher conference. He had an IQ of 146 and could debate just about any issue with anyone. So to call him a drug addict really gave a very one-dimensional picture of my father. I'll admit, he wasn't Pa Ingalls, but we didn't live in a little house on the prairie either, so I don't know why Anjoli always needed to use that tired old characterization with me. The man was dead. Hadn't she already won Parental Survivor?

Anjoli burst into laughter. "I must say, darling, you certainly did inherit his comedic delivery." Every time I am convinced she is nonmaternal, she does something incredibly warm and nurturing. Just as I'm convinced she's trying to body slam a dead man, she acknowledges that Sammy was quite funny. This woman was so infuriatingly inconsistent I wanted to scream. She smiled, and I adored her again.

"How long do you intend to live this way?" Anjoli asked, again brushing the hair from my eyes.

"Will you stop with the hair?!" I snapped.

"I want to see your eyes."

"Then look at them. There's no hair blocking your view. Why do you keep brushing my hair away? What do you want, to just pet me like a cat?"

"Maybe I do. Is that such a crime?"

I moved next to her on the couch and put a pillow on

her lap. I was about to rest my head on it when Anjoli protested. "You're not planning to put your head on my legs, are you?"

"Problem?"

"Darling, my circulation. Please, rest your head next to my legs, not on top of them. I'll get varicose veins."

The doorbell rang. My mother glided to the front door to greet the traveling waiter from Zen Palate. I overheard that his audition went well, but that he wasn't sure he looked Russian enough to play one of the Cossacks in *Fiddler on the Roof*. With that, I glanced around the corner to see the most beautiful Puerto Rican young man I'd ever seen. His brown eyes were so wide and piercing, I almost floated from my seat toward him. I think Anjoli's apartment has some weird effect on guys because every man who passed through those doors in the last three weeks was quiver-worthy.

I heard Anjoli tell the guy that *West Side Story* was coming back to Broadway next season and that she knew the director. Of course she could get him an audition, she assured. "You *are* coming to my New Year's Eve party, aren't you? You'll meet Tommy then."

New Year's Eve party? What New Year's Eve party?

Chapter 9

Never let a comfortable environment fool you. It's those times when you think you're in the absolute safest place when disaster strikes. I'd claimed a favorite spot in Anjoli's living room—the far end of the sectional facing the fireplace and Christmas tree. A bright light craned over my seat so I could always read, even when Anjoli decided to dim the main lights so the tiny white holiday lights would sparkle. And just off to my left was a wooden table just big enough to hold my mug, book, and cell phone.

The sun had set and it was officially New Year's Eve, a night filled with the promise that tomorrow was another year. A clean slate. A fresh start. Anjoli and Alfie were at Jefferson Market picking up some last-minute items and I was curled up on the couch finishing the last few pages of a lovely novel. I felt a rare sense of peace. Then I felt a sharp cramp that made me drop my book and shout. I felt warm blood rushing out of me, soaking my underwear and bottoms. Panicked, I reached for my cell phone to call Anjoli before remembering that she doesn't carry one. She believes they cause ear cancer. I inhaled deeply and tried to fight back the tears while dialing 9-1-1. "Yes, I need help. I'm having a miscarriage and I'm home alone," I said as calmly as I could. Tears rolled down my cheeks as I continued answering the dispatcher's questions. "Eight months . . . Yes, I'm bleeding and cramping . . . Sixteen West Eleventh Street, it's just west of Sixth Avenue . . . Yes, of course I'll stay on the line." Was she kidding?! My husband dumped me and my mother was making a prosciutto run. The disembodied voice said she was sending an ambulance that should arrive within minutes. I could tell she was a mother because she kept telling me to breathe deeply and that everything would be fine. But how could it be? My fifth baby had come so close, and now he was leaving too.

Anjoli and Alfie arrived at the same time as the paramedics, so I didn't have to struggle to answer the door. "What in God's name is going on, Lucy?" Anjoli cried, rushing in to the apartment. "Why is an ambulance here?"

With that, I burst into tears. "I'm having a miscarriage," I bawled.

"Oh, Christ!" Alfie rushed over to me.

The paramedics brought a gurney to the couch and pulled back the blanket covering me. "Why do you think you're miscarrying, ma'am?"

"Because I'm bleeding all over the place, and my stomach is twisting in knots," I managed to say between sobs.

"Not again! Not again!" Anjoli shouted. "What kind of wretched karmic retribution is this?" she shook her fists at the sky.

"Um, ma'am," the paramedic said. "You're not bleeding."

"Yes, I am!" I insisted. "I'm soaked in blood. Can't you see the blood all over me?" I looked at my pants, which were soaking wet, but not with blood.

"Ma'am, your water broke. You're in labor."

"I am?" I wiped my red nose.

"Yes, ma'am."

"Are you sure?" I asked. He nodded. "I am absolutely, positively not having a miscarriage?"

"No, ma'am."

"But I'm not due till February," I protested.

"Ma'am, you'll be delivering in December," he said. "Or January."

"Hallelujah!" shouted Alfie. "Can she still take the ambulance or do we need to call a cab?"

"We'll take her," said another paramedic.

"The hospital's just across the street," I reminded them.

Alfie rubbed his hands with glee. "This baby's a drama queen already!"

For the first time, I smelled the food from Anjoli's shopping bags, and remembered her party. "What about your party?" I asked.

"We'll be back by then," Anjoli assured. "How long can a simple delivery take?" Anjoli always acts as if extended labor is a matter of laziness. She delivered me in less than two hours and firmly believes that if women just set their minds to it, they could do the same. She had some sort of bizarre fantasy that before the clock struck midnight, the kid would be dressed in a fabulous sequined tuxedo and be serenaded by Alfie.

"Call Jack, please!" I requested of Alfie as I was placed on the gurney.

By the time I got checked into the labor and delivery ward, it was dark and the rest of the world had moved into New Year's Eve celebration mode. The staffers were watching the New Year being rung in somewhere else in the world.

"Lucy, Lucy, Lucy!" Alfie rushed into my room. "No one's answering the phone at your house. What's Jack's cell number, hon?" I gave it to him, disappointed in the knowledge that, with party traffic, it would be another two hours before he arrived.

Anjoli was generous in spirit. She was genuinely trying to be helpful. It's just that listening was never her sharpest skill. Despite numerous attempts to convince Anjoli that I was neither hot nor sweating, she insisted on wiping my brow with a cool rag every few minutes. Three times she asked if I was thirsty. Each time I told her I was not, yet she kept slipping ice cubes in my mouth. After a while, she stopped asking, and just kept feeding them to me like coins in a parking meter.

Our nurse, Betsy, came in to check on me every now and again, but basically labor was a bunch of sitting around and waiting, while nurses charted contractions. "Six minutes apart and seven centimeters dilated," nurse Betsy said, checking a strip of paper from the monitor. "You should be a mommy very soon, Mrs. Klein."

Should?!

"Should?" I shot.

"Yes, *should*," nurse Betsy said. "It could take a little longer." She smiled and shrugged as if to say, "We'll see."

"Do you know my history?" I asked our nurse. As she tilted her head down to read my chart, a mass of wavy brown hair fell over her un-made-up face. She shook her head no. I wasn't a patient at this hospital. My doctor was back in New Jersey undoubtedly enjoying cocktails.

"I've had four miscarriages, one was quite late in the pregnancy," I told her.

She scrunched her face with discomfort and held my hand. "This baby is healthy as they come," nurse Betsy said.

Anjoli deposited another ice chip in my mouth as she passed by my bed. "When is Jack going to get here?" She looked at her watch.

"Your party!" I remembered. "Mother, go home and take care of what you need to. I'll be fine here. What could happen in a hospital full of doctors and nurses?"

Anjoli's head whipped around and her eyes narrowed with fierceness. "Plenty. I'll stay. Besides, my guests won't arrive till ten. We have plenty of time. Alfie, be a love and start the aperitifs, darling?" She tossed her key ring to him.

An hour later, nurse Betsy returned. "How are you doing in here?"

"Exhausted," Anjoli replied.

"I'm fine between contractions," I smiled as I answered the nurse. Betsy gave me a knowing look as though she might have the same type of mother at home. She glanced at the strip that monitored my labor and assured me the baby was doing well. The phone rang. Finally, Jack was calling to say he would arrive shortly. Or at least, that's what I'd hoped. It was Alfie who had some questions about menu preparation for Anjoli. I handed the phone to my mother, who sat straight in her chair and listened carefully.

"No, no, no, darling! The caterer knows I won't serve foie gras. Do you have any idea how cruel they are to those poor little geese? I'll have nothing to do with it. Philippe knows I need *faux* foie gras." She paused. "It's soy-based, Alfie. You'll never know the difference."

Anjoli continued chattering a bunch of French names I assumed were her champagne selections when Betsy whispered, "Would you like to take a shower?" I knit my brows. "It's very relaxing. It takes the edge off the contractions."

"Okay," I nodded. "If you really think it will help."

"Has he lost his mind?!" Anjoli shrieked. "Did you tell him this was for *me*?"

"Mom, we're going to go—"

"Hold on a second, darling," Anjoli said to Alfie. "Where are you going, Lucy? To get more ice?"

"Yeah, I need more ice," I said, clutching Betsy's arm.

"Let the girl get it," she shooed with her hand. "Never mind, it's probably good for your circulation for you to take a little walk. Anyway, Alfie, tell Philipe I need the soy-based foie gras or Kiki will have my head. She was the one who told me about those wretched feeding tubes they use on those sweet little geese."

When we arrived at the shower, I stepped into a small room with yellow bathroom tiles and a small bench where the father was supposed to sit. "Can I take my cane in with me?" I asked the nurse.

"It's handicap accessible," Betsy replied. "Grab the rail and you'll be much safer than trying to balance on a cane. How long have you had the Bell's palsy?"

I told her it was about a month and was pleased when she said I was having a remarkably fast recovery. "It's hardly noticeable," she said. "You're lucky."

"Luck, nothing," I snapped in a friendly defense. "I've been doing forty minutes of face exercises every day for the last month."

"Wow, impressive. Okay, press this button when you need me to come around and help you back to your room."

I wasn't sure how long I'd been in the shower, but I believe I came dangerously close to using the entire hospital hot water supply. When Betsy came to help me back to my room, I looked at the clock and saw it had been forty minutes. Something about the hot water was a sedative and muscle relaxer. And feeling clean is always so rejuvenating.

When I arrived back at the room, Jack was there and Anjoli had returned to her apartment. He explained that she had an entertainment emergency and had to get back to the apartment to assist Alfie. Apparently, the party supply store delivered horns that guests would have to squeeze, like the ones clowns use for their unicycles, instead of the traditional foil-fringed blower. Quel horror!

"Hey, kiddo," Jack said warmly. "How're you doing?"

"It's like the worst period cramp I've ever had, over and over, every five minutes," I said, realizing that gave him absolutely no way to relate. "Very bad, but not as bad as I expected."

"The nurse said the baby's doing exactly what he's supposed to be doing in there," he said.

"He's well behaved already."

"Your face is almost back to normal," Jack said.

And yours is beautiful, I didn't say. I'd forgotten how handsome Jack is, with his chiseled features and dark brown hair. He has a baseball player's body—tall and muscular with wide shoulders and a thin waist. He has an olive complexion that highlights his green eyes exquisitely. But his best feature is his lips. The bottom lip is thin and uneven, the right side a bit fuller than the left. Unlike my Bell's palsified face, Jack's asymmetry worked to create a sexy, inviting look.

"The face workout worked," I said awkwardly, hoping he wouldn't notice I was a bit nervous to see him. "Did I interrupt your night?" I said, referring to the fact that he was dressed in a tuxedo.

"Yeah," he laughed. "You can guess how well this went over. My date's sitting there, like your *what* has gone into *what*?"

I burst with laughter at the thought of Jack having to explain to his girlfriend that he had a pregnant wife. What a piece of shit, she must have thought him. God knows, I did on several nights as I lay awake in my old bedroom, wondering what my sort-of-single husband was up to. "You'll explain it to her in the morning," I reassured Jack.

"I doubt it. Sheila made it pretty clear that she didn't want to hear from me again."

Sheila?! Sheila?! What kind of name is Sheila? Probably some type of, of, of ahhhhhhh!!!! The pain is back. It's Sheila. She's made a voodoo doll of me and is sticking pins in the belly.

"Jack, get the nurse!" I shouted.

He rushed out of the room and returned with Betsy, who lifted my gown and announced that it was time to push. But before any pushing began, she rolled my bed into a different room, one with forest wallpaper, bright lights, and surgical tools. "Focus on the trees, Lucy," Betsy urged when she saw my look of horror. There had to be some sort of joke about not being able to see the forest for the trees, but for the life of me, I couldn't figure out what it was. "Breathe in deep through the nose, out with the mouth," she said. Jack started repeating everything Betsy said as he held my hand at the side of the bed. "Let me get the doctor," Betsy rushed out.

"This is it, Lucy," Jack said, wrapping both hands around my one. "This is what we've been waiting for. It's all come down to this moment. You got what it takes to deliver this kid into the world and be the best mom ever."

I know he meant well, but I started to feel like an athlete going into the big game. My heart pounded, but not with fear, exactly. With performance anxiety. "You can do this, kiddo. A couple pushes and we're in there."

A couple pushes turned into a couple hours and pretty soon I heard Dick Clark's voice on the television, announcing that the ball would drop in Times

Square in less than a minute. I pushed one more time before nurse Betsy leaned in close and whispered the greatest piece of maternal wisdom I'd ever heard. "Push like it's a bowel movement, honey," she said. Now, no new mother likes to think of her child as a vaginally delivered piece of shit, but I had to admit there was something to this.

The doctors and nurses all started chanting for me. "Ten, nine, eight, seven . . ." Okay, maybe they were watching the ball drop, but I found it very inspiring. "Three, two, one!" And as they blew horns and shouted "Happy New Year," the small voice of my son let out a tiny wail.

Chapter 10

Ilifted my head to see a light coat of white fur covering the back of a grayish-blue baby curled in a small ball. He was slick with blood and goop and a ropy cord hung from his belly, disproportionately larger than any of his other features. He had a full head of brown hair like Jack's that made him look as though he was in one of those boy bands where the kids over-gel their hair so it stands in every direction. "Is he healthy?" I asked.

"Ten fingers, ten toes," Betsy said.

"What about his face?" I asked.

"He's a looker," Jack answered.

"On both sides?" I asked.

Betsy leaned in and placed her hand on my shoulder. "Both sides of his face are crying."

Thank you, God. I will never, ever ask for another thing as long as I live.

"Care to cut the cord, Dad?" asked the doctor. I did not know it at the time, but this was the official start of our son's doctors referring to Jack and me as "Dad" and "Mom." Jack stepped forward without hesitation, as though our son's umbilical cord was all in a day's work.

If it were me, I'd be so nervous, I wouldn't be able to follow through. Jack seemed entirely at ease as he snipped my son loose from my body. I knew then that, whatever hesitation I had about this whole co-parenting deal, it would be the best arrangement for the baby. He needed a levelheaded parent around the house. The inevitable slips and falls that drew blood from kids would be ably dealt with by Jack. Jack and I would provide a good balance for the baby. Of course, I would have preferred a husband who was madly in love with me, but this arrangement beat going it alone.

"What about the cord blood?" Jack inquired. At first, I thought this was some sort of weird Angelina Jolie kind of thing where Jack wanted to wear a vial of his son's cord blood around his neck. Rather, he'd heard about preserving the cord blood, which contained the baby's cells, so they could be reproduced down the line if the baby should encounter a genetic disease or serious injury.

"We can do that," the doctor said. "It's pretty pricey and the chances you'll ever need to use it are exceptionally rare."

"We'll do it," Jack and I said in unison. When I say we didn't have extra cash to burn, I mean, we really truly did not have a dime to spare. We hadn't been on more than a weekend vacation in ten years, our home was only half furnished, and we both drove early model jalopies. It's not that we were poor; it's just that quite a bit of our money was tied up in Jack's business and, though we bought our home at a steal, we still carried a $250,000 mortgage on it. The house was actually one of our better investments, but it was also one of the economic realities that kept us bound. We could sell the house for a hefty profit, but not enough of one to manage two households. When the doctor uttered those two horrible words, "exceptionally rare," we both knew we'd find a way to pay for the umbilical cord preservation.

Nurse Betsy immediately placed my detached baby on my stomach and wrapped us in a warm cotton blanket fresh from the drier. His arms splayed across my body and melted into me like a pat of butter sinks into a warm muffin. His ten little toes pressed against my thigh as though they were taking root. I looked at his little face with its spider of purple veins on his right eyelid and giggled.

"What's so funny?" Jack asked.

"I don't know." My eyes welled with tears. "He's just so cute. And he's here. God, Jack, he's *here*," I sighed. No one but Jack knew what the hell I was talking about, but nurse Betsy was sobbing too. I wondered if she cried at every delivery, or if my son was just especially, touchingly beautiful.

"This is the sweetest baby I've ever seen," she continued sobbing.

"Bets, you say that every time," the doctor laughed.

"It's true every time, you cynical old fart." She swatted him with a cloth.

My baby's face reminded me of Mr. Magoo at his angriest. All facial skin seemed to gather at his nose.

Nurse Betsy said her shift was ending, but she wanted to get me started breast-feeding. "He should nurse within the first hour of life, so let's get him washed up and I'll get you started."

"I'm so glad you were our nurse, Betsy," I smiled. "Thank you for thinking my son is beautiful." She hugged me with one arm as she held my son in the other.

"I don't think it; I know it." She gave a giggle of a hiccup as she began washing her hands at the basin.

Jack and the doctor stood facing each other awkwardly. They shook hands and bristled something at each other that sounded like a thank you, and an acknowledgment of thanks. The doctor stood motionless in front of Jack for a few more seconds, seemingly waiting for something. *Are we supposed to tip him?* I wondered. "All right then, if that's all. It's been a pleasure," the doctor said, dismissing himself.

When Betsy returned, Jack excused himself to make telephonic birth announcements. "Wanna see something neat?" Betsy asked.

"Well, I don't know, Besty," I said lightly. "I just squeezed a baby from my body. I don't know what could possibly top that."

"This'll come pretty close," she returned. She placed the freshly scrubbed baby on my stomach and instructed me to resist the urge to lead him to my breast. "Open your gown all the way so he knows they're there. Watch how he instinctively crawls to your breasts to nurse." And sure enough, like a little inch worm he wiggled right up to my right nipple and clamped onto it. Motherhood was so easy, I thought, relaxing into my pillow. It's so beautiful and natural . . . My miracle-of-birth, natural-wonders-of-the-universe dream state was interrupted by the last thing in the world I expected to see—a television camera and a reporter wearing more base makeup than the drag queens at Lips.

My left breast was completely exposed while my son's head covered my right nipple. His head was little bigger than Janet Jackson's Super Bowl pastie, so I hardly took comfort in this shield. Before I could say, "What the hell is a TV camera doing in the maternity ward?" the reporter was in my room. They were there to see me, or more specifically, my son, the first baby born in the New Year.

"This looks like my exit cue," Betsy whispered. "My husband has a bottle of bubbly chilled at home, so time for me to fly." She kissed my forehead and told me it was an honor to be part of my "birth experience." And with that, she flew out of my room, like an angel.

Posing a stark contrast to Betsy's ethereal presence was a man with a plastic helmet of black hair and creases in his pancake makeup that looked as though they'd been cut with a knife. "We're live at St. Vincent's Hospital in Greenwich Village with the first New York baby of the New Year. Born—get this—at exactly the stroke of midnight. Not a second earlier, not a second later. How's that for perfect timing?"

Far better than your intrusion into my first ten minutes of motherhood, sir. Can they just burst in here like this, unannounced? Don't they have to get my permission to film me and my baby? They're lucky I'm not too vain and concerned about the fact that my hair is a big knot on the top of my head, I'm wearing no makeup, and my face is functioning at half capacity! They're lucky I'm not in the witness protection program or some ultra-private Greta Garbo type, or they'd be in big trouble.

"Congratulations, Mom!" the reporter spoke his first words to me.

"Um, thanks," I pulled the bedcovers over my exposed breast. "You're not getting my boobs on film, are you?"

He burst into forced laughter and looked into the camera. "What a kidder! The things you get with live TV, eh, Frank and Jackie?" *Who the hell are Frank and Jackie? Where the hell is Jack?* "So, Mom, tell everyone how it feels to deliver the first baby of the New Year? Pretty crazy, isn't it?"

"I wouldn't put it that way."

"Okay, then, why don't you tell our folks at home about how it feels to have New York's first baby of the Neeeeew Year!" *Where is Jack?*

"I guess if I had to try to articulate it, I'd have to say

I feel several different, conflicting emotions that are at the same time completely congruous, if that makes any sense at all. First, I feel such enormous relief and gratitude that my baby is here in my arms with me." With that, my eyes flooded. "We had such a tough time, and so many disappointments, and now that I'm holding this baby, I still remember, but all the pain has washed away. I am so, so amazingly grateful that this beautiful, healthy baby is my son. I feel humbled, really just so humbled, but also proud, too. The human body and the human spirit are really so amazingly resilient. This is my fifth pregnancy," I sniffed. "My *fifth* pregnancy. And it's my first birth. I just want to fall to my knees and give thanks to whatever divine spirit rules this world, because I am so grateful to finally be a mother. I'm terrified too. This baby is so small and so vulnerable. All of his first choices are in my hands, and I want to make the right ones. I don't want to make any mistakes, and yet I know I will. I just hope that everything I have and every ounce of my love are enough to make him happy. I'm so afraid that I won't be a good enough mother, and at the same time, I feel such assuredness that I will because every bit of me instinctively knows that this is my little soul mate, and we're going to be just fine. After everything, and after all the heartache in getting here, I know that we're going to have a beautiful life together."

That went on a bit longer than I'd originally planned. Not that I had much time to plan. "Was that too long?"

"Too long *and* too heavy," the reporter said. "I told them to cut to a Chevy commercial right after all the stuff about your miscarriages. No one wants to hear that kind of thing on New Year's Day, lady. They want something more upbeat, more—"

"Crazy?" I asked.

"Exactly."

"Lucy!" Jack burst into the room. "I was calling my parents and I saw you on television. You were great! You know, everyone in the lounge is crying and hugging each other. It's like a scene out of *It's a Wonderful Life* down there. Mothers are asking their grown children if every ounce of *their* love was enough and if they knew how much they loved them."

I turned to the reporter. "I thought you said I was cut off for a truck commercial." Turning to Jack, I asked, "What was the last thing I said?"

"That, despite your intense trepidation about the monumental responsibility and vulnerability of motherhood, you instinctively knew everything would be all right. Lucy, I'm telling you, you really hit a nerve. Frank and Jackie at the news desk were getting misty. They had to cut to a commercial because Frank couldn't talk about tomorrow's college bowl games without getting a flutter in his voice. He actually asked if they could take a break so he could call his mother."

"Frank the Tank?" asked the reporter.

"You know it, man," Jack said.

"Whatever," he said. And with that, they left.

A new nurse entered the room with a decidedly different demeanor than nurse Betsy. She had a slit of a mouth that never curled up in the slightest, even as she spoke. It was as though she had a wired jaw. Her natural blond hair was pulled in a tight bun and her icy blue eyes completed the look of the Aryan poster child. She walked with such a military cadence that I swore I heard Darth Vader music accompany her every time she approached.

"I've come to take the baby," Fraulein Helga announced.

"I've decided to keep him with me in the room," I said, looking to Jack for support.

"Your hospital offers the rooming-in option," he told

her. It did? There was a name for keeping the baby in the room with you? Thank God for Jack. As long as I remained completely oblivious to his athletic good looks, his sweet charm, and his encyclopedic knowledge, this arrangement would work out just fine.

"The baby needs quiet to sleep." Helga would have none of our nonsense.

"I passed the nursery ten minutes ago," Jack told her. "The place was lit like a refrigerator and every baby was crying hysterically. Our baby's asleep."

"Babies need to learn independence," Helga shot.

"He's forty-five minutes old," Jack countered.

I fell in love twice that night. First with the baby that had taken years to find its way to me. And second with the husband I'd spent years drifting apart from.

Chapter 11

Later that morning, I opened my eyes to see Jack asleep in a chair beside my bed, and our son sleeping in a Lucite bassinet beside him. The hospital dressed him in a tiny white undershirt, a blue knit cap, and a pair of diapers that looked too big. His legs were like little twigs curled into his chest where his head was also protectively tucked away. I knew babies didn't sleep with their hands stretched behind their heads like Jack was positioned, but I didn't expect my newborn to still be in the fetal position.

Jack opened his eyes, looked at his watch, and smiled. "Morning, kiddo. Two hours, that's pretty good," he said. I actually felt pretty well rested and hadn't remembered being awake two hours ago, but then again, everything was a bit hazy.

"Were we up at six?" I asked.

"The men in the family were," he winked. "I hope you don't mind but when you told me about that trick nurse Betsy did with the breast-feeding, I figured I could just hold him to your boob and let him latch on without waking you."

"Wow, and he just did it?"

"A nurse came in and did this little tickling his cheek deal, which made him open his mouth wide, and I put your breast right in his mouth, like the nurse told me," Jack said.

I giggled, a bit embarrassed about being manhandled in my sleep, but more grateful for the six-hour block of rest. "So what did she do, just tickle his cheek?"

Jack nodded. "You know, Luce, that's something we need to figure out today—what his name is going to be. We keep calling him, well, him." We hadn't discussed names because every time we had before, it made the loss that much more real. Whenever Jack dared to connect with my bulging tummy, he always referred to it as "buddy" or "little guy." Now it was time for little guy to get a real name. "Hey, by the way, Lucy, the kid scored a perfect ten on his Apgar," Jack said proudly. I already knew I was going to be one of those obnoxious boastful parents because, though I had no idea at the time what an Apgar test was, I was beaming.

"Do you have any ideas for a name, Jack?"

"I was kinda thinking Adam."

"Your grandfather's name," I said.

"Unless you want to name him after your father," Jack offered.

"Adam's a good name. Let's go with Adam."

"Lucy, this is going to mean the world to my grandfather," Jack said.

I sighed with regret that my own father wasn't with me for Adam's birth. Even with Jack, and the fast-approaching staccato of my mother's heels in the hospital corridor, I felt incredibly alone without him. Not alone, I suppose, but incomplete. Anjoli burst into the room like a firework with gifts in wildly colored wrapping paper and curly ribbon exploding from every side.

"What a fabulous baby!" she pronounced upon seeing Adam. "What are we calling him, darling? My numerology consultant said Oyl would be a good name for his birth date and time."

"Oil?" Jack asked.

"O-*Y*-L," Anjoli spelled.

"It's pronounced oil, though?" he asked.

"We've named him Adam," I said.

Anjoli looked at Adam asleep in the bassinet. "That feels right," she said. Jack shot me a look of relief that she wasn't going to lobby for naming our kid Oyl, however it was spelled. He and Anjoli get along just fine, but like anyone else, Jack doesn't particularly like having a disagreement with her. Anjoli never gets particularly contentious. Rather, she calmly piles on endless servings of New Age philosophy till you can't help but surrender just to make the chatter stop. Jack calls Anjoli "the vapor" because she occupies every corner of every space she's in. It's not just the bags of assorted seeds, sprouting jars, and vitamins—it's her energy. It's everywhere. She's in the corners of the kitchen ceiling, where streams of cobwebs need to be cleaned with a broom.

Kimmy's entrance with a giant stuffed panda was followed by Zoe, who came bearing giant mums with blue ribbon wrapped around the ridged glass vase.

"Flowers!" Anjoli exclaimed. "What a lovely gesture, darling, but I'm allergic to flowers."

Zoe, one of the few people who was not intimidated by Anjoli, told her that mums have no scent.

"It's not the scent. It's the pollen. My eyes are going to start burning any moment now."

"That's odd, because I specifically chose mums because I saw them at one of your dinner parties last year," Zoe said, placing the vase on my nightstand.

"Let me see this little cutie pie!" Adam was in my arms nursing again. He'd just woken up, but as soon as I put him to my breast, he dozed off again.

Kimmy asked if it was okay to watch me nurse. She felt awkward staring at my boobs, although a million homebound New Yorkers had seen a similar sight the night before. "It's okay, except I'm a little nervous that no milk's coming!"

"Colostrum, kiddo!" Jack laughed. "Your milk will come in a few days."

"He's from La Leche League," I told my visitors, never imagining that in a very short while I'd desperately call on that very group.

Our first few days back in Caldwell, I felt as though Adam and I were in our own private universe. I woke up every two hours to the sound of Adam's little squeals for milk. While the rest of the world slept, I sang songs through an almost fully functioning mouth, changed diapers, and nursed. On my third day home, I wondered why I insisted on feeding Adam while sitting in a glider chair. I brought him to the bed with me and we both fell asleep while he nursed. Much better. While the rest of the world was drinking coffee, jogging, and leafing through the morning paper, Adam and I were out. As kids walked home from school, we were on our third nap.

On my fifth day home, I'd spent an hour pacing, rocking, and cooing Adam until he finally drifted off to sleep. Then the phone rang. Adam screamed like a siren, and I nearly burst into tears that we were both jolted from our much-needed nap. I heard the familiar delay of a telemarketing call after I answered. Crackle, crackle, crackle . . . "Hello, is Lucy Clean dere?" the voice of sheer stupidity asked.

"Who is this?" I snapped, knowing it was no one I wanted to speak with.

"Is this Lucy Clean?"

"Who are *you?*"

"Oh, dis Angela," she said. "Can you put Lucy Clean on da phone, please?"

"Angela," I lost patience. "Who the hell are you and what do you want?"

"Is this Lucy Clean?"

"No, it's not," I said, truthfully. After six days of motherhood, clean isn't exactly the mispronunciation of my name that fit best.

"When would be a better time to call Mrs. Clean?" she asked. I suddenly had an image of a muscular bald chick with her arms folded across her undershirt.

"There is no Mrs. Clean! Don't call here again."

"Is this the person authorized to make the long distance phone service decisions?"

I fumed. Didn't she hear my baby crying in the background? I wanted this woman dead. "If you ever call this house again, Angela, I will hunt you down and kill you and feed your dismembered limbs to wild animals and . . ." She hung up. Strangely, I found the conversation extremely cathartic, as I was getting less patient and more furious with every sleep-erratic day.

Jack was helpful in his own way, but no one else could do the night feedings. Plus, Jack was now the primary breadwinner, so it was my job to let him sleep through the night, get to his gallery every day, and sell lots of art. When I was well rested, I could see the logic in this arrangement. Other times, I heard him humming in the shower and vividly imagined recreating the Bates Motel. When he was done, he'd pop his head into my bedroom and say, "Morning, kiddo." This new nickname was getting so old. And in just one week, I felt I was, too. I walked like my eighty-year-old aunts and was as cranky as the hundred-year-old man who had his window smashed by an errant baseball one too many times. Even through the cloud of sleepy haze, I could see that Jack looked good wrapped in a skirted towel. Damned good.

After our first week home, I decided it was time to revisit Desdemona on the cobblestone road. "She was weeping uncontrollably," I wrote before realizing it was actually me crying at my keyboard. The whole world was bustling about doing important, creative things. I hadn't been dressed in three days and couldn't get past my first sentence of the novel I claimed I'd always wanted to write.

Though I had an easy first week of breast-feeding, it was starting to feel like there was broken glass in my breasts. The pain was so intense, it stung my skull. I called Anjoli and asked for her advice.

"I haven't the slightest idea what you should do, darling. I bottle-fed you," she said.

"You did?"

"I refuse to feel guilty about this. I was very young and naively listened to my doctor, who said formula was best," Anjoli said. "I refuse to apologize for it. I did the best I could with the resources I had at the time, and merely—"

"Okay, okay! I was just a little surprised, that's all. It's hard to imagine Miss Health Food buying Carnation instant formula."

"Darling, my mother told me to put whiskey on my fingertip and let you suck it off to get you to sleep longer. I broke the cycle of alcoholism. Formula's certainly better than what I got."

My grandmother was a trip. As flamboyant as my mother, but an alcoholic instead of a New Age workshop addict. Years ago, my cousin's three-year-old daughter returned from a month stay with Grammy, and went back to preschool asking for chardonnay during snack time. We think Emma simply heard the word a lot, instead of having actually acquired a taste for wine, but with Grammy you could never be certain.

"Mom, I'm having a tough time managing," I said softly.

"Motherhood is exhausting, darling," she sighed in solidarity. "I remember when you were learning to walk, I thought I was going to lose my mind with the way you pulled every record out of its case, every cereal box from the cupboards, and every—"

I couldn't help interrupting. "Mom, that was nearly forty years ago. I'm having trouble today. Can you come out and help me?" If she said no, I'd simply collapse in tears. We couldn't afford to hire a nurse. Jack was in the city most of the day, and I hadn't made a single friend in Caldwell since we moved. "Please come out and help me."

I waited for what seemed an eternity as she contemplated the logistics. "Alfie could open the shop and we could always hire one of the kids from one of the stage crews. God knows they always need a little extra day work. Hmmm, this could work, this could work. Are you sure you don't want to come into the city and stay with me? You could bring all of your baby stuff here. It won't get in my way, darling."

"Mom, please. I want to be in my home. Can't you just come to me this once?"

When Jack came home that night, I informed him that Anjoli would arrive on Saturday to help with Adam. He laughed. "Is she going to *help* or create more work for you?"

"Jack." I didn't have the energy to scold with more than one word.

"Why so blue, kiddo?"

"I miss my dad," I said. "I wish he was here to share this. I wish he could see Adam and be a part of his life."

Jack put his arms around me as though we were in a Life Savers commercial. "Don't be sad, Luce. Think of all the good times you had with Sammy and be grateful for that."

I hated this trite platitude people shot out when they were uncomfortable with another person's mourning. It was really a manipulative ultimatum. I *was* grateful for the time we had together. I was also grief-stricken by the loss of it. It would be better if people would simply say, "Know what? I can't deal with seeing you in pain, so can you just take it out of my sight, please, and come out of your room when you're ready to slap a pretty little smile on and tell me that everything is just peachy?"

Chapter 12

As Jack predicted, Anjoli wasn't much of a help around the house. She and I stared at Adam's scab of a belly button in a state of mutual puzzlement. "How did you remove mine?" I asked.

"I can't remember. I don't think you had one of those, darling," she said, looking disgusted with it. I had to admit, it was a pretty awful sight. But I didn't want to yank it off prematurely simply because I was uncomfortable looking at it. Then I remembered that Adam had a pediatric appointment that afternoon.

"We'll ask the doctor," I suggested. Anjoli rolled her eyes as if to say, *Ah yes, let us all bow to the altar of the medical establishment, for they know all*. Yet she was as clueless as I was about what to do with this grotesque belly scab.

Changing gears, Anjoli told me that in a few days some of her friends would be coming to see the baby. "Oh, um, okay. That's fine." I liked all of Anjoli's friends, but I knew my mother prided herself on entertaining properly—a task I wasn't up to in the best of circumstances. Plus, I knew she wouldn't be any help while she was fluttering around pouring herbal tea and regaling her drama posse with tales from the crib. She would characterize herself as the overworked grandmother, when the truth was she had yet to even hold Adam. She certainly hadn't changed a diaper, nor had she volunteered to watch him so I could take a nap or go to a movie. And Jack was right—she was creating more housework. All of her clothing needed to be washed separately in the gentle cycle (by me). And every time she was finished preparing a meal (for herself), she left vegetable scraps all over the kitchen floor. She had her moments where she tried to help, but on these rare occasions, the assistance was utterly worthless. Once, while she toiled away at the kitchen sink, I overheard Jack ask Anjoli why she didn't wash the backs of the plates. "The backs don't get dirty, darling," she lilted.

"They do, Anjoli," Jack returned. "When I cleared the table, I stacked the dishes on top of each other, so you see, there's a pat of butter stuck to the back of this plate and a bit of corn on this one."

"Hmmm," Anjoli said, noticing Jack had a point. "So they do." And yet, she changed nothing. The next morning, there was a drying rack filled with butter-backed plates perched on a counter sprinkled with stray seeds.

As we drove to Dr. Comstock's office, Anjoli asked what type of pie people eat.

"What?" I asked.

"*Pie.* What type of pie do people eat?" She repeated the question, giving me no more information.

"What are you talking about?" I asked.

"Thursday, Kiki, Felix, Alfie, and Fiona are coming out to see me. I need to put a little coffee and pie out to serve." *Oh God, here we go.*

"I don't know, Anjoli. What kind of pie do you normally serve people?" She already knew exactly what kind of pie she planned to serve. We were going through this ritual so she could remind me that she was from this non-pie-eating species, and had no idea what *people* ate.

"Remind me that we need to pick up pie on Thursday morning. They're coming all the way out to New Jersey, the least we can do is serve a decent pie. Where can we purchase a pie, darling?" Mother always seemed to think that the trip from the city to Caldwell was somehow longer and more burdensome than the other way around.

"A bakery, I guess," I rolled my eyes. "Mom, Jack is going to be home on Thursday. How long are your friends visiting for?"

She put her hand to her chest, hurt by the question. "Do you have issues with my friends visiting?"

"No, it's just that Jack is taking the day off to be with Adam, and I want to figure out when he can get some father-son time."

"Oh good, Jack can drive me to the pie shop that morning!" Anjoli said. The poster child for adult attention deficit disorder, my mother looked out the car window and offered, "Look at those kids waiting for the bus, Lucy. Where are they going?" This wasn't some sort of creative improvisation game where we'd make up stories about where we thought the kids were headed. She actually expected me to know. "Chicken Joe's," she read the sign from a fast-food restaurant. "Do they make good chicken?"

"I really don't know, Mother," I said flatly. "I haven't eaten there."

"International House of Pancakes," she lilted. "How very cosmopolitan. Tell me, darling, do they only serve pancakes or is there more on the menu?"

"What are you talking about?"

"The International House—"

"I heard you. Why are you acting as if you've never heard of IHOP? I'm your daughter, you don't have to impress me with how disconnected you are from mainstream culture. I happen to know that you know exactly what an IHOP is."

"Darling, I have no idea! You certainly are moody these days."

"Mother, Daddy told me that on your honeymoon you two ate every breakfast at IHOP and that he'd never seen anyone shovel in quite as many waffles as you could."

"I was a dancer," she humphed. "I had to eat large meals."

"At IHOP! My point is *not* that you ate large meals, it's that you ate at IHOP, you know good and well what the International House of Pancakes is—and that they serve waffles, eggs, bacon, and even grits in the South—not just pancakes."

"Oh yes, now I remember. Honestly, I don't know what you're so huffy about, darling. I came out here to help and you're downright abusive. I'm simply trying to make conversation."

"Well let's see. So far, we've talked about pie, where kids are going on the bus, Chicken Joe's, and IHOP. Riveting. How 'bout asking me how I'm adjusting to motherhood? How 'bout asking if I'm dying inside watching Jack go off to his separate bedroom and call me 'kiddo' every morning? Were you at all curious why we're going to the pediatrician this afternoon? Might you want to know why I'm sweating and gritting my teeth every time I nurse, which just FYI is every two hours?"

After a few minutes of silence, Anjoli returned from gazing out the passenger window and asked, "So, darling. How's it going?"

I laughed. It was impossible for me to stay angry with my mother. "Promise me something, okay, Mom?"

"Anything, darling. You know I'd do anything for you."

"Do *not* be rude to Dr. Comstock."

"Rude?" She looked seriously perplexed.

I lifted Adam from his car seat and placed him in a baby sling that Zoe gave me as a shower gift. All this kid ever did was sleep, but at our last checkup, Dr. Comstock assured me that this was normal and my son was not bound to be a lazy, good-for-nothing slacker as I'd feared. I suppose I should have done more in terms of educating myself about infants, but I always felt that in doing so, I was tempting fate.

When Dr. Comstock entered the exam room, his eyes shot directly to my mother. I was used to this. She was a stunning-looking woman who drew even more attention to herself by wearing colorful scarves, feathered hats, and low-cut blouses. "Well, hello, Mom," he said, more excited to see me than he'd ever been. "I see you brought your sister with you today." *Oh God, how cheesy!* He glanced at her left hand and I saw the beginnings of a smirk on my mother's face. She glanced at his wedding ring and smiled dismissively at it. *Oh no! I smelled pheromones in the air. Gross.*

"My *daughter* didn't tell me she had such a charming pediatrician," Anjoli leaned forward in her seat and extended her hand. "Anjoli L'Fontaine." God strike me dead if the old white-coated geezer didn't kiss her hand.

"What an unusual name," he said, still holding her dainty hand in his.

"I'm an unusual woman," she shot back immediately.

"I can see that."

"Okay, so anyway, Dr. Comstock, nursing has become extremely painful and I'm not really sure what to do about it," I said.

"Nor am I," Dr. Comstock said. "I gotta be honest, I don't know a whole heck of a lot about breast-feeding. Have you tried calling La Leche League?"

"My, my, Dr. Comstock," Anjoli said. I swore the next words out of her mouth were going to be "I do declare" as she hid behind a lace hand fan. Instead, she finished, "A doctor who admits he doesn't know everything. How very unusual *you* are."

"So anyway, Adam is still peeing about eight times a day and pooping four times, so he's right on track with the chart you gave me." I said, though it got absolutely no response. "He didn't have any reaction to the vaccine, so that was a relief."

"Yes," Dr. Comstock said. Finally, I'd reclaimed the pediatrician's attention. "I try to empower my patients by not leading them to believe I have all the answers." *What? Just last week, I asked a question and you said, "You came to the right place. When it comes to babies, I have all the answers."*

"We got the meconium poop just like you said," I struggled. "But my mother and I were wondering how we remove the umbilical cord scab."

"Excuse me." Dr. Comstock finally turned to me. Then he asked my mother what she was wondering about.

"That dreadful-looking scab, darling," she said. "Whenever can we stop looking at that thing?"

He burst into laughter. "You are so refreshingly honest, Anjoli. May I call you by your first name?"

"Certainly . . ." She paused for his.

"Edward," Dr. Comstock answered. "I can't tell you how many grandmothers come in here and pretend they're charmed by every bowel movement their little ones make. You are so genuine." *Ask her about IHOP!* Never breaking eye contact, he assured Anjoli that the scab would fall off on its own in a few days.

"So how are you doing, Mom? Are you breastfeeding?"

On the drive home, we avoided talking about the unbelievably gross spectacle she and Dr. Comstock, oh excuse me, Edward, made of themselves. Instead, Anjoli asked if we should buy our pies that evening. "Will they keep for two days?"

"We can buy them fresh Thursday morning," I said. "I'll take you to a nice little bakery where they have everything from apple to mincemeat."

"Oh, Kiki's a vegetarian."

"Mother, mincemeat isn't meat and besides, all I meant was that they have a large selection."

"What do people like best?" *Again with the people. What planet did she fancy herself from?*

"People like apple pie," I declared, absolutely certain my suggestion would be rejected.

"Not pumpkin?" she asked.

"People like pumpkin pie too. We should absolutely get the pumpkin pie."

"What is mincemeat if not meat, darling?" Anjoli asked me.

"It's an apple-raisin thing. It usually has meat in it though and Kiki's a vegetarian, remember?"

"She's wheat-free, too."

"Well, Mother, pies have wheat in them."

"I want to go look at the pies myself," Anjoli said. "Does the pie place open early?"

"Mom, it's a bakery! They open at, like, five in the morning."

"We don't need to get there *that* early."

"Okay, my point was that they will be open for pie inspection earlier than we could ever, possibly, in our wildest dreams imagine going there."

"You are so cranky. I have an idea. Why don't we drive there now and bring home a pie for you and Jack? That way, I can take a look at the pies they have *and* I can treat you two to a little dessert. I really think a little something sweet will cheer you up. What's Jack's favorite kind of pie?"

"Fuck pie!" I exploded. "Enough about the goddamn pie, already. How 'bout you take the wheel and drive so I'm not sitting straight on this fucking peanut-sized hemorrhoid dangling from my ass? Give me a break and change a diaper! Hold the baby so I can take a shower! I haven't slept a full night in a week. Let me take a nap. I feel like I'm pissing razor blades and no one seems to give a shit that every time I nurse I feel like someone's grinding glass into my breasts. Every time you prepare a meal—for yourself, I might add—you leave my kitchen floor looking like a chicken coop with your lettuce leaves and vegetable scraps all over the place," I shouted insanely. "And all I hear is your incessant, ceaseless, unrelenting chatter about fucking pie! Pie, mother, you are singularly focused on pie! Do you know what that makes you? Absolutely, indisputably in-fucking-sane!"

"Well," she said, as if to ask if I was quite finished. "You certainly are in touch with your rage, darling. This is why you'll never get cancer."

"Take me back to the hospital," I begged no one in particular.

Chapter 13

By Saturday morning, the first snowfall of the season began. It was nice, thick, white snow that clung to the branches of the three trees in my front yard. Before noon, my lawn was carpeted in white and neighborhood children took to the streets with bright-colored saucers and old-fashioned Radio Flyers. Jack stood beside me at the window with Adam swaddled in his baby sling. Anyone driving past our home would've mistaken us for a real family.

"Are your aunts going to be able to drive in this weather?" Jack asked.

"Too late," I answered. "They left Long Island over an hour ago. They either need to finish the drive here in the snow, or drive home in the snow. I'm a little worried too."

"They'll be all right, kiddo. Which one of 'em's at the wheel?"

"Bernice," I told him.

"Better than Rita. Hey, where's Anjoli?"

"Meditating."

"Nursing getting any easier?"

I couldn't understand what the problem was. I called the La Leche League, and they told me to come to their upcoming meeting, which was in a few days. In the meantime, the group leader suggested I use lanolin cream. This provided no relief. When Adam nursed, it didn't feel as though the sucking itself was the problem. My breasts were the epicenters of pain that extended from the tips of my toes to my eyebrow hair. My ob-gyn had no idea what it was. The lactation consultant at her office was puzzled, and Adam's pediatrician was only interested in one set of breasts in my family and they weren't mine.

"No, but I'm going to that support group on Tuesday and maybe someone will be able to give me some tips," I said. "I don't know if I can make it another day like this."

Jack patted me on the back and assured me I could do anything I put my mind to. He went into our kitchen and offered to make a cup of hot chocolate with marshmallows. As I watched him wipe down the gold-speckled white counter, I dreamt of remodeling our kitchen. I saw a thinner version of myself bustling about a rich cherrywood, modern rustic kitchen with a stainless steel sink and a double-door sub-zero. I imagined the yellow Maytag being replaced by a brushed silver Bosch, and granite floors to replace our linoleum that curled at the corners. I shouldn't have hot chocolate, I told myself. The day I had Adam, I stepped on the scale and was horrified to see that I'd only lost five-and-three-quarters pounds upon delivery, which was even more disturbing considering the baby weighed six. Of course everyone had told me it would take a few months to get back to my pre-pregnancy weight, but I secretly thought that the momentum of delivery was going to help shed not only the pregnancy weight, but an extra ten with it. You know, kind of like my body would feel the removal of the baby and all my blubber would come along for the ride. I thought it would be one great flush toward the exit and I'd be left with the Pamela Anderson body I had in my fantasies. But birth was not the fat vacuum I'd hoped. My hips and belly were far from ready to sport the *Baywatch* red Speedo, but my breasts were a wonder to behold. I couldn't believe how scrumptiously full and round they were. Prior to a feeding, I looked as though I had implants.

"Thanks, Jack," I said, looking at him filling the silver kettle Zoe bought for our wedding. He seemed to make the transition from spouse to friend seamlessly. Though I missed having him as my husband, I must confess, our relationship was far less tense this way. In fact, there was no tension between us at all. I wondered if there was hope for us. If our interactions were amicable as friends, why couldn't they be this easy as lovers? On that note, the doorbell rang. Bernice and Rita made it in one piece.

"Oy," my father's sisters said in unison. "Who made it so easy for any maniac to get a driver's license?" Rita shot in her thick Long Island accent. "Maniacs, lunatics, and imbeciles, all of them," she spat.

Taking their coats, Jack answered, "In the forties, Congress made an economic decision that what was good for GM was good for America, and lowered the standards for driver's licensing to encourage car ownership."

"Don't you love him?" Bernice stamped his cheek with Estée Lauder lipstick. "Married to you all these years and still thinks your family wants answers to their questions," Bernice laughed. "Let me see that gorgeous baby, Mista What's-Good-for-GM-Is-Good-for-Lee-Iaccoca." That was second only to my all-time favorite phrase-butchering of Bernice's. "Try this new oleo," she once offered. "It's called, Would You Believe This Isn't Buttah?" Bernice lifted Adam out of the baby sling and cooed something that sounded like dolphin talk.

"What kind of contraption is that?" Rita asked, pointing to the sling.

I saw Jack stop himself from answering, then offered them hot chocolate instead. "Bernice, bring that baby over here," Rita demanded, parked in her chair. "Has it occurred to you that I'd like to see the child, too?" Our living room was decorated in the early seventies, like the rest of our home. We purchased the house from the estate of a deceased widow whose decorating included seven La-Z-Boy chairs and nothing else. Three were lemon yellow, two were avocado, and the other two were brown and beige paisley. We had a few ugly plywood end tables and one ultra-pedestrian brass floor lamp, but no couch. The pièce de résistance was the Rice-a-Roni brown shag carpet which, now that we had a child who would soon crawl, must go no matter what the price. Jack and I spent every last penny we had on the down payment for the home, so we gladly took the furniture as part of the purchase price. At the time, we were focused solely on the school district, and were quite sure we'd decorate very soon. Instead, very soon, we just stopped caring—about our marriage or our home.

Rita and Bernice were twelve and fourteen years older than my father. They lived within four blocks of each other in Merrick, Long Island, the Promised Land for second-generation Jewish immigrants, and now, their kids. The main street was lined with trendy clothing stores, and take-out restaurants with bravado names: the Bagel Boss, King of Siamese Food, and the Sushi King. There's really very little humility among Merrick business owners.

Rita could find fault with a twenty-one-gun salute in

her honor. "Too noisy," she'd complain. "All that gun powdah makes me cough." Bernice, on the other hand, was overjoyed when a salesman from the cremation place informed her that her ashes would weigh about six pounds. "Thin at last!" she shrieked.

In fairness, Rita had a tougher road of it. She was diagnosed with polio when she was six weeks old and had too many operations to count. She always walked with a limp, which Bernice said looked like a sexy Mae West swagger. This annoyed Rita, but then again, most things did. As much as she complained, though, everyone loved Rita. It was partly fear, but she was also hilariously funny in her ongoing running commentary on the world. To add to Rita's lot, she and Bernice were teens when the Holocaust was destroying European Jews by the millions. Their parents had a plan for if and when Hitler's Third Reich came to America. My father, a toddler at the time, was to be adopted by the German family in the apartment downstairs from theirs. Bernice would go to a convent that had enough space for nine Jewish girls. But Rita had polio so there was no hope for her survival, even if she were a blue-eyed blond German. That's a heavy trip for an eighth grader.

Rita coped by shopping pathologically. I don't mean she bought lots of pretty things for herself and loved ones. She purchased things for people we didn't even know. She anticipated parties, weddings, and showers years in advance. We once braked for a garage sale and she snapped at the seller, "I don't even know what an edgah is!" Bewildered, he informed her that an edger is a gardening tool used to create edges on lawns. "Why would I need that when my gardnah takes care of all of that nonsense?!" Now mind you, Rita pulled over for this garage sale. The man wasn't barking her in or trying to hard-sell the edger once she arrived. He never even suggested she look at it. He simply had it out with all of his other things. "Uch, twenty-five dollahs for a ridiculous edgah. Who needs it?!" She was outraged.

"So don't buy the edgah!" Bernice suggested.

"Not for twenty-five dollahs, I won't!" Rita said. "This crook would never get ovah twenty dollahs from me."

"I'd take twenty for it," the guy said.

Rita raised her eyebrows as if to show us both that she'd revealed his scam. She handed him a crisp twenty dollar bill, gestured for me to load the edger into her car, and walked off muttering that she knew that "piece of crap" wasn't worth twenty-five.

Rita's husband died five years ago. Bernice's passed away last summer. Bernice took to funeral crashing. No one really understood why, least of all her. "I don't know, it's always so lovely to see all the beautiful flowahs and hear the nice things people say about the deceased. Sure, there's crying, but people also have so many stories about the person. I really feel like I get to learn a lot about people," she explained.

Rita rolled her eyes. "*Bernicil,* you're getting to know someone who's dead. What good does it do to know someone who's dead?"

"Rita," Bernice said in her sweet, calming voice. "It's always wonderful to meet someone new, even if they're not around for it." Bernice combed *The New York Times* obituary section and attended two or three services a week. She always read the prominently featured obituaries because the more attendants at a funeral, the less likely she'd be recognized as a crasher. And she never attended funerals of anyone under seventy.

"My sistah says any death of a person youngah than seventy is too sad, like the eighty-year-old ones are a regular Mardi Gras," Rita teased.

As my aunts made themselves comfortable in our living room, my mother emerged from the guest room. She wore a peach silk kimono with an embroidered green dragon on the back. "I thought I heard you two!" She rushed to kiss Rita, then Bernice. "Was the traffic abominable, darlings?"

"Not really," Bernice answered.

"A horror!" Rita contradicted. "Every other car skidding all over the freeway, but you know my sistah, 'lovely, lovely, everything is lovely.'" Rita laughed. "How are you, *mamaleh*? You look stunning."

"You know how it is with a new baby in the house," Anjoli sighed. "No one gets any sleep, but they're precious gifts from the universe that we cherish."

Jack shot me a glance. I wasn't sure if he was commenting on Anjoli's characterization of herself as the sleep-deprived grandmother, or her gifts from the universe mumbo jumbo. Or both.

"We're here to help, Anjoli. Lucy and Jack, you just tell us what you need and we'll take care of everything!" Bernice chimed.

"What are we taking care of? We've been here five minutes," Rita corrected.

"That's sweet of you," I finally spoke. "I'm going to bring everyone a nice slice of pie and coffee. Or would you prefer hot chocolate?" From the kitchen, I shouted, "What I really need is some advice on breast-feeding. It's hurting like hell."

"Breast-feeding?!" my aunts responded at once. "What makes you think we breast-fed?" Rita finished, spitting to her side.

"You didn't nurse?"

"Why would we do that when we had formula?" Rita asked. I saw Jack inhale as though he were going to answer. Then he deflated as my aunt continued. "Don't be such a martyr, Lucy. It's not like you're living in the jungle and there are no supahmahkets to buy formula. I would never breast-feed. I listened to Doctah Spock."

Puzzled, Jack couldn't contain the question. "When did Dr. Spock say women shouldn't breast-feed?"

"Not in so many words," Rita replied. "He said to trust your instincts. My instincts said breast-feeding was disgusting."

Chapter 14

Adam barely made a peep during my aunts' four-hour visit. Bernice said he was very considerate. Rita feared he might be deaf. Jack took Adam to his room to read him *Green Eggs and Ham* for the fifteenth time in his two weeks. I thought it was cute that Jack was already concerned about our son's education. Ridiculous, but sweet. Jack's mother mailed us an article about a study where a group of infants was broken into three categories—babies who heard an average of 3,000 words per hour, 1,500 words, and 500 words. The sociologists followed up on the kids fifteen years later and found that the high-word kids were high achievers in school, bright, articulate, and well-mannered. The average-word kids were doing okay, nothing remarkable either way. And the low-word kids were flunking in school, getting into trouble, and on the wrong track in life. In the days after we received this news clipping, Jack talked to Adam almost nonstop. I saw no harm. I just hoped that he didn't expect our two-week-old son to retain the lecture on earth's major bodies of water Jack gave during bath time.

"How's that lunatic of a friend of yours, Lucy?" Rita asked while Jack was undoubtedly following up his Seuss reading with a discussion of whether *Green Eggs and Ham* was primarily a story about trying new things or persistence. "The one doing the confession show? What's her name, Zuzu?"

"Zoe," I corrected.

Zuzu?

"Whatever her name is," Rita continued. "That girl's out of her mind." I also thought *True Confessions* was doomed for failure, but I didn't like Rita's characterization of my best friend as a lunatic.

"I think it's clevah!" Bernice defended. "I'd be very interested to hear what these Catholics are confessing about. You tell me when that television program has its premiere and I'll tune in."

Rita switched gears to her favorite topic—sex. Her philosophy: What a mess, but so pleasurable. "Speaking of confessions, tell us, have you and Jack been intimate again?" I cringed. "When I had your cousins, the doctahs told us not to have relations with our husbands for six weeks!"

"So we had to call our boyfriends!" Bernice quipped.

"You stole my punch line!" Rita exploded.

"I did no such thing. I thought of a clevah thing to say, so I said it."

"I was about to say the same thing!"

Anjoli interrupted by telling them that they should seriously consider a two-woman show together.

"Really?" Bernice bit.

"Of course, not really, you maniac. She's trying to distract me from the fact that you stole my punch line," said Rita. And with her accusation that my mother was trying to distract her, Rita scanned the room and noticed that Adam was no longer with us. "Where's the baby?"

"With Jack. He's reading to him," I said.

"Reading to him? Tell that moron we didn't drive from Merrick in the snow to have him disappeah with the baby. I want to look at the baby. That baby really should cry more. You need to have his hearing checked, Lucy. I'm telling you, the sooner you know, the faster you can learn sign language." Bernice added, "Like in that beautiful movie, *Mr. Holland's Music Class.*"

After my aunts left, Anjoli asked Jack to give her a lift to the movie theatre. I settled into my glider chair, took a deep breath, and endured the pain of another nursing. I grabbed a copy of *The Womanly Art of Breast-feeding,* but wound up cursing at the pictures of the serene looking women pictured on the pages. They smiled contentedly, almost smugly saying *I'm nursing just fine, why can't you?!* "Liars, frauds, and lunatics!" I accused, not surprisingly, in a Long Island accent.

I picked up the phone to call Mary, the La Leche League leader who urged me to call her "anytime." Nine at night didn't seem too outrageous. By the grace of God, she answered and actually sounded happy to hear from me. "What if I used formula just for tonight and tomorrow, then come to the meeting on Tuesday morning?"

"I'll be there in ten minutes, honey," she said.

Over the past few days, everyone had gotten sucked into my nursing drama. The word "you" became synonymous with "your nipples," as in "How are your nipples this fine morning? . . . Can your nipples have lunch next week? . . . Hey, have your nipples been able to make any headway with the novel?" I even bought plastic protective shields so my bra wouldn't touch my nipples. These hubcaps made me look like Xena's older, fatter sister, Lactatia, the Nipple Warrior whose secret weapon was a milk spray of four feet.

Jack was great, reading a list of benefits of nursing, urging me to "hang in there, kiddo." Still, I needed more practical advice than what Jack could offer.

Mary arrived at my house minutes later in a boob-shaped car with a nipple siren on top. Okay, maybe it was really an early model VW bug, but it looked like a breast to me at the time. With her, Mary carried a yellow page-sized book of questions about breast-feeding. After I explained my problem, she asked if she could look at my nipples. Before her question was articulated, the snaps of my blouse crackled open so fast they sounded like fireworks exploding.

"I can't diagnose anything, you understand, honey, but this looks a whole heck of a lot like a fungus to me," Mary said.

"That's what you said when we talked on the phone," I said.

"And now that I can see your nipples, I'm even more convinced."

"So how does she get rid of it?" Jack asked.

"You've already tried every natural remedy, so why don't you call your doctor tomorrow morning and see about getting a prescription for Diflucan."

We thanked Mary, who told me I wasn't off the hook in coming to her La Leche League meeting on Tuesday. "Don't forget, Lucy! You're going to love meeting other nursing mothers. Unitarian Church at ten. See you there."

I did not want to go to this La Leche League meeting, but felt indebted to Mary. What did we need to meet about? How long could we talk about breast-feeding? But my Jewish guilt would not allow me to simply take Mary's free advice and ditch her meeting. La Leche League it was. I could survive one meeting. But first, I needed to survive the next feeding.

"Jack, I think I'm going to bottle-feed tonight. Just till I can get my doctor to fill the prescription."

"That's not an option, kiddo," he said. He informed me that Mary swept through the kitchen and made Jack hand over all of the baby bottles. "She seemed very serious about it, Lucy. She kept telling me I'd thank her for this someday."

That day was not today. Jack explained that my milk supply would diminish if I took even one day off. How Jack suddenly became a lactation expert was beyond me. Between Jack and his mother's mailings of articles on infant care, he was becoming more of an expert on mothering than I was.

For the next hour, Jack and I tried unsuccessfully to convince the doctor on call to phone in a prescription to the all-night pharmacy. "No can do, *amigo*," he kept saying in a surly Texas accent that suggested he did not consider us amigos at all. A red sports car pulled into our driveway and its headlights shone into our living room. We heard music turn off and voices chatter. Dr. Comstock was sitting in the driver's seat and Anjoli was his passenger. I'd never been so conflicted in my life. On one hand, I hated my mother for making me an accomplice in her adulterous affair with my infant son's pediatrician. On the other hand, Dr. Comstock could have me on my way to the pharmacy in minutes. "Dr. Comstock!" I burst onto my front steps. Saying his name created a cold fog from my breath. Were life equipped with a rewind button, I would've done the second take with slippers on my feet and a sweater tossed over my t-shirt. The pain from the snow on the soles of my feet was minimal compared to the crushed glass beneath my bra.

"Hiya, Lucy!" Dr. Comstock said like a jolly old guy with nothing to be ashamed of. "How'd you two kids get along without Anjoli holdin' down the fort tonight?"

"I need Diflucan!" I shot with no pretense. He looked puzzled. "I have a fungus. I need you to call in a prescription for Diflucan."

"Good God, darling. Let the man in the house before you jump all over him like a dog that hasn't seen his master all day," Anjoli said. They giggled. Anjoli hung her coat in the front closet and offered Dr. Comstock a cup of coffee as she took his coat. "We saw a fabulous film tonight," she began.

Like all of Anjoli's best boyfriends, Dr. Comstock tried to make an ally of me without alienating my mother. "We did," he smiled. "It was great luck bumping into your mother at the Cineplex." *Oh please, even my son wasn't born yesterday.* "What do you need the Diflucan for?"

"I have a fungus. I can't go on another day with this pain. *Please* call the pharmacy so Jack can run and pick up the Diflucan tonight?!"

"Why didn't your ob-gyn write a prescription when he diagnosed you?" Dr. Comstock asked.

"Lucy, darling, I'm not crazy about your taking antibiotics. Why don't you let me try to Reiki your nipples tonight?"

Dr. Comstock raised his eyebrows to question her term.

Jack answered for Anjoli. "Energy healing through the hands." Jack gave Dr. Comstock a subtle eye roll, but he didn't return the gesture. Instead he let out a hearty guffaw and claimed that my mother was "refreshing."

"Who diagnosed you then?" the doctor asked.

"The La Leche League lady," Jack answered.

"They shouldn't diagnose," he said indignantly.

"And why not, darling? You said you don't know

enough about breast-feeding to help my daughter. Her ob-gyn said the same thing. So if you doctors can't help her, why shouldn't she turn to these Leche people?"

"Anjoli," Dr. Comstock said as he sat at the kitchen table. "If I let patients tell me what type of prescriptions they need, I'm basically a drug dealer." No one made a move. It looked as though Jack, Anjoli, and I were frozen as we waited for Dr. Comstock to talk himself into writing the prescription. "Well, I suppose there's no harm to be had from a little Diflucan."

The next morning, the infection had cleared up almost completely. No pain. No sweating. No gnashing my teeth. I was fit for my own page in the nursing book. I was so proud of my new skill, I wanted to share it with everyone. I told my letter carrier about how my nipples were in top form again. He was thrilled for me, really. That day, I was such a show-off I had to resist the urge to lie down on the supermarket floor and squirt my milk into the air like fountains. I thought I had such a choice piece of entertainment, I imagined spending my spring afternoons in the park collecting tips in a tin cup for my milk-producing excellence. I considered opening a game park for milk-shooting wars among new mothers, like paint ball or laser tag. Forget Desdemona and her stupid walk through the rain. I'd produce a *Nipples of Steel* video.

Chapter 15

There's a story from Anjoli's collection of greatest hits that goes something like this. (There's an unspoken rule in my family that you can tell someone else's story for them if you've heard it more than ten times. This policy is not just about ensuring accuracy; it's payback. Like a rewards card for listening to the same blasted story year after year.)

I was twenty-one years old, living with three roommates in Greenwich Village. It'd been two years since I'd run away from Newark, from an oppressive family in an oppressive city in an oppressive state. I was just starting to explore my spirituality, and saw a little ad for a meeting of the Young Metaphysicians on West Thirty-Fourth Street. Fabulous! I showed up and I said to the guy up at the front, "I'm here for the meeting." So he said, "Next door to your left." I went in and the first thing I noticed was all of the great-looking, fabulously dressed men. A few freaks too, but mostly very sharp-looking businessmen in suits. So I sit down, and I suppose I must've been a tad late because there was someone up front talking about his life, and how after

*he divorced he started drinking more heavily, blah,
blah, blah. The first thing I thought was how wonderful
it was that these men were so connected to their feelings. He went on a bit longer, then everyone started
clapping and he sat down. So my second observation
was that these young metaphysicians really needed to
learn to tell a better story. This one was so depressing.
Not even a hint of a kicker. I mean, really, of all places
to have an uplifting ending, you'd think it would be
among a group of spiritualists. So the next guy got up
and he was stunning, obviously gay, but delicious to
look at nonetheless. And believe it or not, his road to
metaphysics was also paved with alcohol.* At this point,
she raises an amused, but suspicious brow. *I didn't want
to be rude and just walk out on this guy's testimony because I know how sensitive these alcoholics can be, but
obviously this was not the meeting I came for. I waited
until he finished, picked up my coat, and stood to leave
when the leader said, "I see we have someone new today."
And all eyes were on me. So I told them how wonderful
it was that they were in recovery and I wished them
well, but that I was in no way, shape, or form an alcoholic. "I don't even drink socially," I told them. "I'm a
dancer. With the Joffrey."* There's a fifty-fifty chance she
actually referred to the Joffrey Ballet Company, but it's
always thrown in for the story to let her audience know
she was with the Joffrey at one point. If Anjoli did actually say this, I have to wonder what the AA folks
thought of her comment. Were ballet dancers somehow
immune to alcoholism? *Everyone looked at me as if I
was to be pitied, as if I were in such heavy denial that I
couldn't even admit to social drinking. "I thought this
was the Young Metaphysicians meeting. Obviously, I'm
in the wrong place."* A woman in the back shouted, *"We
was all in the wrong place once, lady."* Ten-to-one that
never happened but it always gets a laugh. *They were*

so concerned, they didn't want me to leave. Of course, no one blocked the doors or tied me to my chair, but they were so earnest in their desire to help me that I couldn't just brisk away. The more I tried to explain that I was not an alcoholic, the more invested they became in my taking the first step and admitting that I had a problem bigger than myself. There was no escaping these do-gooder teetotalers. I couldn't help wondering if they weren't more fun in their drinking days because after about a half hour of this, I must admit, their persistent charm wore thin. In any event, it was time for me to either make a huge fuss, which admittedly I'd already been doing quite unsuccessfully, make a run for the door, or simply admit that I'm an alcoholic. If people weren't already squealing, "You didn't?!" Anjoli pauses so they can. "You didn't?!" her audience says on cue. *What else could I do? I stood up there, took a deep breath and said, "Hello, my name is Anjoli and I'm an alcoholic."* Now this part I know is made up because back then she was still called Margaret Mary. Name discrepancy notwithstanding, she does quite well with this story.

My mother also has a story about the time she went to a Chinese cooking class and wound up at a Nation of Islam self-defense class. Don't ask me how it took her so long to figure this out. No woks. No Chinese people. No food! Just a half dozen brothers in bow ties and gym shorts talking about Elijah Muhammad. Yet she stayed for an hour, thinking she just might be in the right place. The men assumed she was a reporter from *The New York Times* who was scheduled to do a story on them. "Did you see the fabulous story on organic stir fry in the Sunday Styles?" Then she points to herself as though she was at the center of an adorable little mix-up. Alfie called her "Farrakhan's bitch" for months after that.

But I digress. Quite a bit, in fact. My point in the "Anjoli goes to AA" story was that I'm not quite sure how Anjoli always seems to wind up at the wrong meeting. And once she gets there, why it takes so long for her to figure it out. Because when I entered the community room of the Unitarian Church, there was no doubt in my mind that I was at a La Leche League meeting. My first clue was that every child—not just every baby—was breast-feeding. One kid walked up to his mother's diaper bag, yanked out a book, unbuttoned her blouse, and started reading a little Tolstoy at the breast. Okay, maybe it was a book of shapes and colors, but the kid was a full-on, walking, talking, blouse-unbuttoning toddler.

I saw three species of mother. First, there was the crunchy contingent with rainbow knit skull caps, long braided hair, and hemp necklaces with a single shell in the center. Rope mesh purses rested beside their Birkenstocks. I could easily see any one of these three mothers scooping organic grains from barrels at the health food stores. I imagined they hand-made rag dolls for their babies and mashed their own baby food. The next group was the one I fell into. Two tired-looking mothers in sweatpants and oversized t-shirts who put their hair in unbrushed, low-hanging ponytails. One had socks that didn't quite match. The other looked as though her idea of a morning shower was running a baby wipe under her armpits. The other two mothers at the meeting surprised me. They were the tidy twins, more suited for Junior League than La Leche League. These women were impeccably dressed with immaculate toddlers playing calmly with natural wood blocks. Both wore ironed jeans. One wore an Ann Taylor sweater set in icy blue, while the other donned a snowflake sweater over a winter white top. Icy Blue Top had straight black hair, cream skin, and chipper blue eyes. She wore Ugg boots and a cute suede jacket with lamb's wool trim. My savior, Mary, was one of the granola girls.

Helene, one of my fellow-slovenly moms, complained that her parents were constantly asking when she was going to wean her son. *Note to self: Cross this question off your list. Helene does not seem happy having to answer this inquiry.*

"Ohmigod, he's only two!" a crunchy mom exclaimed. "Do they realize how healthy it is to breastfeed?"

For two years?! That seems a bit long. I think at that point it has more to do with . . . Helene jumped in again. "If I hear one more person say that my nursing has more to do with me than my son, I'll scream."

Note to self, part two: Anything I am thinking should be kept to myself around Helene.

Mary took out a bunch of articles and said that Helene's comment was well timed because this month's topic was the benefits of extended breast-feeding. "I hate even calling it that because throughout the world, the norm is to breast-feed well into the toddler years," Mary said, passing out article after article listing the health benefits to nursing past a year. I was just feeling victorious for making it through the first two weeks. These marathon lactators made me feel thoroughly inadequate.

Candace, previously known as Icy Blue Top, placed her hand on my knee and whispered, "Don't worry, no one says you have to nurse that long. Mary just doesn't want new moms to dismiss it out of hand because they don't realize it's a legitimate option."

"Oh, okay," I whispered back, wondering how Candace read my mind. At the break, Candace asked if she could hold Adam, then took him over for her toddler, Barbie, to see. "Do you live around here?" she asked.

"Right in Caldwell."

"Me too!" Candace said with delight, though I couldn't really understand why. "How come I haven't seen you around? Is Adam your first?"

My first? No one had referred to him that way yet. I knew what she was thinking. I looked older than she did by about ten years, so she probably figured I had another few in junior high. "Yes, he's my first."

"Barbie's my fourth," she said proudly. "Breast-fed them all."

"And you're still at it with her, huh?" I said, hoping she wouldn't be offended like Helene. She nodded, nonplussed. "Do you mind if I ask how old she is?"

"Three in another few weeks."

"Wow, and you don't mind nursing her that long?" I treaded lightly.

"Sometimes I do, but I'm committed to it, and I know how good it is for her immune system, so most of the time, I'm happy to do it. But I'd be lying if I told you that some days I am not at all in the mood for it. At this point, she's down to once or twice a day."

Well, that certainly made a difference. I'd cringed at the thought of her nursing a child every two hours. As I spoke to Candace, I was struck by a double whammy of guilt. First, she was so slim and pretty. I felt I'd somehow failed in the looks department. She had four children and yet she looked so clean and put together. The second guilt trip was brought on by Candace's invitation to Barbie's birthday party. I had no invitations with which to reciprocate. I was also quite sure that her party would outshine anything I could ever hope to put on for Adam. I heard Anjoli's voice in my head: *Release guilt. Guilt leads to punishment. Punishment leads to suffering. Suffering leads to . . .* "Okay, what time?" I asked.

Mary asked the mothers to please return any books they borrowed from her nursing library. "Remember next month's topic is keeping the romance alive in a marriage with young children. We'll have some super ideas to share right in time for Valentine's Day," she said with excitement. I looked around the plain white room with its circle of folding chairs, and everyone else seemed tickled by this topic as well. Afraid to be exposed as the imposter I was, I blurted an uncomfortable, "Right on to that!" When will I learn to just keep quiet?

Chapter 16

It was with mixed emotions that I drove Anjoli back to the city after her week with us. Sure, she can cause drama and lunacy in our home, but the benefit of her visiting is that she can cause drama and lunacy in our home. As she stepped out of the car, Anjoli blew a kiss to sleeping Adam in his car seat and reminded me that Kimmy's wedding was in just three weeks. "How much weight do you plan to lose by then?" she asked.

It was hard enough for me to look at my post-pregnancy body. Knowing that it was also disappointing to my mother was sinking. "Mary says nine months on, nine months off."

"Is that the Leche woman who's breast-feeding her three-year-old?" Anjoli asked.

"No, that's Candace. Mary has the two-year-old."

"My point, darling, is that your friend Mary isn't exactly a model of discipline, is she?"

"Good-bye, Mother," I blew a kiss at her body bent at the passenger window. "You're sure you don't want help with your bags?" As if on cue, two guys in formfitting jewel-colored sweaters descended the front stairs of the building, overjoyed to see her. The air-kissing began and muscles flexed as the guys lifted my mother's arsenal of clothing and cosmetics. As they turned their backs, I heard laughter and snippets of their conversation. *Catch-up party* sounded like a suggestion that went over well. Then, if an exaggerated eye roll had a voice, it would have been the one Anjoli used as she muttered the words *New Jersey*.

I decided to spend the day in the city with Zoe, who I hadn't spoken to in weeks. I suppose that's normal in the first few weeks of being a mother, but I missed chatting with her about the mundane little things that fill our days. For me, it seemed I'd been out of touch with the outside world for years, but for someone like Mary, my few weeks of solitude probably seemed hurried. She suggested I take a "babymoon" with Adam, which is essentially spending the entire day in bed sleeping and gazing at him. Don't get me wrong, there were times I'd stop dead in my tracks and watch his sleeping little mouth phantom nursing, his tiny lips pulsing in and out. I loved the way one of his little cheeks fattened when it pressed into the mattress. I melted at the sight of his wrinkly fingers balled into fists. I knew I'd have to break myself of the habit of shrieking "Look at that little acorn penis!" whenever I changed his diaper. My adoration of him was constant. The desire to sit and stare at him lasted about ten minutes. I tried the babymoon because it sounded like a sweet idea. It seemed like what good and virtuous mothers would naturally want to do. But after about an hour and a half, I couldn't help getting up and making a list of things we needed at Costco.

"Hey, girlfriend," I said into my cell phone. "I'm about to very gladly pay forty dollars for a parking spot for our play date. Y'ready?"

"Our what?" Zoe asked.

"Play date," I said. "It's jargon. Picked it up at a La Leche League meeting. Whaddya think?"

"The *milk* league?" Zoe asked. "Hey, how's your face?!" she switched gears.

"Judge for yourself!" I said, thrilled that the Bell's palsy had gone away. I still felt a difference and people who knew me well could still see traces of it, but for the most part, my face was back to normal.

I decided when we went to lunch I'd drop the new mommy vocabulary. I recalled Zoe telling me that she was terrified that I'd become absorbed into the land of the children once Adam was born. She'd seen it happen before, she said. One moment she had a friend who could talk politics, books, and fashion. The next minute it was all Diaper Genie, car seats, and Baby Einstein videos. I remember laughing at the absurdity of the idea of buying a videotape of geometric shapes floating to classical music in hopes of boosting a baby's IQ. Now, I wondered if there might be something to it. I mean, if there was no harm in it, maybe I should get one of these. If every other mother was amping up her baby's brainpower with this magic video, would Adam be at a disadvantage if I turned my nose up at it?

At first I felt guilty for being so competitive, but after Zoe and my excursion to the puppet show, I realized I was an amateur. On the ticket line for the show, Zoe shot me a terrified look as we heard clips of mothers' conversations comparing how old their kids were when they first spoke, potty trained, and split an atom. Of course, it was all done very politely, under the guise of exchanging information, but the subtext was clear. Mothering was an Olympic sport. I thought it was pretty cool that I was exposing Adam to live theatre at three weeks, but I was strictly a bronze medal mom for this. There was a pregnant woman sitting alone in the theatre, who I thought I saw holding her cell phone to her belly after the show so Daddy-to-Be could have a discussion with his future Ben Brantley.

More frightening than the one-upsmomship going on in the line for the puppet show was the constant chime of hyper-soprano voices crying, "Good job!" Zoe's look implored, *Don't let this happen to you!* "Good job, Olivia!" was immediately followed by another voice exclaiming, "Good job, Pete!" Thirty seconds later, we heard a different voice claiming that her child had also done a "good job!" What the hell were these kids doing that was so damned magnificent anyway? I glanced over to see that a four-year-old had picked up a toy that he'd dropped. Isn't that what kids are supposed to do? Why the vocal parade every time a kid wiped his nose? There was no way I was going to be able to keep up with this. I like spells of silence so I can think and worry about things. There was no way I was going to remember to chirp "Good job, Adam!" every time he demonstrated the slightest sign of competence. I didn't have the emotional energy to build a verbal fortress of self-esteem to protect my son from feeling that he wasn't doing a "good job" at absolutely everything.

A three-year-old started screaming that she wanted a cookie. Her mother calmly responded, "Wouldn't it be great if we had sixty *million* cookies and could build a cookie castle to live in?!" Had this woman lost her mind? A cookie castle?!

Zoe was a sport to come along to the puppet show with us, especially since she thought it was ludicrous to take a three-week-old to a puppet show. "He'll never remember it," Zoe told me. The truth was I thought Adam would hear a lot of words and I could honestly report to Jack's mother that our baby was on the fast track to Harvard.

"I know, but he'll enjoy it while we're watching," I

said. "Oh! I'm having a Zen parenting moment! I'm so excited. My new friend Candace lent me a book about being in the moment. She thinks I'm a little high-strung, I think."

"Candace isn't Jewish, is she?" I shook my head that, no, Candace Anderson wasn't even one sliver Jewish. "Well, that's good, Lucy. It's great that you're trying to be more in the moment now that you have Adam. That'll be good for you." She smiled, "Good job!"

The puppet show was not quite as dreadful as either of us feared. I'm sure I wasn't the only mother who realized that Tim Johansen, the man behind the marionettes, was a certifiable babe. His dirty-blond hair was casually swept to the side, and his piercing blue eyes felt like they were looking right at me. Now, that's a set of eyes I could take to Tantra Yoga. I took some comfort in knowing that most of these women were here in part to gawk at the puppeteer. As kids cried out in delight about the aqua-blue sequined gown the roller-skating cat wore, mothers like me wondered what else Tim could do with his nimble fingers. I looked around the theatre and the moms were more mesmerized than the kids. All of the polite mothers who sang "good job!" now snapped "shhh!" when their children made a peep. I felt their pain. I too found it very difficult to maintain a sexual fantasy while kids kept yammering "pretty kitty" or some such nonsense.

I treated Zoe to lunch since she was kind enough to come to the puppet show with us. "That puppet guy was hot," she said as tall glasses of fruit-infused iced tea were placed on a white tablecloth. Thankfully, Adam decided this would be an ideal time for a nap. For the time being at least. "Did you see Tim after the show?"

"No, what was he doing?"

Zoe brushed part of her neat blond bob behind her

ear and leaned in conspiratorially. Her skin was flaw-less in a way that only women with time seem to be able to pull off. Zoe was not the most naturally beautiful woman I'd ever seen, but she pulled herself off exquis-itely. She'd cultivated a professional Manhattan look about her that screamed *Don't fuck with me.* Her eye shadow was expertly applied to look daytime smoky, while a thirty-dollar lip liner framed her even more ex-pensive lipstick. Her purposefully ragged-looking pale-green skirt and blazer bore slightly darker green leather straps at the side seams, giving her an artistic and whimsical look. Artistic and whimsical while still being able to kick your ass. I wondered what it would be like to look like that again, before I realized I never did. So then I wondered what it would be like to again have the option to look like that. I looked at her small purse in wonder. I was packed like a mule with a Loony Tunes bag stuffed with diapers, wipes, a first-aid kit, a small blanket, Elmo, and a change of clothes. No lip liner for me.

"After he finished chatting with the moms," she paused to make a gagging gesture, "he slapped on the black helmet with flame painted on, and jumped onto a motorcycle." Zoe had a thing for guys on bikes. I had a thing for this guy on a bike. I imagined wrapping my arms around Tim's waist as his bike growled beneath me. "A sexy puppet guy, go figure."

The waiter brought us Chinese chicken salads, which looked entirely different from the ones I'd been picking up at Lo Fats near Caldwell. Despite its name, the restaurant couldn't seem to get that putting mayon-naise in the chicken salad added quite a few fat grams. This one was a masterpiece, with green and purple leaves artfully fanned across a plate topped with hu-mongous slices of mandarin orange, peanuts, and bean sprouts. I hated to disturb the presentation with my fork.

"So what are you doing lusting after puppet guys when you've got Paul at home?" I said lightly, knowing full well that an attached woman was more than capable of a wandering eye. Even when Jack and I were married for real, I noticed good-looking men. Just not quite as often as I do now.

"You haven't seen Paul in quite some time, have you?" Zoe asked. I shook my head. She continued. "He's gotten so fat that the last time we had sex, I tried to get on top and I couldn't keep my balance on that tub of his." I burst with laughter. "It's not funny. I kept rolling off his big, fat belly."

"Gross! You mean it stayed round?" I asked, oddly compelled by the story of Paul's blubber. "Didn't it get mushy when you put your weight on it?"

Zoe slapped her hand onto the table and exclaimed, "You'd think so, wouldn't you?!" Though I felt for Zoe, I was also comforted by the fact that I wasn't the only one with a stalled love life. We couldn't all be as fabulous as Anjoli and Kimmy.

"When does your show launch?" I tried changing the topic. Hearing about Paul's naked fat belly didn't go well with my haute cuisine salad. Zoe told me that *Real Confessions* aired next month and FOX expected it to be a top-rated show within weeks. Real confession number one: Forgive me, Father, but I think my friend has lost her mind.

Chapter 17

Jack was getting on my nerves. I had been up most of the night with our crying, vomiting, snot-dripping son while he snored away, absolutely undisturbed. At seven on Friday morning, Jack woke up fresh as a bird and started whistling in the shower. I could've stabbed him. It wasn't just that he was making noise during my first two hours of uninterrupted sleep since Thursday. But he sounded so damned happy it was annoying. I wondered why he was so chipper, but dared not ask for fear that he would tell me what I already suspected— he had a new girlfriend.

Fatherhood looked good on Jack, whereas I wore motherhood like a dishrag. He was sleeping full nights, showering every morning, and going into the city every day. And very possibly dating. Meanwhile whenever I wanted to pee, I had to chart out a game plan like Knute Rockne at the chalkboard. I actually fantasized about being in a coma for just a few weeks. There would be no guilt about sleeping all day. People would play nice music for me. No one would expect a thing.

And with no temptation to gorge snacks all day, a coma would be an ideal way to lose weight.

I shared my ambivalence about motherhood with Candace, who told me that motherhood would make my life more rich, more beautiful, and far more interesting than it'd ever been before. She really could make a person feel like crap. I know her heart was in the right place, but the comment made me feel as though I was completely ungrateful for this wonderful experience. Why was it impossible for people to accept that humans had room for completely conflicting emotions, and one did not detract from the other in the slightest? Of course I loved my son. And of course I saw the beauty in motherhood. But I also felt depleted and burdened by my onslaught of new responsibilities. And I resented the hell out of Jack for moving on with his life and making it better without me as a wife.

Sometimes I wondered why I stayed in this sham of a marriage. Why not just run away from New Jersey and live with my mother until I got back on my feet again? Sure, our suburban community was lovely and had excellent schools, but Greenwich Village had a lot to offer a kid as well. Why was I so willing to subscribe to what Jack thought was a good place to raise kids? Years ago, it was because he was my husband, and I wanted to accommodate him. Plus, back then I didn't know that suburban life was not for me. I was a city kid. For all I knew, I'd love life in Caldwell. Four years later, I realized that while this community offered a wonderful life to many people, the suburbs weren't for me. When Jack returned home every night and held his son in his arms, I knew that Anjoli's home could never offer what I had here. Here there was hope.

Adam was a month old when Candace's daughter Barbie had her spectacular Barney birthday party. By spectacular, I don't necessarily mean good. I hate to say this because I know Candace worked very hard to throw a perfect party for her daughter, but it was sort of a relief to see that no matter what I did for Adam's parties, they could never turn out more disastrous than this one. It showed me that no matter how good a plan is, life could always throw you a curve ball.

Candace's home was a brick McMansion with a hilly lawn covered with snow. A brick curving walkway led to a red door with an enormous and elaborate winter wreath. Inside was decorated like a page from *Country Living* magazine. In her family room, Candace had a light oak entertainment center, which matched perfectly the trim on the blue-and-yellow-checkered couch, as well as the coffee and end tables. The table cloth, valances, and wallpaper on the bottom half of the walls were the exact same pattern. Everything was obnoxiously well coordinated. There were at least a hundred ducks around the house, from the wooden carved ones sitting on the immaculate eggshell-colored carpet to the crystal collection in a lit glass display case. Candace had a large oak toy chest where every board game was stacked neatly. Certainly there were no missing pieces. She served peanut butter (not Jif) and preserves on crust-free wheat bread to the kids, and subs and a salad that rivaled my Manhattan lunch to the adults. I noticed her glancing at the grandmother clock next to the "Home Is Where The Heart Is" sampler.

"Everything okay?" I saw Candace's husband ask.

"Barney's late," she whispered.

"If he's late, we'll do something else," he offered.

"What if he doesn't show?"

I was having an influence on my new friend already. I was already two steps ahead of her, imagining Barney dead at the side of the road. I imagined parents honking their horns and cheering at the sight of the purple roadkill. In retrospect, this may have been a better course of events.

"He'll show."

Candace continued to fret. "Manny, you have no idea how important it is to her that Barney's here."

It seemed a little odd that this character could make or break a birthday girl's day. There were fifteen little kids, tons of party games, and a huge cake of what I later learned was a creature called Baby Bop. Then again, I remember how upset I was when Cher had to bow out of my ninth birthday party last-minute. I had such high hopes of her appearance catapulting my social status. Instead Emily Weintraub and Gail Barker said I was lying and that Cher never was scheduled to sing "Half-Breed" at my sleepover. So, I guess I could understand a three-year-old's attachment to this dinosaur character.

Nearly a full hour late (that's seven hours in kid time), Barney rapped on the door and shouted, "Open up, birthday boy, and let's get this party started with a bang." It sounded like more of a threat than an opening line for a children's entertainer. There was something not quite right about Barney from the get-go, but it was tough to pinpoint because of the thick layer of purple fur shielding the actor from inspection. As his fat purple legs clunked into the family room, I could see that his fur was matted down on one side, as though he'd been sleeping in his costume. I swore I saw Adam lift an inquisitive eyebrow as he sat on my lap. "Who's Barney?!" the dinosaur blasted in a raspy voice. All of the adults immediately stopped what they were doing, and turned to look at Barney. "I said who's Barney?!" he shouted again. It had the feeling of a hijacking.

Like the Grinch's Cindy Lou Who, Barbie stepped forward and in her soft squeaky voice said, "You're Barney." Her father placed a protective hand on her shoulder and pulled her back.

"Not me. I mean the birthday boy. Barney. Barney, the kid!" he shouted. We needed no Breathalyzer to tell that Barney had blood alcohol level 2.0. "Is anyone gonna answer me?" No one knew what to say. I clutched Adam close to me for fear that this dinosaur had evil intentions for the child Barney.

"It's not Barney, silly," said Barbie. "I'm Bar*bie* and I'm three," she said holding out three fingers.

"Well blow my fur back if it ain't a little girl. The agency said I was doing a boy party."

"Okay, thank you very much for coming, Barney," Manny put his arm around the dinosaur and started walking him toward the door. "It was nice of you to stop by on your way back to—"

Barney swatted away Manny's arm as if he was getting ready to fight. It was surreal body language to see from the character best known for his vapid song of mutual love and familial glad tidings.

"You want a piece of me?!" Barney held up his fists at Manny. At this point, the mothers started scurrying the children into the kitchen by promising them birthday cake, while several of the dads went to aid Manny. How many fathers *would* it take to bring down a drunken dinosaur? Barney laughed that hoarse, drunken chortle that drunks let out when nothing funny has happened. "You want a piece of me?!" Barney laughed hysterically. The odds that Barney was packing heat were exceptionally low, so I stayed put for the show.

"Barney, I'm going to call the police if you don't leave right now," Manny said in a voice that would one day be used to let his children know he was not messing around.

"You rich fucking bastards always think you know the deal," he slurred.

What?

"You don't know shit!" Barney shouted. By now a

few mothers and a toddler were peeking out from the kitchen.

"That's enough," said one of the other dads, who marched over to Barney and grabbed his thick, purple arm. Barney misjudged how hard the father was holding him and jerked back with the strength of an actual dinosaur. He lost his footing and stumbled back a few steps before crashing through the screen that separated the family room from the indoor swimming pool. He didn't fall into the pool right away. First Barney fell back, lost his purple head, and hit his human noggin against the pool edge. Then like mud sliding off a hill, Barney fell into the pool, where his floating purple dinosaur head was under the diving board. Seconds later, blood colored the water around Barney's human skull.

"Cut the cake!" a dad shouted into the kitchen. "Barney's fine! Crazy dinosaur decided to take a swim." Wrong thing to say to a group of kids. They all rushed to see their favorite character goofing around in the swimming pool, and quickly started screaming that Barney was bleeding. "Is Barney going to die?" Barbie sobbed. This was so much worse than my Cher no-show.

"Why is his head in the deep end?!" shouted a five-year-old.

"Manny, go in and get him before he drowns!" shouted Candace.

Freeze for a moment and imagine the perfect mother in her perfect home wearing an apron with ducks. Now imagine she's shouting to her husband that he should jump in the pool to save a decapitated, bleeding, and inebriated purple dinosaur. Who said the suburbs were dull?

Manny dove into the pool and pulled out a muttering, bleached-blond guy with horrible teeth wearing a dinosaur body completely disproportionate to his own.

At that point, Candace started crying, which was

when the party stopped being fun for me. She was quickly rushed into the kitchen by two Paxil-ized women who remained smiling through this whole encounter. I lifted Adam, who seemed genuinely irritated to be removed from the scene. It was like a reality show for kids—*Real Fucked-Up Birthday Parties.*

"Candace, are you okay?" I said. *Okay, stupid question.*

"What can I do for you, honey?" Patty Paxil asked. *Show-off.*

Candace sniffed and handed her friend a business card. "Tell him we need an emergency session. Now!" Her friend turned on her charcoal leather boot heel and sauntered to the kitchen phone as if she were on the catwalk.

Mothers corralled children into the formal living room and led stilted rounds of songs, including, "If You're Happy and You Know It Clap Your Hands." We heard Barney punctuate a round with "Ah, fuck!" This is how the mothers learned that Barney was still alive, but also gave the kids an entirely different version of the song they'd learned in preschool.

Ten minutes later an ambulance had taken Barney off on a gurney. As the kids waved and wished him a speedy recovery, Barney shouted, "What are you little fuckers staring at?!" Candace buried her head in her hands. "Enjoy your stupid cake 'cause from here on out, life's a piece of shit. Got it, Little Barney?"

"Okay!" Barbie shouted back happily.

Adam held out his hand and pointed at Barney, smiled, and gurgled.

Moments later, there was another knock on the door. Who next, crack-addicted Muppets? It was even worse. I stood motionless as I saw him at the door. I wondered if he'd remember me, and if he did, what he would say. Why was he here anyway?

"Excuse me, but is that who I think it is?" I whispered to another mother.

She confirmed with a nod. "It's so Candy to make sure everyone has the chance to process this ordeal. I really give her credit for thinking on her feet on this one."

Candace clapped her hands to get everyone's attention. "One, two, three. Eyes on me!" she said. I made a mental note of that one to lend to Anjoli. She'd love the sentiment. "We've all shared a traumatic experience together here today. First, I must express my deepest regret about Barney's, um, behavior. The paramedics say he should be fine. He'll need a few stitches . . ." *And rehab . . .* "but he'll be good as new lickety-split! In the meantime, I'd like to introduce Dr. Collin Lee, family therapist. Dr. Lee is going to facilitate a discussion and help us talk about our feelings about today, okay?"

After an hour, we learned that kids are amazingly resilient and therapists are highly overpaid. Dr. Lee recognized me and quickly averted eye contact.

Four-year-old Kyle thought it was cool how Barney's mom let him say bad words. A few children said they never knew that there was a "people head" under a dinosaur's. Little Kisha said she felt sorry for Barney because he seemed "super-di-dooper mixed-up." And Barbie said that she still loved Barney, even though he couldn't remember her name. I shudder to think of her future relationships.

For the first time in my four weeks as a mother, I believed what Candace told me. My new life as a mother really was more rich, interesting, and wonder-filled than ever before.

Chapter 18

_____

A week later, Adam was still attached to the stuffed Barney that Candace gave the kids as a party favor. Dr. Lee said that since none of the children seemed particularly traumatized by Barney's head injury, there would be no harm in sending them home with a memento of the event. The first time we left it behind at Lo Fats, Adam cried hysterically for twenty minutes before I figured out that Barney was missing. I changed his diaper, played the Baby Einstein video, gave him a pacifier, but nothing would soothe him. I even tried nursing him, which was my trump card. Adam was always comforted by nursing. Not this time. Not until we had Barney back in our possession. "That's very unusual," Jack said. "Infants don't attach to toys at five weeks." *I really needed to buy a parenting book and read it. How did Jack know every developmental milestone?*

"I know!" I bluffed. "I don't think he's this attached to me and we sleep in the same bed and are together twenty-four/seven. God knows his first exposure to Barney wasn't a pleasant one, but he loves the thing!"

Jack and I sat at the table sharing a rare meal together, discussing the appeal of Barney. When we were first dating, I would have thought his musings on Barney were his attempt at humor, but now I know better. He was genuinely curious about why the purple dinosaur was adored by millions of kids. "If you take a look at fertility goddesses and symbols of motherhood throughout the ages, the figures always have that rotund belly and soft arms like Barney. Across virtually every cultural divide, it's the soft fleshy body that represents nurturing. I wonder if that has anything to do with it."

And he really did. My first instinct was to jokingly shoot back, "Yeah, Jack, kids are thinking, 'Gee, that Barney reminds me of the fertility goddess of Zulu.'" A moment later, I thought he might have a point. "There's something about Barney." *There's something about Barney.*

The next day, I scoured the Internet for images of fertility goddesses and symbols of motherhood, and sure enough, they all looked quite a bit like Barney. I felt a bit guilty about leaving poor Desdemona out in the rain on the cobblestone street for all these weeks, but for the first time in months, I was actually inspired to write. I began pecking away at the keyboard about the Barney phenomenon and hypothesized that the popularity of this dinosaur is not a social commentary on the dumbing-down of today's kids. Rather, any generation of kids in any part of the world would love Barney for the very same reasons the Greeks worshipped Demeter. Adam and I would play silly games while he was awake, then as soon as he nodded off, I was back at the keyboard. I watched Adam for signs that he might try to nurse from Barney, but no such luck of any breakthrough anecdotal evidence to support my theory.

By the end of the week, I finished "There's Something About Barney," which admittedly would have been better timed with the release of the Cameron Diaz movie, and mailed it to the editor of the Mothers Who Think column at *Salon* magazine.

Jack agreed to watch Adam all day Saturday while Zoe and I treated ourselves to a day of pampering at Narcissa Day Spa. It was one week until Kimmy's Valentine's Day wedding and I wanted to feel cosmetically refreshed.

I must give Kimmy credit for being the least uptight bride I'd ever seen. I've been a bridesmaid three times, and brides are the biggest pain-in-the-ass group of women I've ever seen. They act as though the world really just might come to a screeching halt if their flower arrangements aren't perfectly coordinated with the pattern on the salad fork. Kimmy was almost laissez-faire about the whole thing. We went to the florist together a few weeks ago and she whipped out a cigarette and started smoking right there in the flower shop. This ultra prim swan in an orange suit asked Kimmy to kindly preserve the health of her blossoms and lungs, and extinguish the Camel Light. She clasped her hands together and leaned in to Kimmy and me conspiratorially. "Where is Mr. Right today?" she asked.

"If you know, clue me in, 'cause I'm marrying a controlling son of a bitch in a few weeks," Kimmy said. She sounded so unlike herself (and so much like me) that I actually checked my body to see if we were having some sort of *Freaky Friday* experience. When I later asked if everything was okay, Kimmy said she was just experiencing last-minute jitters. But she didn't sound nervous. Just angry. She hadn't said anything negative since, but then again, she hadn't said much at all about the wedding. She was the world's coolest bride, but then again why wouldn't she pull this off perfectly too?

In any event, since there was no chance of my outshining the bride, I asked the good people at Narcissa to give me the once-over and recommend a beauty day. The reception area of Narcissa was completely mirrored, and had a koi pond as a centerpiece to the room. I found it comforting that we could be unapologetically vain there. I appreciated the sentiment of Candace and Mary when they told me I "glowed with the beauty of motherhood," but I wanted to glow with the beauty of actual beauty. I tried yoga, Pilates, weights, and aerobics, but couldn't seem to lose weight at the rate I wanted to. A half pound a week was always so little that, after I weighed in, I figured I'd pick up the routine the next week. After all, why suffer for eight measly little ounces? Plus, these exercise classes all had hidden hazards. In yoga, when I lay on my back and placed my legs up in the air perpendicularly, an avalanche of thigh came close to suffocating me. In step aerobics, my ass arrived on and off the step a full two seconds after the rest of me.

Zoe and I were taken from the sea-foam green reception area and into a welcoming room. We were given two ultra fluffy terry-cloth robes and told to join our concierge of beauty in the orientation room. The room was lit with vanilla-scented candles and softly in the background played music that sounded like it was composed by stoners in Area 51. If this were a cult, I would have signed up on the spot. There was no threat of baby screams. No one expected mc to feed, bathe, clothe, or care for him in any way.

After a salt scrub, seaweed wrap, and Vichy shower, I was bored out of my mind and ready to go home. My breasts were ready to explode with milk so while my fellow narcissists ate lunch, I pumped in the hot stone massage room. Zoe said she had a massage from Adonis who kneaded her inner thighs so skillfully, she feared she may have started speaking in tongues. She said she was so zoned-out, she honestly couldn't remember if she just thought it, or if she actually requested a full-on horizontal massage. She also had a scalp massage and a cellulite treatment that actually seemed to work. Meanwhile, I got spiced, wrapped in seaweed like a piece of sushi, and hosed down like a zoo elephant.

In the afternoon, I was scheduled for an eyebrow, leg, and bikini wax. "Am I allowed to have hair anywhere?" I joked with a Narcissa employee with burgundy leather pants and eyes made up to look Asian.

Without a bit of friendliness, she replied, "You can do whatever you want." She closed a large appointment book and walked away from me without a glance. The combination of erratic sleep and blatant dismissal created a lump in my throat that alerted me tears were coming. My mother would say I needed to confront this woman or my pain would turn inward and create some sort of horrible disease. She'd go berserk if she thought I was suppressing anger because according to her heal-thyself heroine, Louise L. Hay, unexpressed anger manifests itself in the form of cancer. Most of the time, my mother's ideas sounded pretty absurd, but I had to wonder if there wasn't an ounce of wisdom in them. If all feelings are their own energy, where do they go if they are unresolved? Or are they just fleeting, intangible thoughts that simply dissolve into thin air? Not that I thought anger causes cancer, but it definitely causes frustration.

In the waxing room there was a paper-covered table like the ones in a doctor's room. On a rolling, metal table was a pot that looked a lot like Pooh's honey jar. Beside it were hundreds of Popsicle sticks, cotton, a magnifying glass, and tweezers. Why was I doing this anyway? The eyebrows I could understand, but it was not as though anyone touched my legs or saw me naked.

In walked the burgundy pants woman, smelling like she'd just stepped out for a smoke. "Hello," she said coldly. "I'm Jaiyne."

"Yes, I believe we met a few minutes ag—"

"Let's do your eyebrows first, then move down."

"I'm Lucy."

"Mmm," she glanced down to her bowl of wax.

"I'm a little nervous about this," I said. Jaiyne said nothing. "Is it going to hurt a lot?" Again nothing. "Do you hear me?"

"Your question is ludicrous," she said as I stared incredulously at her. "You're nervous, so what? What am I to do with that? Will the waxing hurt? Yes."

"You know, on second thought, I'm going to skip it," I said, hopping off the table and onto my feet.

"Why's that?" Jaiyne asked, barely moving her face.

"Well, Jaiyne, to be honest with you, I'm not crazy about the thought of having a total bitch tear the hair off my body."

"Excuse me?" she raised her perfectly arched eyebrow.

I inhaled for courage. "Which part was unclear?"

"The part where you'd let someone else stand between you and what you want," she said icily. "I assume you came here because you want beautifully shaped brows to change the look of your face."

"Well, I—" I muttered.

"And I assume you want your legs to feel smooth and sexy for four weeks, correct?"

I nodded. I liked her tactful exclusion of mentioning my bikini area.

"Then what does it matter if I'm a bitch? Look, frankly, Lumeta—"

"Lucy," I corrected.

"Whatever. You don't want some sweetie puss in here yanking out your pubic hair. This is a job for a bitch."

I stared at her agape, completely at a loss on how to respond. "I, um, I don't know. Maybe you're, um, maybe you're right."

"Be happy I'm a bitch. I'm going to get every last piece of hair off your—"

"Okay, gotcha. Let's just get this over with." I sat back on the table, then rested my head on a pillow. The wax actually felt soothing as Jaiyne brushed it on my eyebrows. As she tore the muslin sheet off, I was shocked at the places I felt burning, excruciating pain. Why would I feel pain in the back of my neck? Why did my nose feel like someone kicked it with a pair of size twelve Doc Martens?

I tried to make small talk with Jaiyne during the bikini wax, since she seemed to find this part of her job distasteful. "I just had a baby," I said.

"Mmmm," she said, looking utterly disgusted at the prickly muslin sheet she just stripped. "You're very hairy."

"A boy," I tried again. "Adam. He's five weeks old. Born on New Year's Day." Jaiyne tore another strip. The pain actually made me sweat this time. Jaiyne put on a pair of glasses with a magnifying glass attached to the front of it. She made an irritated tsk-tsk sound and grabbed her tweezers.

"Stubborn hair," she said, glaring at me as though this was all part of my evil plan to keep her at the muff longer than she'd planned. "Lift your leg," she snapped. "Hold this for me," she said, grabbing a pair of latex gloves.

This was more complicated than gynecological surgery. She was unfolding so much skin and going places I didn't even knew existed, much less grew hair. "I wish you could pull my pregnancy pounds off with those strips. Now there would be a spa treatment."

"Hmm," she nodded. "When was the last time you waxed?"

"I've never waxed."

"I can tell."

Then why did you ask? "Do you have kids?" I asked Jaiyne.

"I hate children," she said flatly.

"Oh, well then you shouldn't have any. My friend Mary says it took her nine months to get back to her pre-pregnancy weight, but I just read an article that said Cindy Crawford was modeling just three months after she gave birth."

"She should chip a tooth," Jaiyne said. Finally, I felt a moment of solidarity from this bitch. But just for a moment. "I have to charge you extra for all of this hair," she said. "It's not supposed to take this long. My clients aren't usually this hairy." She handed me a mirror to inspect her work. I couldn't help gasping. "What?" Jaiyne said, annoyed.

"I didn't realize you were taking off so much," I said, horrified. Jaiyne left me with a postage size stamp of hair that sat a half inch over my completely bare lips. Wow, I hadn't seen them since before puberty. "I thought you were just doing the bikini line so I'd have a neat little triangle. This looks like, like Hitler!"

Chapter 19

Zoe couldn't believe my experience with Jaiyne. Of course she had some sort of naked-body-nibbling therapy performed by Colin Farrell until she had multiple orgasms and white chocolate truffles served from Ben Affleck's abs. Over dinner, we recalled the first night we met at college, how we stole a realtor's "For Sale" sign and put it in front of the snootiest sorority. The finishing touch was the teaser on the sign that read, "Foreclosure." Zoe and I were always in some sort of trouble, together and on our own. One semester, I was busted for reverse plagiarism, which basically meant I was too lazy to research a paper for my psychology class so cited false references to support my own theories on deviant behavior. Zoe failed a Shakespeare class for trying to bluff about *Twelfth Night* on a final. Her essay strictly referred to the video she checked out at the library.

"Listen, I hate to drop this bomb on you, but there's something I need to tell you," Zoe said, changing the mood of dinner. "Rich Cantor passed away."

"Why would you say something like that?" I gasped.

"I'm sorry. I saw his obituary in the alumni news. I wanted to tell you before you heard it from someone else."

I deflated. My first real love was dead. I could see him plainly in front of us, approaching Zoe's and my table in the dorm cafeteria. He had a scruffy, unpretentious cuteness about him that had me way before hello. "So what do you recommend here?" he had asked.

"The thinly sliced veal delicately bathed in a white wine and caper glaze is excellent," I suggested.

He smiled. "I was trying to find a way to meet you all last semester, so my New Year's resolution was to do it first thing when we got back to school."

Zoe smirked. "It's March."

Rich said if I went out with him he'd make it worth the wait.

I did. And he did. For the next two years we were inseparable best friends with incredible chemistry. We always said we wished this could last, which might sound as though we were making plans for the future. But actually, it was a realization that while we had something special, it was a relationship on a meter that expired upon graduation. After college, I was going to stay in Ann Arbor for my MFA and Rich was going to teach English in Japan. We wrote for a while, but then I met Jack and I heard through mutual friends that Rich married a Japanese woman and lived in Kyoto with two children. Last I heard he was a software engineer and started a few dot-coms, some of which were actually viable. Now Zoe was telling me he was dead.

"How did he die?" I asked.

"Cancer." And with that one word, a small part of me died too. That always sounds so dramatic when people say it, but it felt so true right now. A part of my youth, my love, my history was gone. Suddenly I felt a slap of guilt over making his death somehow about me.

Frighteningly, I was becoming my mother. I forced my-self to imagine a Japanese woman holding his hand through chemotherapy, then dressing two little boys for their father's funeral. God, he was such a good guy. I knew my mother's theory about cancer being unex-pressed anger was a crock of shit. Rich had the most insane temper I'd ever seen. When he was pissed about something, he'd curse, throw things, and scream for hours.

As I drove up to my home, I saw an unfamiliar car parked in the driveway. A perky sports car with no in-fant seat or baby gear packed in it. I unlocked the door to a burst of voices on the television screen. Jack was watching a movie, but he wasn't alone. "Oh hey, kiddo." Jack sat up and reached for the remote control. He paused the film to introduce the woman sitting be-side him—on my chair. "Natalie, this is Lucy. Luce, Natalie," he gestured with his hands at each of us. Na-talie looked a bit like Alanis Morissette, with long, wavy brown hair and clear pale skin. She wore a loose-fitting, embroidered peasant top with well-worn Levi's and a silver skull ring on her middle finger. It nearly crushed my finger as we shook hands. Her shoes were strewn across the floor next to her tote bag. Everything about this setup screamed fifth date. They'd already had dinner at a restaurant, done their quirky off-beat date like chasing the grunions at midnight, and had sex. Now they were renting videos and dressing com-fortably. "I thought you were at the spa this weekend," he said.

"It's a day spa," I said.

With that, Natalie got up and started collecting her things. "Jack, why don't I call you tomorrow and we can take Adam to the park like we planned?"

They were going to take my son to the park? Every-one would look at the three of them and think she was his mother. This woman was going to take my breast milk out of the freezer, pour it into a bottle, and feed my son?! I think she had an excellent idea when she suggested leaving.

"Don't be silly, babe," Jack said. *Babe?! Babe?! I'm kiddo and she's babe?!* "Lucy doesn't mind if you spend the night, right?" He looked at me for assurance.

"It might be confusing for Adam," I offered.

"Lucy," Jack laughed. "He's five weeks old." *You arrogant, condescending rat fuck.*

I laughed along. "I guess you're right. Natalie, that's fine. I'm sure Jack has explained our living arrangement to you."

"I think you are an exceptional woman," Natalie said. "Not a lot of women would put their child first like this. You know, a lot of mothers are quite self-centered."

"Fathers too," I added.

"Absolutely," she agreed. "Slap on the hand for me for that sexist exclusion."

"Natalie's a teacher," Jack explained.

I liked her. After being called a hairy gorilla and finding out that my sexy Richie Cantor was dead, I liked the sound of her voice telling me I was exceptional.

"Wanna watch the rest of the movie with us?" Natalie asked.

"Is it any good?" I asked.

"Crap," she answered.

"Natalie, this is a great movie!" Jack said with mock outrage.

"I'll leave the two of you. I'm going to have a threesome with two hot guys," I held up my grocery bag. "Ben and Jerry."

"Oh," Natalie looked disappointed.

"Is something wrong?" I asked.

"No," Natalie said unconvincingly. "Mind if I ask what flavor?"

"Chunky Monkey."

"Oh," she said.

"Something wrong with Chunky Monkey?" I asked.

"No, I love Chunky Monkey!" she paused. "And I hate this movie."

"Did you want some ice cream?" I asked incredulously. *Look bitch, if you're not going to date my husband, I will!*

"Would you mind?!"

"Um, okay, I guess."

"Are you jumping ship on me, babe?" Jack reached for the remote on the coffee table.

"I am," she said with the giddy giggle of a schoolgirl. She was far too perky to be Alanis Morissette.

I scooped ice cream for my husband's new girlfriend into a glass dish we got as a wedding gift fifteen years ago. I imagined the person who bought these for us never in their wildest dreams thought this would be the context in which their gift would be used one day. "Caramel sauce?" I asked Natalie.

"Oh yes, please!"

I sat at the table with her and asked if anyone ever told her she looked like Alanis Morissette. "Oh, all the time," Natalie said. "You know who you remind me of?" I shook my head to prompt her to tell. "Renée Zellweger," she said. Before I had a moment to thank her, Natalie finished, "in *Bridget Jones' Diary.*"

"Oh," I said, putting down my ice cream spoon. "I just had a baby five weeks ago, Natalie. I'm sure as a single woman you have time for all kinds of self-indulgences like dieting and exercise."

Natalie clutched her hand to her chest. "I didn't mean—"

"Natalie, I've had a long day." *At the spa*. "I've been

name-called by some crazy fake Asian salon bitch, then I found out my college boyfriend died of cancer two months ago. So I really don't have the energy to deal with your little backhanded comments about my weight."

She laughed. "You don't pull punches, that's for sure, but Lucy, you are completely misreading me. I think Renée Zellweger is beautiful at any weight. Okay, she's a little heavier in *Bridget Jones* and you look more like that Renée than her skinnier incarnations, but I think she looked great in that movie." Either she was sincere or the most adroit phony I'd ever met, but Natalie's explanation rang true.

"Oh, sorry. It's just been a long day," I said. Then hoping she would let me off the hook by switching conversational gears, "So how did you and Jack meet?"

"At his gallery. I was actually on another date. Blind date from hell. Nice guy, but a complete bore. We finished a dreadfully dull lunch, then I suggested we stop in the gallery to pass some time. You know how it goes? You feel as if you've got to put two hours on the clock to convince everyone that you gave it a fair shake. Anyway, so we walk in and boom, there he was. We talked for like a half hour and it felt like five minutes. The exact opposite of the date I was on. So Jack asks if Cliff is my boyfriend and I shake my head no. And the rest is kind of history." Natalie was sweet. It was hard making silent, snide comments because she seemed like such a genuinely decent person. But come on, three weeks together is hardly "history."

Over the next hour, I got my primer on Natalie. She was originally from Ohio and went to Oberlin College before she moved to New York to teach junior high school. A quick mathematical estimation said Natalie was just under thirty. How was I supposed to compete out there in the world with these little pop-tarts who have time to waste on bad blind dates and consider a three-week relationship a historical, epic event? In grad school, Jack had worked on paintings for longer than three weeks, and ended up hating them. I don't think Natalie realized that she and Jack had different perspectives on the investment of time.

I wanted to hate this woman sitting in my kitchen, and every time I was right on the brink of loathing, she'd say something that made me laugh, or at least smile. I hated her utter lack of detestability. "So do you think this whole setup is pretty weird?" I asked Natalie.

"At first I thought Jack was full of shit. I mean, who hasn't heard the married guy telling her that he and his wife *have an arrangement*, right?" she said.

I haven't. No married guys have ever hit on me, even when I was single.

"Oh my God, tell me about it," I rolled my eyes in disgusted solidarity. "Men are such pigs."

"Jack wasn't, though. He kept asking if I wanted to talk to you, or get a note or whatnot."

He what?! He offered to have me sign an infidelity permission slip?

To Whom It May Concern:
I, Lucy Klein, being of questionable mind and body, give my blessing to any woman of consenting age to engage in romantic and/or sexual relations with my estranged husband who just so happens to live with our infant son and me.

"That's Jack. He's forthright through and through," I said.

"Do you mind if I ask what went wrong between you two?" Natalie asked. I actually did. Not just because it was an intensely personal question to ask of someone you just met, but because I didn't really know the answer. What did go wrong between Jack and me? Other couples survived multiple miscarriages. They made it through relocations that weren't ideal. At what point did our marriage go from troubled to fated? And if we were both asked that same question, would our answers be the same, or was Jack harboring secret resentments of his own?

"I'm not really sure, Natalie."

"Oh," she seemed disappointed.

"Sorry I don't have any great insights for you."

"Oh, it's not that," Natalie said. "It's just that when I asked him, he said the same thing."

"Dumb and dumber, I guess," I shrugged. "At least we don't hate each other, right? That's got to be of some comfort to you."

"Oh, no," said Natalie. "Quite the opposite."

Chapter 20

"What in good God's name is that dreadful smell, darling?"

"Mother, surely you knew there would be flowers at the wedding," I scolded. "Didn't you take your allergy herbs?"

"Look at this place! There are six thousand flowers. I'll never survive the evening. Never! How am I supposed to walk Kimmy down this gauntlet of pollen?"

"Anjoli, let's try to make this Kimmy's special day. You can have the remaining three hundred sixty-four."

"What is that supposed to mean?" Anjoli turned the wide brim of her hat so quickly, she nearly took out one of the floral assistants who was still hanging orchids from every pew in St. Patrick's Cathedral. She wore a form-fitting cream silk gown with pearls sewn into the bodice, and had a hat specially made to match. What made the dress so dramatic was the way it clung to Anjoli's shape until it hit her calves. Then it blossomed into layers of open, overlapping cream silk in varying textures. Were Anjoli outside, her hat brim would've cast a shadow over her entire body. I'd seen umbrellas less cumbersome than Anjoli's fab chapeau. She was the perfect mother of the bride except for one small detail—she wasn't. Kimmy's mother had been institutionalized with Alzheimer's disease for the past twenty-some years, and her father was killed in a car accident a year later.

"How cute does Adam look?" I asked, holding my tuxedoed baby out for everyone to see.

"Can you believe I found a tux in a baby size?" Anjoli asked. "When will Jack arrive? Oh look, Rita and Bern are here. An hour early; how unlike them. Is Jack going to wear the matching cummerbunds I bought for him and Adam? How incredibly precious will that look? Who's your favorite Grammy?" she leaned in to Adam.

"Mother!"

"What now, darling?"

"Don't pit yourself against Susan."

"You're so right. There really is no competition, is there, my little Indigo child?!" *Her what?* "Your other grandmother hasn't even been out to see you yet, much less bought you your very own tuxedo. Maybe Grammy will take you to the Tonys this year." We watched Rita struggle as she walked. Anjoli continued. "Jesus, poor Rita is going to need an hour to get to her seat at the rate she's going, poor dear. Oh that reminds me, I want to take Adam to *Avenue Q* next week. Sam will get us tickets."

"*Avenue Q?* Isn't that a little adult?"

"It's a puppet show, darling!"

"Mother, don't the puppets have sex and talk about Internet porn?"

"He's two weeks old," she protested. "He'll never understand what they're talking about. He'll just see the adorable muppets, darling. Trust me, I took you to Tracedero when you were five."

"Tracedero?"

"The drag ballet," Anjoli reminded me. *Oh yes, how could I forget?*

Rita stumbled, and Bernice struggled to assist her.

"Mother, I think Rita needs help. Bernice can't manage on her own."

"She'll be fine."

"Hold Adam, I'm going to see if they need help. Adam's six weeks, by the way."

I handed Adam to Anjoli, who was waving her hands as though the baby were shooting paint. "Not today, darling. If he vomits on this dress, I'll die. I have to look perfect walking down the aisle."

Snapping Adam back into my grasp, I walked away. "Susan would hold him," I shot.

"Susan doesn't wear six-thousand-dollar dresses, darling," was her retort. I heard a cough echo from behind the altar. Surely a nun having a seizure over the price of Anjoli's attire. "I'm not in competition with Susan. I have my style and she has Sears."

"*Gavalt*, this is a death march!" snapped Rita. "Who needs an aisle that goes on for two miles like this? Showy *goyim*."

"Why don't you use your wheelchair?" Bernice asked.

"Because I'm not a cripple!" Rita shouted, creating another echo.

"Have it your way," Bernice said, scanning the cathedral. "I was at the loveliest funeral here last summah." Bernice floated into her memory. "Flowers forever, and what a eulogy! It was the best funeral all season."

"Oy, thumbs up from the Rogah Ebert of death ovah here," Rita said. "We're early, aren't we, *mamaleh*?" she asked Anjoli. Without waiting for a response, "I told you we were early, Bernice. She insisted it started at four, even though the invitation says foive."

"Better early than late," Bernice shrugged.

"Better on time and not sitting around in a church for an awah," Rita snapped.

As they slipped into a middle pew, I offered to bring my aunts water before I went to help Kimmy get into her dress.

"I'm starving. How 'bout getting me a few of those Jesus wafers?" Rita asked.

"Rita!" Bernice chided. "Those are special to Catholics. It's not a snack food."

"It was a joke! I was being funny. No sense of humor."

"Not a bad idea, though, Rita," Anjoli piped in. "It's one of the few things I miss about being Catholic—taking the Holy Eucharist. They're so light."

Holy Communion Snack Chips by Nabisco. Not just for Mass anymore! Now in low carb, so His body won't go to yours.

"Mother, we need to get Kimmy into her dress," I reminded her as I went to get water for my aunts. "Two-minute warning."

A nun told me I couldn't bring food or drinks into the chapel, but when she caught a glimpse of my aunts in their fragile, elderly state, she made an exception.

As soon as my mother and I entered the bridal dressing room, it was clear that something was very wrong with Kimmy. She wrapped her arms around her folded legs and wore a sick expression as a woman did her hair. Kimmy's makeup was Cover Girl perfect, but her face looked like it could be featured in a special section on anxiety disorders in *Psychology Today*. "Don't you look like the most fabulous bride ever?" Anjoli said as she swept in to kiss Kimmy. Other than the look of horror on her face, she really did.

"What's the matter, Kimmy?" I asked. Anjoli shot me a look urging me to cease and desist with this line of questioning.

"Kimmy has the wedding day jitters, darling. It's perfectly normal. In fact, it's an extremely healthy form of stress release." Kimmy was silent for the next thirty minutes as her hair was twisted and pinned to the top of her head.

"Kimmy," I waved my hands in front of her glazed eyes. "What's going on? Did you take a tranquilizer or something?" I remembered during our teen years, Kimmy could never get to sleep without serious pharmaceutical assistance. A few years later, she couldn't do much without some sort of chemical regulation.

"No," she said flatly. I couldn't read anything into her expressions.

"You look perfect!" her hairdresser said as she pinned the final tendril to the top of Kimmy's head. She shot up in her white lace bra and panty set and snapped, "I do *not* look perfect!" This was the sort of high drama you hear about models in gossip magazines. It was so unlike Kimmy to say anything negative, much less rude. This wedding brought out the worst in her. Then I got it.

"Kimmy, you do look perfect. Is the problem your hair, or the wedding?" I asked.

"Lucy, what kind of thing is that to ask ten minutes before Kimmy and I are walking down the aisle?! Give her a little credit, darling. Certainly, Kimmy's given this marriage a great deal of deliberation, which is why she's—"

"Lucy's right, Auntie!" Kimmy collapsed into her chair. "My hair is fine," she turned to the hairdresser to apologize. "I'm sorry, it's not you. The hairstyle is lovely. It's *him*." She pointed her finger straight out. *Adam? Oh, she meant Geoff.* "I'm so sorry, Auntie. I know you spent a lot on the wedding and your dress and everything, but I can't do this."

"Why not, darling?!" Anjoli exclaimed.

"Because the thought of being Geoff's wife makes me want to totally barf," Kimmy sobbed. Maybe it was just Anjoli clinging to her chest in shock, but it sure looked as though she were shielding it from Kimmy's threatened sickness. I'll give Anjoli credit for this. When she's on your side, she can spin anything so you feel as though everything—no matter how disastrous— is part of some spiritual growth process.

"This is a breakthrough for you, Kimmy!" Anjoli said. "You've always been such a people-pleaser. For you to disregard the feelings of your fiancé and disappoint the three hundred guests who came to see a royal wedding is monumental. Finally, you're putting your own needs ahead of others—and on such a grand scale too. This is worth five years in therapy!"

"You're not angry?" Kimmy looked up from her lace handkerchief.

"Angry?!" Anjoli waved her hand. "I've never been more proud, darling."

They hugged and Adam's hands reached up to my mouth. "I hate to interject reality here, but someone's got to tell Geoff and his three hundred closest friends that he's being jilted. The wedding was supposed to start ten minutes ago."

Kimmy looked at Anjoli, who suggested I'd be the perfect person for the job. "Why me?"

"You're the matron of honor, darling. This is part of your duties."

"Really? Is there a designated person to announce jiltings?"

Anjoli looked impatiently at me. "It can't be Kimmy!" she said. "If she goes to the chapel, the organ will start playing and everyone will think she's there to *marry* him."

"Imagine that!" I laughed. "It's not like they weren't sent engraved invitations to a wedding."

"You're angry with me, Lucy. I can tell," Kimmy said. "I'm sorry, but he's such a creep. You don't want me to marry a creep, do you?"

"I don't want to break this to him," I whined.

"Stop being so selfish!" Anjoli said. "Kimmy needs our help. This is her special day!"

"Mother, you just applauded Kimmy for being selfish! And I'm sorry, is it still your special day if you jilt the groom?!"

"I'm going to climb out the window and I don't care who tells him!" Kimmy stomped her ivory shoe.

"Kimmy, there's no window here. You'd have to go into the chapel, throw a rock through the stained glass, and climb out that way."

"Then that's what I'll do!"

My mother shot me a look begging me to de-escalate this situation. I just needed my sixty seconds of selfishness before I would concede to being the bearer of bad news. "Kimmy, stop for a second and think about how utterly ridiculous that would be. Just put some clothes on and Anjoli will walk you out the front door. I'll tell the guests."

"Can you tell Edward that I'll meet him back at the apartment?" Anjoli asked.

"You brought a date?" I shrieked. "Adam's pediatrician?!" She shrugged as if to ask why not. "He's married. It's a wedding. Do you *not* see the irony?" I threw my hands in the air. "Fine, I'll tell him. Any message for Geoff, Kimmy?"

"Tell him this is for the best," Kimmy said as she and my mother finally unpinned her veil from her head. Kimmy slipped on her white pantsuit—appropriately enough, her getaway outfit—and slipped out the door with my mother.

It's for the best, I muttered silently. I'm sure he'll find that deeply comforting.

As Adam and I reached the entrance to the chapel, all heads turned to us. I was dressed in a nursing t-shirt and jeans. People began to whisper. Clearly, something was wrong.

"Is everything okay?" Geoff asked as I finally reached him at the altar. This, of course, was the moment Adam decided to test the acoustics of St. Patrick's Cathedral. He screamed like I'd never heard before. Wailing mournful, horrible tears of utter horror. I tried to shout above my son's crying, and just as I got to the part where I said, "It's for the best," Adam stopped. "Best, best, best" echoed throughout the chapel.

Everyone turned their heads in every direction to murmur about what this might mean. But they knew. We all did. Adam began crying again, which was actually a relief because I had no idea what to say to Geoff, who was standing agape with a fresh corsage pinned to his tux. I caught Jack's eye. He offered to take Adam, an offer I gladly accepted. Finally, when Adam stopped crying, I heard Aunt Bernice in a stage whisper say to Rita, "See, I told you that baby wasn't deaf."

"I'm sorry to announce that the wedding has been postponed indefinitely," I said, avoiding eye contact with Geoff's entire side of the chapel. "I know this is a shock, and on behalf of my family, I'd like to apologize for inconveniencing you all today. I hope you will all join me in supporting Kimmy in her decision. I know she feels terrible about everyone wasting their time here today, but I know you'd all feel even worse if Geoff and Kimmy, two very decent people, made the mistake of entering into a marriage they weren't absolutely committed to."

No one except Aunt Bernice looked terribly supportive. "That's very true," she said loud enough for others to join in agreement. But they did not. They all seemed very pissed off—at me. "Alrighty then, as a gesture of apology, my family extends invitations to you and your guests at Marco's, where the reception will not be this evening. The directions are on your invitation. And if you have any favorite Sinatra songs, the band will gladly take your requests, so just try to think of this as a bride-less reception, and enjoy!"

Chapter 21

Believe it or not, Geoff's family took me up on the dinner invitation and insisted that Adam and I have dinner with the jilted groom. It wasn't a friendly "let's all be civilized about this" kind of thing. They wanted answers and since Kimmy and Anjoli had fled the crime scene, and Jack had a Valentine's Day date with Natalie, I was stuck as the ambassador of the rogue nation. I knew Jack would have to leave the reception early with a prearranged excuse about an emergency at the gallery. What I didn't expect was for him to be quite so excited about his early dismissal. I had hoped he might want to stick around and help me deal with Geoffrey's lynch mob, but he had plans of dinner and champagne in Tribecca with Natalie.

"So where is the runaway bride, anyway?" Geoff's sister Anne asked as the waiter placed our menus in our hands. He looked intrigued by the question and slowed his rounds to hear my reply.

"I'm not sure where they went," I apologized.

"They?!" Geoff's mother snapped as she placed a protective hand on her son's shoulder. "Is there another

man involved?" Geoff said nothing as the women at the table took charge.

"No, I mean, I don't think so. I just meant Kimmy and my mother," I explained, imagining one hundred gay men at the apartment for an impromptu altar-jumping party. Alfie was playing piano, revamping the Billy Idol classic to the new and improved "It's a Nice Day for a Non-Wedding." Anjoli was toasting Kimmy's extraordinary courage, and supermodels were sipping champagne from Kimmy's satin shoes. Meanwhile I wondered how in the world I ended up at Marco's with someone else's family.

"I suppose what we'd like to know," began Geoff's mother as she sat erect in her chair with her hands folded like a school principal, "is why did Kimberly wait until the day of the wedding to cancel? It seems in terribly poor form."

Adam started making noises that were not cries, but more like nondescript moans that meant something to him. He seemed to be trying to add to the conversation. I bounced him to try to soothe him into silence, but he would not cooperate. Of course, he chose the moment when all eyes were on me to want to nurse.

"I'm not sure," I stammered. Geoff's mother frightened me. So did his elegant sister and their stern, silent father. Geoff was a sight to be pitied tonight, though under normal circumstances he would have fit right in with this country club family. "I guess she didn't really understand, until she was right about to do it, that she really didn't want to marry Geoff. I hope that doesn't sound too harsh, but it appears to be the reality. I'm not sure. Geoff, you should call Kimmy and ask her yourself. I really can't speak for her."

"He'll do no such thing!" blasted the booming baritone of his father. "Do not call that woman under any circumstances, do you understand me, Geoffrey?" I started to unsnap the flap of my dress to feed Adam when Geoff's mother caught a glimpse.

"You're *not* going to do that at the table, dear," she said. It was not a question.

"Well *we're* eating at the table. Where do you propose I feed my son?"

"Forget about this!" Geoff snapped at his mother. "I want to know where Kimmy is. What did she say, Lucy? Where did she say she was going? I'm going to her."

His father actually stood up from his seat as though he might physically prevent Geoff from trying to leave. "Sit down!" he insisted. *Um, sir, you're the only one standing.* "Do not go groveling to that woman. She's not going to make any more a fool of you than she already has, son. And you! Put your breast away and cease that nonsense immediately."

Put my breast away?! Now, let me be very clear about something. I may have had a little trouble breast-feeding at first, but after six weeks at it, I was a pro. I had bras and shirts that had more secret compartments and trick doors than the Bat Cave. I nursed so discreetly, most of the time, people had no idea I was breast-feeding. It simply looked as though my son was resting comfortably at my chest. Okay, there were times when he'd push off against my stomach to get a little extra pull of milk, but even then, no skin showed. I was pretty pleased to be such a skilled breast-feeder, especially when my mother and aunts were not able to offer me any guidance whatsoever. So this "put your breast away" business pissed me off. I wondered if Geoff was like his father and if this is what she meant when Kimmy told the florist that her fiancé was a control freak. Furthermore, I wondered what the hell I was doing at this dinner table with the jilted, mean family. They did not need me to console them. I couldn't provide them with answers. I was simply the sacrificial lamb, a symbol of Kimmy to be slaughtered at the dinner table. With that realization I stood and told them that my son, my breasts, and I were leaving.

"Geoff, I'm sorry to leave early, but given everything you've been through this evening, I'm sure my skipping dinner falls into the category of small stuff you're not going to sweat. Good evening."

Dramatic exits are always so much more effective when the person leaving doesn't need to pack chewing toys, a muppet, and a case of wipes into a diaper bag, then strap on a baby sling and adjust an infant into it. Three full minutes later, I was ready to walk out the door. "So good evening then," I repeated, resisting the temptation to whip out my right boob and squirt a stream of milk in Geoff's father's face.

On the bus ride home, I asked Adam if we'd ever go to a normal party together. "You always said normal was boring, Mommy," I imagined him saying to me one day. Right now, I'd kill for a healthy dose of boredom. Adam floated off to sleep as I drifted fifteen years back to my wedding to Jack.

In some ways I envied Kimmy's and my mother's complete conviction that they are the epicenter of everything fabulous. I would never presume to ask people to give up their Valentine's Day to attend my wedding. Nor would it ever occur to me to have a royal wedding at the colossal St. Patrick's Cathedral. I would never dream of asking my mother to pay for 300 dinner guests at Marco's. When I was younger and started lightening my hair, I remember seeing those L'Oreal commercials where the gorgeous women would say that the hair color costs a bit more, but they were worth it. So I bought Clairol.

My wedding to Jack suited our style, though, and it was thoroughly lovely. We had fifty guests in Anjoli's backyard on a humid summer night in July. She placed white Christmas lights in the trees and a string quartet played classical music on Anjoli's terra-cotta patio. She hired out-of-work actors to serve tiny hors d'oeuvres like lobster puffs and mini potatoes with sour cream and caviar. More than any of that, I remember looking at Jack and thinking how lucky I was to be spending the rest of my life with my best friend. To finally have found my home. When Jack and I danced together for the first time as a married couple, he whispered that he hoped we died together because the thought of one of us holding the other's body, and not feeling the incredible warmth we shared that night, was too painful to bear. I told you Jack was never light and breezy. I knew that when I met him and he was working on a painting in varying shades of black acrylic, and paving large, dead insects into it.

His marriage proposal was surprisingly upbeat. We were still in grad school in Ann Arbor and one night we were walking home from seeing a movie at the Michigan Theatre. "Stop," he said. He looked at his watch and said, "Kiss me right now." I happily complied. We were underneath the arch of the West Engineering Building as the Bell Tower gonged twelve times. "Keep going," he pulled on my hands when I pulled away. "That will do," he said as the final bell tolled.

"What was that all about?" I laughed, although I secretly knew.

The campus legend was that couples who kissed under the arch at the stroke of midnight would stay in love forever, he explained. "So do you think it's true?" Jack asked.

"I don't know," I giggled.

"How 'bout we find out? Whaddya say? Are you game for an experiment? We'll get married and see about this staying in love forever business." He smiled.

I wasn't sure if he was kidding. "I know it would be a huge sacrifice on your part, Lucy. Having to stay with me for your whole life, but in the name of social science and the love of U of M, might you consider it?" Then he got down on one knee and pulled from his pocket a velvet box with an antique engagement ring that belonged to his grandmother. A few people slowed down their walk onto the Diag to watch the proposal, though no one stopped and stared openly.

"Jack," I knelt down to him. "I already know I'll love you forever, and I'd marry you right this second if I could." Our wedding was the following weekend.

Obviously, I will be suing the University of Michigan for selling a naïve grad student false hopes for eternal wedded bliss. Unfortunately the monetary compensation for a broken heart is quite low. The best I'd get is a Chicago Dog at Red Hot Lovers.

Our first ten years were so smooth and effortless, I remember being quite smug about it actually. People would talk about how marriage was such hard work, and I very arrogantly thought that they simply didn't have as intense a love as Jack and I did. I guess when things really started to unravel was after the second miscarriage. It could have brought us together, but had quite the opposite effect. Jack was so distant. He never said anything about anything, and would've preferred if I didn't either. Every time I shared a feeling with him, he immediately insisted that I deny it. God knows, I understand that when someone says, "Oh, don't feel sad," they really are trying to help. But telling me not to feel what I'm already feeling is not at all helpful. He'd also repeat like a mantra, "It's okay, it's okay, Lucy." Again, I know he was trying to soothe me, but "it" was not okay. Helpful tip for husbands: If your wife is hysterically crying over the loss of her babies, her father, or you, her husband, everything is definitely not okay. Trying to convince her otherwise is emotional abandonment at its worst. I remember a few weeks ago, I was at the park with Adam and a baby in his stroller was wailing at the top of his lungs, and the mom was saying, "You're okay, you're okay, you're okay." Guess what? If the kid's crying, he's not okay, no matter how much you wish it weren't so. Deal with whatever's bothering him.

I wondered what Jack's side of the story was. According to Natalie, he had no idea why our relationship broke down. Perhaps he had theories but didn't want to share them with her despite their oh-so-long history. Was it my weight? Did we simply drift in opposite directions or does he feel I pushed him away? If I asked him where we went wrong, would he think I was trying to reconcile? Perhaps I would tell him I needed closure on our relationship. Oh God, I'm turning into my mother.

Chapter 22

If I hadn't had a six-week-old baby with me, I would have checked into a homeless shelter that night. When I arrived at my mother's home, there was a soiree that surpassed my wildest expectations. Kimmy was body surfing in her wedding gown atop the meticulously manicured hands of her guests. Anjoli was wildly playing the saxophone (she doesn't play). Dr. Comstock gyrated his hips as though he should have dollar bills stuffed in his G-string. Oh God, on second glance, I saw that my son's pediatrician *did* have dollar bills stuffed in what was thankfully not a G-string, but rather, Disney character boxer shorts. And surprise, surprise, Alfie was at the keyboard doing the campiest, gayest renditions of wedding songs ever heard. No one noticed me come. Or go.

An hour later, as I turned the key to my home in Caldwell, I heard the unmistakable sounds of sex coming from the room formerly known as my home office. "Quiet, honey," I whispered to Adam. "We wouldn't want to interrupt Daddy fucking his girlfriend."

The next morning Natalie made pancakes for the

three of us, and asked if I minded if she and Jack spent the day with Adam. The way she moved around my kitchen filled me with rage and inadequacy. I felt as though I was in a gender-swapped American version of *Bed and Sofa*. How did she know where the wire whisk was when I had no clue? Was she boiling water with *my* teakettle?! As much as I tried to find fault with Natalie, the reality was I couldn't help but like her. She was smart, insightful, and pretty in a very unassuming way. (Which was difficult to do considering she was assuming my role as Jack's wife and Adam's mother.)

"Enjoy!" I said, too enthusiastically. "I'm sure you guys will have a lovely day together. And I could use the break myself. I've got a million things to take care of." *Namely screwing the first willing guy that comes directly into my line of vision.*

What was Natalie's agenda anyway? Oh sure, she seemed sweet enough with her schoolteacher calmness and artsy good looks, but beneath the surface was there someone far more evil and dangerous? Might she and Jack have a plan to kill me for my life insurance money? Or was she simply trying on the role of step-mommy and second wife to see how it fit her?

"I've got to tell you, Lucy. I think you're just about the coolest woman I've ever met," Natalie interrupted my silent musings. "Not every mother would feel comfortable with this whole setup, and welcome me into her home like you have. I hope you know how much I genuinely appreciate your generosity." Jack looked up from his newspaper and smiled. He was having his pancakes and eating them too. I wanted to cry. Why couldn't this woman have the decency to be loathsome?!

Adam had no loyalty whatsoever. Whenever Natalie made funny faces at him, he laughed. Whenever she cooed baby talk to him, he gurgled back. If I had a daughter, she'd instinctively know to shun this imposter. I heard the three of them bundling up at the front door, discussing their plans for the day. Natalie wondered if the Natural History Museum still had the frogs. Jack thought the planetarium would be fun. A laser show, he suggested. I got the pediatric appointments, midnight nursings, and toenail clippings. These two get the planetarium. Adam would grow up to hate me, thinking Jack and Natalie were the fun ones and I was the bitch who enforced curfew and homework.

"Good boy!" Natalie squealed. *What did he do?!* I nearly ran from my bedroom to see. Then I heard Adam giggle. *That was my giggle! He should have giggled for his mommy. He's never giggled for me. Ever! When they get home, I'm going to snatch back my child and be the funniest mother anyone has ever seen! The boy will laugh himself into a state of exhaustion, then fall into a deep, eight-hour slumber thinking that he has the most hilarious mother in the whole wide world and that all others are simply cheap imitations.* The door closed and they were gone.

I sat at my computer screen and stared at poor rain-drenched Desdemona. I imagined her turning her coquettish little body toward me and putting her hand on her hip. "I've been in the rain on a cobblestone road for months," she'd say. "How 'bout you do something with me already? At least bring me indoors!"

Desdemona came in from the rain, drenched and dejected. It had been a tough day. Her husband never noticed her come in, much less offered her a towel or a cup of tea. It had been so long since he'd noticed anything about Desdemona. She went to the kitchen to look for her teakettle, and wondered where it had gone. It seemed so much of Desdemona's life had been misplaced recently.

"Thank you," my character said to me from the

computer screen. "Perhaps in chapter two, I will find my kettle, no?"

Thankfully, the ringing phone interrupted my internal chatter. "Hello, I'm looking for Lucy Klein," a woman said.

"Who's this?" I snapped in my telemarketer-defense mode.

"This is Karen from *Salon.* We received your submission for Mothers Who Think, *There's Something About Barney,* and we love it."

I peed. The downside of having recently given birth was the incredibly poor bladder control.

"You did?" I said, hoping she'd spend the afternoon on the phone telling me exactly everything she loved about my piece.

"Yes, it's just what we're looking for. Smart, sharp, and edgy."

"Thank you."

"No, thank *you* for thinking of us. Do you mind if I ask how you came up with the idea?" I told her about the Barney birthday party and how Dr. Lee showed up at the end to facilitate a therapy session for the kids. "Wow, that's pretty bad. I thought the one I went to in Los Angeles was weird," Karen said. "A three-year-old slugged the photographer and called him 'paparazzi.' Prince Charming refused to eat a piece of cake because he was on Atkin's."

"You're kidding?! What about the princess?"

"Oh she had two slices. I'd never seen a porky princess character before," she said.

"Well when you've got all those royal feasts to attend, who can keep trim, right?" I said desperately hoping she wasn't a calorie Nazi who'd snap that Cinderella was a lazy, fat cow who should join a gym.

"Amen to that," she said instead. "Maybe that should be your next article, Lucy. Anyway, my editor asked me to see what else you've got. We like your style. What are you working on now?"

Ummmm.

Desdemona stormed into her room and burst into tears. "Now I will never get my cup of tea!" she cried.

"I actually just started working on a piece called 'It Takes a Village to Nurse a Child,' I bluffed.

"Pitch me," said Karen.

"Traditionally breast-feeding is something that was taught by one generation of mothers to the next, right?" I heard her grunt in agreement. "But our mothers weren't encouraged to breast-feed, so there's this whole gap in knowledge from today's grandmothers to today's new moms. There's a whole community of breast-feeding consultants, though, from La Leche League mothers who will drive to your house and help you, to paid lactation consultants, and hospital specialty shops just for breast-feeding. How 'bout if I write something about my experience struggling to nurse and how this subculture of breast-feeding experts was there to help. The whole village concept in the context of nursing a child."

"Write it," she said.

"Write it?"

"Yeah, it rocks. Give us seven hundred words in two weeks and we'll run it in May. We like your edge, Lucy. There's not a lot out there with your utter lack of treacle sentimentality about motherhood."

I felt pressure to say something that would maintain this image. What unsentimental thing could I say to show her how edgy I am? "Alrighty then, two weeks it is," I said. *Oy!*

Four hours later, I finished my story.

When I was pregnant, the Nature Channel aired a video safari through Africa. I watched the ani-

mals effortlessly nurse their young and arrogantly recalled a friend's suggestion that I take a breast-feeding class. Who needs a class in the most natural thing in the world? Why would anyone waste their time and money on a breast-feeding class? Be careful what you ask, because very soon, you may discover the answer. Breast-feeding may be natural, but it's not always easy. It's a skill passed down from generation to generation of mothers, and as I soon learned, it takes a village to nurse a child.

I went on to tell about Mary and her boob-shaped car, and how the thrush was diagnosed not by medical doctors, but by another mom who took the time to come to my house one night with her *La Leche League Big Book of Answers*. Since I opened with a reference to Africa, and the village proverb was African, I'd continued with this theme. Mary was likened to a chimpanzee while I made Candace into a cheetah. The other women in the La Leche League meeting took on characteristics of other jungle animals. I spared no one the comparison, least of all myself and Adam, mama and baby baboon.

Two weeks later, Karen called to say the magazine accepted my article. "I love the part about the word 'you' being synonymous with your nipples. Our readers are going to love your style," she said. I adored Karen. I couldn't remember the last time someone forecasted my success or said they liked my style.

It was March and Natalie and Jack had kidnapped my child yet again. They took my baby to the playground, so I decided to grab lunch at Lo Fats before attempting to revive the tale of Desdemona the waif whose husband had forgotten her. I'm not sure why I continued to go to Lo Fats when the menu was clearly anything but. I liked the idea of dieting far more than the reality. And truth be told, I loved to watch the chef throw food onto the flaming wok. The kitchen was an open one, so I could always admire his muscular arms and defined chest through his white undershirt. He had brown skin that could have either been Puerto Rican or Native American and black eyes that belonged to no particular race or creed, but were rather a universal feature of sex gods. Every time he saw me enter the restaurant, he'd come to the counter to take my order. He'd shake his black curls out of his eyes even though they were secured under a backward, light-blue Yankees cap. Most of the time, the manager, a miserable scoop of lard, ordered him back to the kitchen, then revealed his inflamed gums as he took my order. Yes, I was chunky, okay chubby, but this guy was downright amorphous. His overall appearance seemed almost defiant. It was as if he was saying, "Look how vile I can be!" He wore greasy blond hair and had pimples on his chin that somehow sprouted hairs from them! And his misshapen red nose had such prominent blackheads, it actually looked like a strawberry. Whoever decided to put Lard Scoop up front and lock the brown-skinned love god in the back was indeed a moron. But on this day in March, the snow had melted, the sky was blue, and Lard Scoop was nowhere to be seen.

Chapter 23

"Forgive me, father, for I have sinned. I'm not Catholic, is that okay?" I saw the priest's silhouette nod that I was welcome to confess at his church. "I'm Jewish. We don't have this kind of setup, but it seems like a good idea. Like therapy where you don't actually need to analyze every little nitty-gritty detail of my psychological makeup, but just do your penance and move on. Anyway, what I guess I'm trying to say, father, is that I think you Catholics are on to something here." I wanted to suck up to the priest before I dropped my adultery bomb on him. "I had sex with a man who's not my husband, which is not the part I need to confess because my husband is actually okay with me having sex with other men. I mean, really, he's had at least two girlfriends over the last year, so he's hardly one to judge. It's just that I feel so violated. I feel like I violated myself by having sex with this stranger. I mean he isn't a *stranger* stranger. I've seen him cooking behind the counter before and we've exchanged a few words. Okay, I guess that would make him a stranger. I just didn't want you to think I just met him *that day.* It's been a few weeks that we've been flirting. But anyway it was supposed to make me feel young and sexy, but I ended up feeling raped. Raped by myself, does that make any sense at all?" I paused. "Father? Father, you're going to need to help me out here. This is my first time at confession. Is this interactive, or do I have to wait till the end to get your feedback?"

"You've been very wicked," he said.

"Well I'm not sure I'd call it wicked, father. My husband and I have an arrangement, you see. He says it's okay for me to, um, to fornicate."

"Your husband is not God," the priest replied.

"Yeah well, someone forgot to give him the memo on that one. Anyway, I'm hoping you can give me a little wave of that ash wand thing or give me a few prayers to say to make me feel better."

"My child, have you ever heard of the show *Real Confessions*?"

"Have I ever heard of it? It's the number one rated show in America! My friend Zoe is a producer. I actually wrote the tag line. *Real Confessions*, missing it is the real sin. Wait a minute . . . am I on TV?!"

Okay, none of this happened, but there are sprinkles of truth throughout my mid-morning horror fantasy. First, by the end of March, *Real Confessions* was the number one hit television show in America. Zoe was raking in the bucks because not only were advertisers clamoring for placement on the show, but everyone knew about it because of the storm of controversy it had caused. They spent almost no money promoting the show because it was covered by news media everywhere you turned. Catholics protested in front of FOX, priests blasted the show in their sermons, and finally the crowning jewel of controversy, the Catholic producers of the show were all excommunicated. Of course, this attracted a flurry of national media coverage. When the Vatican issued a statement denouncing the show, it became headline news. Tabloid shows of rival stations couldn't help but cover the controversy. *Dateline, 20/20*—they were all there to gobble it up. One priest made the mistake of implying that Zoe had an anti-Catholic agenda because she was Jewish. This angered the Jewish community, so the Anti-Defamation League got involved. Within hours the Ku Klux Klan got into the fray, issuing a statement saying that while they hated Catholics, Jews were even worse. Who knows what their position on the show was? Of course, this pissed everyone off, especially when the ACLU weighed in and said that the KKK had every right to voice its opinion. The civil liberties union stood by the white-hooded lunatics, saying that simply claiming to hate Catholics (and Jews) wasn't technically hate speech. For two weeks in March, *Real Confessions* was the hot topic on everything from *Capitol Gang* to the *O'Reilly Factor*. The only clear winner was the show, which had everyone's attention.

The second truth is far less exciting. I did wind up having sex with the Lo Fats chef. Eddie was his name, I found out minutes before my underpants were pushed to the side of my crotch in the back seat of my Ford Windstar. Let me rewind. I was sitting in a booth at Lo Fats, enjoying a book that was so hilarious I felt like an utterly inadequate scribbler of fluff. I sat in my booth giggling with every page when I heard a voice from the kitchen shout, "You getting off now?" The chef was talking to Eddie, and I don't mind admitting that I had a physical reaction to the question about him getting off. I peeked up from my book to see that Eddie had nodded yes. I confess that earlier I called Lo Fats and pretended to be a job applicant. I said I was interested in a position as a cook and asked when the shifts were. When I found out that the day shift ended at 5:00 P.M.,

I made sure to stop by at 4:30 on my free day, and park myself at a booth. I put on just enough makeup to look as though I wasn't trying quite as hard as I was, and squeezed into my pre-pregnancy jeans. I sat, trying to look as casual as I could with the circulation in my legs long ago cut off, and read.

"Hey there, Chicken Salad," he said. Sounds ridiculous, I know, but when you've been sex-deprived for more than a year, you take your opening lines as they come.

"Oh, hi," I said.

"You readin' something funny?"

"Um, yeah, it's called *Sellevision*. It's about this home-shopping network that—"

" 'Cause you crackin' up over there."

"Where?" I wondered aloud.

"Here at the table," he said.

"Oh, *here.*"

"Yeah, that's what I said," Eddie said.

"No, you actually said *there* so I wondered where you meant because we're both *here,* not there." *Jesus Christ, Lucy! End this utterly moronic conversation and say something flirty and fun.* "So, do you know where I can get a car wash around here? My minivan's a mess." *Merciful God, kill me now.*

"You need a car wash?" he asked. Thankfully, since Eddie was legally brain-dead, he didn't notice anything particularly odd about my request.

"Yes, I need a car wash," I said.

"I know a place you can get a car wash," he said. Okay, clearly, this isn't going to be the man I have a deep and meaningful relationship with but, when he wasn't speaking, he was so incredibly sexy.

"And what do I need to do to get this information from you?" I smiled. If this guy asked for payment, I was seriously going to go to the supply room of Lo

Fats, fill a bucket with water and detergent, and stick my head in it until I drowned.

"Aw, you don't need to gimme nothing for that," he said. It wasn't a rejection, but he either was ignoring my flirtation because he was disinterested, or he missed it altogether. "There's a car wash right on the corner here, um, there."

Okay, now what?! Great goddamned plan, Lucy. Step one: Ask for the nearest car wash, proving you're an unaware rube to have missed the one on the corner. Step two: Have him give you the information. Step three: Say, "Oh thanks. Bye!"

"Is it any good?" I asked. *Please God, strike me dead right now. I do not deserve to live! I am simply a waste of food.*

"Yeah, they cleaned my mom's car real nice," he said.

"Great, I'll give them a try!"

"You think you could give me a ride home? I don't mind stopping off at the car wash with you. I need to pick me up some smokes anyways."

What am I doing? I panicked. I'm advancing the flirtation with a short-bus retard, thinking it will actually help me feel good about myself. Tell him no. Tell him I'm in a rush. Tell him I need to just get my car washed and go home. Then he smiled and no words came out of his mouth. "Okay," I smiled.

As my minivan passed the black strips marking the entry of the car wash, Eddie turned to me. Manufactured sheets of rain sprayed the headlights, then hood, then windshield of my minivan. Something about the sound of the rushing water and the absence of Eddie speaking had the effect of a glass of red wine. I ran my fingers through my hair and relaxed my head back on the seat, hoping he would catch my vibe. I glanced at him and smiled slightly, hinting for physical contact.

"Can I ax you somethin'?" Eddie said.

"No," I snapped. I was feeling so sensual and ready for a man's touch, I knew whatever he had to ax me would, well, ax it.

"Shit, I never heard that before," he shook his head, not knowing what to do next.

"Don't ask, do," I smiled invitingly. It took a few seconds for him to figure out what this highly complex sentence meant, but then he kissed me. This man was not a real thinker, but he was an excellent kisser. He was a genius, really. His thick, warm lips covered mine like a blanket as he gently stroked his tongue across my mouth. He was completely and totally in charge without being overbearing. Most guys kiss as though they're in a sword fight with you, lashing their tongues around as if they get bonus points for taking out your teeth. Not Eddie. I'm quite sure I sighed, "Oh dear God," which gave him the confidence to slide his thick fingers through the buttons of my blouse and graze my breasts. Rainbow colored suds began dropping down onto my windshield as a green light flashed, "Move forward."

"Let's go in the back where we have more room," Eddie said.

"More room for what?" I was the idiot now.

"Come on," he urged.

Panicked that the incredible kissing would end, I complied. He unstrapped Adam's car seat and tossed it into the back compartment where I put groceries and silos of laundry detergent. *Oh my God, he wants to . . .* before I could finish the thought, he leapt at me, this time far more aggressively. I landed on my back and heard what sounded like a duck being tortured. It was Adam's chewy toy that quacked when squeezed. I pulled it from under my butt cheek and tried to forget that I was mid-cycle of a car wash in New Jersey, but nothing seemed to help.

"What's your name?" I asked, trying desperately to backtrack.

"Eddie," he said.

"I'm Lucy." I tried to sit up.

At any point, I could have stopped. While crass and uneducated, Eddie was not a rapist, and would have surely complied with my request to put his penis back in his pants and release me from his body pinned on top of mine.

"Lucy, good to meet you," he laughed, struggling, squirming to get his pants down. I wanted nothing more than for this to end, and yet I did nothing to stop it. "Can you slide your panties over for me?"

This is not what I wanted. "Eddie, why don't we wait until we know each other a little better?"

"I can't wait," he said. "You're so beautiful and sexy and I gotta be inside you." And with those final words, I surrendered and he slid into me with ease. "See baby, you want it. Don't worry, I'm going to give you what you need." Not exactly what I would have scripted him to say, but I wouldn't have set my hot sex scene in a car wash either. Could he give me what I needed? What *did* I need anyway? As I tried to convince myself that this tryst was liberating and empowering, I heard Eddie start to grunt like he was lifting heavy boxes. His skin was moist with sweat and his face scrunched up with a strained look. *He couldn't possibly be done so soon, could he?* He let out a final howl that confirmed that Eddie, the retarded cook, was indeed coming inside me. He retrieved his slick flesh from my body and tucked it back into his briefs, and pulled his pants up from around his knees. He wiped his sweaty forehead with the sleeve of his white shirt with the Lo Fats logo embroidered on it. "Thanks, baby. That felt real good." The final rinse of the car wash began and the colorful suds were washed away as my car began to roll forward on its own.

Thanks, baby. That felt real good? What happened to giving me what I need?

Seconds later, I heard the tornado-like wind of the dry cycle of the car wash as the artificial light was replaced by the natural evening sky. Tiny beads of water separated and clung to the window as they were blown toward the edges. A new light-sign read, "Your car has never been cleaner!"

Eddie and I had a silent drive to his house, a trashy white home with expired aluminum siding and broken car parts strewn across the driveway. "Maybe we could do this again sometime," Eddie said as he hopped out of my car. *Maybe?!* Never again in my life did I want to see this revolting creature. But what exactly did *he* need to consider? Why was it a maybe in *his* mind? He got no-strings, effortless sex *and* a ride home. What part of this deal was unfavorable to him? Maybe, my ass! For a moment of insanity, I thought about asking him to dinner that weekend and trying to convince him that I was someone he definitely wanted to see again. I was no "maybe" girl.

Reality appeared suddenly—and rudely. Gravity kicked in and Eddie's wetness escaped from me and was absorbed into my panties. I needed to get home immediately to shower myself with Clorox and vomit my Lo Fats chicken salad. "Good-bye, Eddie," I said, my minivan screeching away.

I walked into my house ten minutes later to find Natalie feeding Adam a bottle of my breast milk as she and my husband watched a DVD. It was some romantic comedy where adorable Kate Hudson was charming her leading man—not being mistaken for a sperm receptacle that a dull-witted cook may or may not want to shoot his wad into again.

Chapter 24

_____

"**M**en are vile creatures, darling!" Anjoli said into the phone. She never bothered with "Hello" or "It's your mother." God knows I rarely heard her start a conversation by asking how I was. My mother immediately launched into her monologue of the day.

I lifted Adam from his bouncer seat and rested him on my hip. His hair was a thick patch, similar to Jack's. He was starting to mimic the facial expressions of Jack and me, which was hilarious to see. Adam also picked up a few mugs from Natalie, which was far less adorable. "Mother, this is not a good time for me," I said, about to explain that we were on our way to a La Leche League meeting.

"Me either, Lucy! That's why I'm calling. I'm in crisis, darling!" She always pronounced "crisis" with a French accent.

"What's wrong?" I asked, deciding I could pack Adam's bag while still carrying on a conversation with Anjoli.

"It's that bastard pediatrician of yours."

"Dr. Comstock? What did he do?"

"Kiki's boyfriend invited us to his place in Barbados next week. Just the four of us in his fabulous seaside villa with an entire staff, and a million nightclubs and places to shop. Guess what Edward said when I tell him about our plans?"

"That he can't go," I said flatly.

"Yes! How did you guess?"

"Mother, he's a married man. You can't expect him to be available to you on a moment's notice like a single guy would."

"He's a bore," she dismissed. "If he had any passion for living, he would find a way to make this trip happen for us. How many times in his boring little life does an opportunity like this fall into his lap?"

"*This* is your crisis, Mother?"

"It's pushing my abandonment buttons," she said. I sat on the couch, resigned that I would be late for my meeting. After a minute, I reconsidered.

"Mother, call my cell phone, so we can finish this chat while I'm driving."

"Isn't that illegal?" she asked.

"So is trading banned Kent cigarettes for Romanian money! So is ignoring a Czech order that you never enter the country again. And believe it or not, so is adultery in some states."

"Not in New York!" Anjoli snapped.

"That's right because nothing matters if it's not happening in New York, least of all in New Jersey."

"Darling, we're talking about your safety. Driving while you're on the cell phone is equivalent to driving under the influence of two cocktails."

"Three if the person's talking to you," I replied.

"I simply care about you. There's no need to get huffy."

"Mother, if you don't want me to drive while on the cell phone with you, then let me go. I will call you later. Dr. Comstock refusing your invitation to Barbados does not qualify as a crisis. I'm late and I need to go."

"Lucy, this *is* a crisis for me," Anjoli pleaded.

"It's not for me, though!"

"Can't you help me, darling? Talk to Edward for me. Tell him what a cad he's being."

"Okay, Mother, I will help you." I took a deep breath and looked at Adam dressed in his jacket and spring hat. "Here's my advice. Stop dating married men. They are not emotionally or physically available to you. You are far too high-maintenance for this gig. I can't remember a single legitimate relationship you've ever been in, and it takes its toll on everyone who has to play a role in it—including me. Especially me. Mother, I am by no means blaming you for every relationship problem I have, and you know that I love you dearly. But I am so tired of your boyfriend dramas. Do you know how many times I've heard this same story? Your married boyfriends always fail you, and guess what? They always will. I think you like it that way because it gives you something to complain about. You know something else, Mother? I think you like that these men are unavailable to you because it gives you an excuse to be unavailable to them. I'm sorry to be so harsh. I love you, but I have real problems to deal with. I like going to these La Leche League groups because I can talk to women who have issues that I can relate to. I like hearing about sore nipples and introducing solid foods because it's something I can understand. And even though none of them has a husband who dumped them the day the pregnancy results came in, they can understand many of the things I'm going through with Adam. I am now ten minutes late for my meeting and I'm not going to make it eleven. I'm going to hang up now, and because you're so concerned about my safety, I will not be call-

ing you from the road. Your problems will be here
when I get home. If not, I'm sure you'll have some new
ones, so I'll call you then. I love you. Good-bye." I
wish I could report that I hung up the phone and strode
out the door without an ounce of guilt. "Are you still
there?" I asked after a moment.

"I'm here," Anjoli said, clipped.

"Are you going to say anything?"

"You're very dramatic, darling. Enjoy your meeting
and call me the moment you return."

"Are you mad at me?" I asked.

"I have anger, but I wouldn't say you were the cause
of it. It's not my style to blame other people for my
feelings."

"Be careful, Mother. Louise Hay says passive-
aggressive behavior causes wrinkles." And then I hung
up the phone and strode out the door without an ounce
of guilt.

As I expected, I was late for the La Leche League
meeting. What was a pleasant surprise was that my ten-
minute lag was considered neither rude nor unusual.
Only three mothers were there—Mary, Candace, and
an overweight hippie who I hadn't seen before, but she
seemed as if she were an old-timer with the group.
Hannah wore a loose-fitting faded t-shirt, corduroy pants,
and utilitarian shoes. Her long, curly, salt-and-pepper
hair was pulled back into a tortoise-shell barrette and
draped over the denim jacket on her seat back. Mary
looked at her watch and said she was expecting another three mothers, and asked if we minded waiting
another ten minutes. We shook our heads that we didn't.

"So anyway, I'm telling you, they're worse than the
tobacco companies," Hannah continued.

"It just sounds as though you're being terribly judg-
mental of women who use formula," Candace countered. "It's hard enough being a mother without these

divisions between the stay-at-home moms and the working mothers, the nursing mothers, and the ones who use formula. I don't know, Hannah. I hate to sound like Rodney King, but can't we all get along? I mean, every month we sit here and talk about how people condemn our extended nursing and chide us for nursing in public. It's hurtful when your friends and family don't support you. It seems like we're simply turning around and doing the same thing to women who formula feed."

"It's different," Hannah's husky voice defended. Mary set out books and pamphlets on a table and handwrote a sign reminding people to return books they'd borrowed the month before.

"How?" Candace asked. I always envied people who could deliver one-word inquiries. I don't have the confidence to be concise.

"I'm not judging the *mothers* who use formula," Hannah said. "I have a major problem with the misleading tactics the formula-makers use. I think mothers are being duped. I'm not pitting us against them. I'm on their side."

"Ah yes, the poor victimized mothers who make a choice you disagree with need you to come educate—read save—them, is that it?" Candace said. "Look, I hear what you're saying. I'm not blind to what Nestle did to those women in Africa. But I have friends who use formula, and my unspoken deal on nursing, and in life, is that I let them do their thing and not try to change them, and I hope they return the courtesy."

"Candace," Mary interrupted. "I think what Hannah is trying to say is that it's the formula companies she has a problem with, not the mothers. Is there something you want to talk about this week? Is your mother-in-law still pestering you about weaning Barbie?"

Mary is one of those people who says very little, but when she does, it's always relevant. I always feel as though if I spout out enough words, sooner or later something will make sense. As it turned out, Candace's friend suggested—well, insisted—that she refrain from nursing at a dinner party. "She said, 'You'll be more comfortable in the den' and stupid me actually thought she was concerned with my comfort, so I said that I was fine. She shook her head no and made this sad little face." Mary rushed over and hugged Candace.

"I was told to 'put my breast away' at a wedding reception. Well, a jilting reception," I said, hoping to get in on the act. Catching my Anjoli tendencies, I stopped and offered, "That's terrible."

"I really don't know what the middle ground is," Candace said. "I know some people are uncomfortable with my nursing, and it would've been fine if she didn't shake her head like she was disgusted with me."

"It's not fine!" Hannah shouted like a battle cry. "People need to get used to seeing mothers breast-feed. Why are you so damned conciliatory, Candace?! These people would never ask you to bottle-feed in the den."

"Well, it is their home," I offered.

"And it's Mother Nature's planet!" Hannah shouted.

Hannah was militant, but there was something I liked about her. Beneath her bravado and breast-thumping, I saw someone very wounded by the fact that her politics and intellect had alienated her from mainstream culture. I couldn't see where she fit in the world, but hoped she had a community of peaceful, angry people to share her life with. She didn't necessarily want to be accepted by mainstream culture, but at the same time was frustrated that she wasn't. I must also admit that part of my affection for Hannah was that her comment about formula companies using tobacco-industry-like tactics sparked my interest.

While Adam napped, I surfed the Internet and found thousands of articles supporting her theory. Dozens of obscure left-wing papers and even medical journals documented some pretty unsavory strategies used by formula-makers. I found that they spent an average of $8,000 per pediatrician per year supplying free gifts to offices. Not a bad thing to do until you consider that everything has logos and is a tacit endorsement of formula. I read about a formula company that offered to build a new maternity ward at a hospital, provided it was far away from the nursery. The author explained that the farther the distance between mother and newborn, the more difficulties the couples experience nursing. I read dozens of other examples of shady deals and unethical tactics used, but the one I found most disturbing was the funding of emergency room television dramas where babies died from "insufficient milk syndrome." Nursing women were characterized as selfish flakes who were responsible for their babies' deaths by refusing to use formula. Brought to you by the good people of the formula industry.

Hannah was right. There was a vast right-wing conspiracy to undermine breast-feeding. It was all about economics. And mothers and babies were being sacrificed at the altar of corporate greed. The problem was that Candace was right too. It was time for a cease-fire in the mommy wars. I wanted to do a piece that exposed the formula industry for exploiting mothers, while still being respectful of women's diverse life-styles and choices.

Without even thinking through my pitch, I called the editor of *Mothering* magazine, which I discovered through the La Leche League traveling library. The magazine catered to women from Hannah to Candace and everyone in between who expressed some level of commitment to "natural" parenting. That could mean anything from simply buying organic fruits and veggies to homeschooling and having a family bed. As the phone rang, I drifted into thought about the arts community Jack and I never started. We'd planned to grow our own fruits and vegetables and toss our scraps in a compost heap located just beyond the horse stable.

My fantasy was interrupted by a lovely woman who listened politely to my pitch. At first, I thought the line had disconnected because she was so quiet. Then I realized she must've hated the idea. After a seemingly eternal pause, she told me my timing was perfect. *My husband asked for a divorce the day I discovered I was pregnant. My timing is anything but perfect, but please continue.* "We were talking about doing an investigative piece on the ties between the formula industry and the American Academy of Pediatrics," she explained. The woman asked me to send her samples of my writing and explained the scope of the piece. Three days later, she called back and asked me to write the piece for their summer cover story.

Thrilled as I was to be writing all of these articles about mothering, I felt guilty about not working—not even wanting to work—on my novel. Poor Desdemona. Ignored first by her husband, then her creator.

Chapter 25

"I have to cancel lunch today, Lucy. I'm sorry." In the background of Candace's apology was the cacophony of a household of multiple children. "Everything's crazy right now. Manny's been working late, I'm having family in this weekend, and Barbie's having a fight with her imaginary friend."

"A fight with her imaginary friend?" I said, laughing.

"It's kooky, I know, but what can you do? Last week, Nina wasn't speaking to Barbie. Last month, Nina punched Barbie right in the face."

"Nina?" I asked.

"The imaginary friend," explained Candace matter-of-factly. An operator interrupted our call with an emergency breakthrough from Anjoli. "Oh dear!" Candace shrieked. "You'd better get that. I hope everything's okay."

"It's fine," I said, sure I sounded like the daughter with no compassion. It'd been decades since I was startled by my mother's emergency breakthroughs. Once she interrupted my phone call to ask where I put the salad dressing. Another time, she wanted to know if I was hungry and wanted to grab a bite. (She lived in the same apartment building at the time, mind you.) Sometimes her motives were less selfish. A few times she'd called because she was at a sale and wanted to know if I'd like her to pick up an item she claimed was "to die for." Then she'd ask if I was still a size twelve or if I'd "slimmed down any." Back when I protested these interruptions, she reminded me that she wouldn't have to break through if I just got call-waiting. I suggested she call my cell phone, but she said she loved me too much to contribute to my ear cancer. In all probability, her phone book doesn't have room for a second telephone number entry.

"Darling, it's Mommy," she sobbed into the phone. I knew this was for the benefit of the operator connecting the call. "There's been a terrible, terrible emergency in the family," she recited between sniffles. "Thank you, operator, that will be all."

"What's up?" I said, biting into an apple. Today reminded me of my days in grad school. Jack and Natalie were out with the baby so I had no childcare responsibilities. My morning of researching my article was highly productive. And my calendar was free for the next several hours.

Anjoli's voice perked right up. "I did it!" she said.

"Did what?" I played along.

"I dumped Edward," she sang. "I wanted to tell you just as soon as I hung up the phone with him because I knew you'd be proud of me. Oh, Lucy, I was so empowered. You should have seen me. I was magnificent." And there I could see my free time being sucked up into the black hole of my mother's ego. As I settled back into one of the avocado La-Z-Boys, I realized that every time Anjoli monopolized my time with her drama, I allowed her to. But I didn't have to. Part of me wanted to hear her Edward story. And truth be told, I enjoyed feeling self-righteous and put upon as Anjoli's one-woman audience.

"Mother, that's wonderful," I began. "I have about ten minutes for you, so give me the highlights."

"Ten minutes?! Where are you going?" she demanded.

After a few moments of deliberation, I told her the truth. "I didn't say I was going anywhere. What I said was that I have ten minutes for your story."

"Since when are you so stingy with your time, darling? All your life I listened to your stories without putting time limits on it."

"Mother!" I could not help jumping into her fray. "You had me tell stories to entertain your friends. Plus, you are the mother. You're supposed to listen to me."

"God, how I wish you had a daughter so she could visit this type of cruelty on you some day!" Anjoli shrieked. "I can't be held to some ludicrous deadline simply because you've taken some sort of boundaries workshop. I get quite anxious with time limits."

I sighed, exhausted just by the thought of where to begin. "Mother, first, I haven't been to a boundaries workshop, though now that you mention it, it seems like a good idea. Second, you deal with deadlines every day. You run a business in Times Square, not some little sweat lodge in North Dakota. Get on with it and tell me about dumping Dr. Comstock!"

Less than one second after I'd finished, Anjoli obliged. "So, as you know I'm off to Barbados this weekend, and Edward says he can't go because his wife is on the committee for this Burn Victims Society Gala or whatnot, and the event is Saturday night. Now I care about burn victims just as much as the next person, but he's already bought a table so what does it matter if he's there or not?"

"But his wife is on the—" I started.

"This is about choosing *her* over me," she said. "It's about making one relationship a priority and the other some little side dish on the side!"

Side dish on the side?

I hated when she made me explain to her the rules of an affair. I'd been faithful to my husband since our first date, and yet I was always called upon to give her the lowdown on the rules of adultery. "His family *is* his priority. You *are* a side dish on the side. I'm sorry, but it's true."

"So I gave him an ultimatum. I told him to come with me to Barbados or we were through."

"Oh my God! What did he say?" My mother's account of her dumping my son's pediatrician was obviously just spin. He broke her cold, demented heart. Oddly, I felt protective of Anjoli.

"He said he was sorry I felt that way and that he wished things were different," she sighed as if to say *Can you believe the nerve?* "Like I haven't heard that one before!" *Uh, sorry, but whose fault is that?! Grown weary of your married lovers' excuses? Cry me a river. My husband and his girlfriend now have a joint account at Blockbuster Video.* "Then he calls back after two hours and says he can't stand to lose me and he'll go. He confided in his partner who promised to vouch that Edward needs to go on some impromptu trip with Doctors Without Borders to do cleft palate repairs on kids."

"Oh my God!" I shrieked. "This is the most awful thing I've ever heard."

"I know, talk about being a day late and a dollar short!" Anjoli added.

"What?"

"How dare he jerk me around like that, making me think he couldn't go when obviously he very well could have if he only was resourceful enough the first time I asked. It wasn't until I threatened him that he even tried to make this happen for us."

"Mother, do you have any idea how horrible this sounds?"

"So I dumped him right there and then, darling. I said, 'Edward, I refuse to be treated this way by you. We are through. Go have your little dinner for the burnt people and don't ever call me again.'"

"Maybe he'll spend his weekend actually helping kids with cleft palates," I said.

"Oh no," she replied, missing my sarcasm. "That was just an alibi, darling."

"Well, I'm proud of you," I said and meant it.

"I am too. I cannot wait to tell my Pilates class about this."

You tell your Pilates class about this kind of stuff?

"Which reminds me," Anjoli continued. "One of the girls in the class says she lost four inches from her waist just from Pilates. Do they have Pilates in New Jersey?"

"Yes, but it's illegal," I whispered. "Don't tell anyone, but we have to go to the Pilates speakeasy because anything that hip and cool is banned from New Jersey."

"Just make sure it's a real Pilates studio, not some second-rate gym trying to put one over on a bunch of uninformed suburban housewives."

"Alrighty then," I interrupted. "Gotta run, darling! Stay humble. And leave the married guys alone. We poor dumb suburban housewives don't stand a chance against you."

"I didn't mean that—" I heard her voice from the receiver as it was en route to its cradle.

Desdemona's journey through the rain left her cold and sick. It was four days before she felt ready to face the world again. She promised herself she'd never walk in the rain again. As she closed her eyes to sleep, her mother burst into the room and decried her daughter's foolish actions. "Never do this again, silly child!" Desdemona's mother demanded. "I will walk wherever I please," Desdemona replied defiantly. She muffled a cough and said she was fine.

The following week, I drove into the city to meet Zoe for the Blubber Flush class at the Ninety-Second Street Y. It was April and the winter snow had melted, giving me greater comfort in driving the evening highway and city streets. Still, I wore a knit poncho and boots to camouflage my weight as well as protect me from the slapping night air.

Zoe had saved us seats in a packed room of nearly 200 women ranging in size from two to twenty. The two women who taught the class sat motionless in the front of the room, like puppets waiting to be enlivened. In the back was a table with dozens of books written by the course facilitators. *Flush Your Blubber* was a *New York Times* best seller. *Flushing Blubber in the Kitchen* was their cookbook coupled with *Flushercise,* an entire book dedicated to flushing blubber by jumping on a trampoline. Later that evening the woman announced the upcoming release, *Flush This!*

The first woman looked like a porcelain doll. Her pale face was without a pore and was utterly motionless even as she spoke. It was not like my Bell's palsy, but rather like someone Botoxed her entire face. Atop her freakish head was spiked ebony hair that was as frozen as her face. Olivia was the nutrition guru and standing beside her was her fitness counterpart, Randy. Like Olivia, Randy was in her forties, but taking every desperate measure to reverse the signs of aging. Their bodies were absolutely devoid of any fat and they both wore clothing that highlighted that fact, but there was something bizarre-looking about Randy's eyes. She claimed to run one hundred miles a week and I wondered if this was why her eyes were bulging out of the sockets. As Olivia began speaking, Randy stood by her side, nodding her head and echoing choice inane phrases.

"Welcome to Blubber Flush, where miracles happen," Olivia said, moving only her bottom lip.

"Miracles happen," Randy repeated, nodding frantically and smiling like a game show contestant on a winning streak.

"If you want to shed blubber, live a healthier lifestyle, and look like a million bucks, you have come to the right place!"

"Oh, you *have* come to the right place."

"I am so excited to be here with you ladies tonight," Olivia continued with the enthusiasm of a mortician on Prozac. "We are going to flush blubber right off your body and you are going to love looking in the mirror."

"I like looking in the mirror," Randy added. The more she spoke, the more she looked like a mole rat begging for food. Her short red pigtails bounced around as she nodded in agreement and her hands were even clawing under her chin.

For the next half hour the women showed us before and after photos of some of their Blubber Flusher success stories. "We have a cruise every holiday season where we literally take you away on a ship so you're not tempted by cookies and cake." Zoe shot me a look as if to apologize.

"We literally take you away on a ship?" I whispered, not able to control a laugh. "Is that unusual for a cruise?" She elbowed me, urging me to behave.

"No cookies, no cake," Randy said, nodding to every corner of the room. "You're on a boat."

"And we have Camp Blubber Flush, which is our spa," Olivia said, advancing the next slide to their fat camp. "Remember her?" she asked Randy as they showed an unbelievably unflattering photo of an obese woman.

"Oh yeah," Randy snickered. "Blubberella."

The next photo was a studio portrait of the same woman after she lost twenty pounds at the three-week Camp Blubber Flush. And on and on the slide show went until I looked at my watch and noticed that forty-five minutes had gone by without their imparting any of their blubber-flushing wisdom on us. It was the closest I'd ever come to sitting on the set of an infomercial—and paying one hundred dollars for the privilege. No one else seemed bothered by this. They were all taking copious notes. Of what, I'll never know.

"You're probably asking yourself, okay so how do I become a Blubber Flusher?" Olivia noted.

"You want to do it, don't you?" Randy added. I'd never understood the impulse to kill another human before this evening.

"It's all about food-combining, drinking enough water and longevity cocktail, the right vitamins, and eliminating no-no foods," Olivia said.

No-no foods?

"We can leave at the break if you want," Zoe whispered.

"Shh, they're finally getting to the good stuff," I assured her.

"To flush blubber you need to cut out all dairy products, wheat and gluten, fruits, and carbohydrates," Olivia said.

I had to raise my hand. "What *can* we eat? I mean, can you give me an example of a blubber-flushing dinner?" I couldn't believe I was using this ridiculous terminology.

"It's in the book," Olivia answered.

Another woman shot up her hand. "You mentioned

we need to take vitamins. Can you tell us which ones, please?"

"In the book," Olivia snapped again.

"All in the book," Randy echoed.

Another hand shot up. This woman looked pissed-off to have spent one hundred dollars to keep hearing that she'd have to buy a book. "Uh, yes," Olivia smiled and pointed to the tough-looking woman.

"Don't tell me this is in the book. I want to know what the hell a longlivity cocktail is."

"Longevity," Randy corrected, nodding her head. I realized that the constant head bobbing had injured her brain. "Means long life. Lon-gev-ity."

"What fuckin' ever. What's in the shit?" the woman returned.

"Okay, calm down. Deep breathing is also a part of flushing blubber so let's all take some deep, blubber-flushing breaths."

"You bitches better tell us what the fuck is in this cocktail!" The woman stood. I was seriously rooting for her to go and knock an expression onto Olivia's face. Preferably replacing it with one that communicated *Ouch!*

"A longevity cocktail is a patented weight-loss formula consisting of . . ." Olivia said, pausing for us to take notes, "hot purified water with lemon juice and psyllium husks. Stirred briskly."

Randy added, "You've got to stir briskly."

Zoe leaned in and asked, "Isn't that Metamucil?"

The chubby gangster girl heard Zoe and demanded to know if this was accurate.

"Metamucil is a brand name," Olivia said.

"It's a *kind* of psyllium husk," Randy said, adding her usual nothing to the discussion.

"This is what you bitches call a miracle diet?" the

gang girl shouted. "Your book says we can only eat nine hundred calories a day."

"Then we're supposed to drink constipation medicine twice a day?!" barked another participant as she leafed through the book.

"Please don't touch the books unless you're planning to buy one!" Olivia said. I despised this woman, but had to admire her boldness. It was pretty clear that at least one of these very pissed-off women was packing some sort of weapon, or at the very least could crush a windpipe with her thumbs. And yet, the only thing that seemed to register with Olivia was that she was getting her garage-greased fingers on the pages of her twenty-nine dollar book.

Randy giggled. "You read, you buy. This is *not* a library."

Suddenly I was overcome with a need to join in. "Yes, but it *is* a class and we all paid one hundred dollars to be here tonight under the assumption that we would actually learn something. All we've learned is that you're selling books. I didn't even know we weren't supposed to exceed nine hundred calories a day until that woman opened your book."

"I told you the no-no foods!" Olivia shot angrily.

"How 'bout some of the yes-yes foods so we know what the hell we can eat," another woman shouted.

Zoe beamed. "It's a Blubber Flush riot! Where the hell is a camera crew when you need one?"

"Look, you bitches better knock the fat outta this bullshit class right now and tell us what we can eat, and give us the names of them vitamins we need to take," the gang girl shot.

Another woman joined in. "Excuse me, but does it concern anyone that a nine-hundred-calorie-a-day diet and regular use of laxatives is basically what anorexics do?"

"No one here's anorexic, bitch," the gang girl shot. "I got weight to lose, so sit down, shut up, and let this freak show get on to the part where we find out what we need to eat to get skinny."

"Okay," said a startled Olivia. "Sounds like you're all ready to move on to the step-by-step Blubber Flush plan." It was satisfying to see her look this terrified.

"Let's do the plan," Randy said, nodding at double speed.

Chapter 26

Three weeks after taking the Blubber Flush class, Zoe lost six pounds. Her hips jutted like spears from her low-rider jeans. I, on the other hand, shed a pound and a half. It was no fault of the program, though. At the very end of Olivia and Randy's presentation, one of them remembered, "Oh yeah, if you're pregnant or nursing, you shouldn't be a Blubber Flusher." Still, I felt so motivated hearing about their principles of weight loss that I incorporated a few into my lifestyle. I figured cutting out candy and capping my calories at 2,500 a day couldn't hurt my milk supply. I also joined Candace's stroller club, which was a group of about six women who met twice a week to push strollers and gab for four to five miles.

It was May, so I had no more excuses not to exercise. The weather had finally warmed enough where I actually wanted to be outdoors taking a walk.

Adam looked more like a little baby boy than an infant, crawling and cooing back at strangers who said hello to him.

It was funny, but the busier I got, the more I was able to do. I'd written four pieces for *Salon's* Mothers Who Think column, was in the midst of editing and fact-checking my cover story with *Mothering*, and even had contracts with a handful of online parenting magazines, which paid surprisingly well.

Zoe was at the house on Saturday night. We'd planned to catch a movie while Jack and Natalie played house with Adam, but a hotly sought-after artist finally returned one of Jack's numerous calls and said he'd be willing to meet to discuss representation—right then. Ever the supportive girlfriend, Natalie immediately agreed to meet Jack later that evening and cook him dinner "whenever" he arrived. Even I was starting to fall in love with her. I wondered how I used to respond when similar situations arose in our marriage. I was pretty understanding, though visibly disappointed. Is that what went wrong between us? Was I not self-sacrificing enough for Jack? Then I looked around my house and realized I was living his suburban dream, not mine, and gave myself a break. After thirteen years of marriage, even St. Natalie might stomp her foot with disappointment once or twice.

"I have a confession to make," Zoe said, leaning in conspiratorially over the kitchen table.

"Roll 'em," I joked. When she didn't laugh, I urged her to continue. "Want a longevity cocktail?" I offered.

"Why not?"

After mixing the sour grit and returning to the table, I placed the drinks on the table. "Remember when we used to drink things like fuzzy navels and sex on the beach? Now it's Blubber Flush juice."

"Doesn't that seem like forever ago?" Zoe sighed.

"I can't believe Richie is dead." I nodded.

"Puts things in perspective, doesn't it?"

"What's going on with you, Zoe?"

She said that, compared to Richie Cantor's, her problems were small.

"This is true, but it doesn't make yours irrelevant either," I said. I always hated when Aunt Rita completely negated my feelings by telling me how much worse off she was at my age. In grad school, I was rejected from a summer writing workshop in London, and Aunt Rita immediately started in with a story about how she was rejected three times from the Brooklyn College Masters in Education program before she was accepted. I think her point was that persistence pays, but the message I got was that my disappointments were so small compared to hers, they didn't count. And if they didn't count, how could I indulge in nurturing them? Anjoli, on the other hand, always seemed to choose my lowest points to tell me how charmed her life was. When the exchange program didn't work out, Anjoli chimed, "London is beautiful in the summer! When I was with the Joffrey, we toured London, Paris, and Rome and it was the most culturally awakening and exhilarating summer of my life." Gee, good to hear.

Zoe said she met someone else, and was thinking about leaving Paul. They'd been together four years, so their relationship was as significant as many marriages. When I pressed for details, Zoe said that she was sad to see the relationship with Paul peter out, but what really bothered her was her cheating on him. "I know we're not married or anything, but I feel like shit, sneaking around behind his back," she said. "God knows I can't stand him these days, but I can't stand to hurt him either," Zoe continued. "I'm not even sure I love Tommy. I think I just love the way he makes me feel." I wondered what the difference was between loving someone and loving the way he made you feel. "Or, God, I hate to admit this, but sometimes I think I just like the attention from someone new. Is that awful?"

"Please," I shooed my hand. "A dog sniffed my crotch in the park this morning and I was flattered."

Zoe burst into laughter. Encouraged, I added that sometimes I bought things on eBay and paid quickly in order to get good feedback from the seller. My mother regularly showed up on Page Six. I was thrilled that there was a buzz about my quickie with PayPal.

"I'm so glad I have a friend I can be honest with, and not worry about being judged," Zoe said. *Gulp.*

"Zoe," I said meekly. "When we finish talking about you and Paul . . . or you and Tommy . . . I mean, when we get done talking about you, there's something I need to come clean with you on."

With that, Adam began screaming, demanding to be fed. When I lifted him from his crib, Adam looked like a drunk recovering from a bender. Half of his red face was covered with drool and the left side of his hair was standing up. And like a drunk, he was disoriented, confused, and wailing. But also like a typical intoxicated male, his cranky tirade was nothing a little C cup couldn't fix.

"So dish," Zoe said as I returned to the table with Adam latched onto my breast. "Are you cheating on Jack?"

"No," I said, inhaling to gain the courage to tell Zoe about my pseudomarriage. "Jack and I aren't really married anymore. I mean, technically we are, but we've emotionally divorced."

"Emotionally divorced?" Zoe repeated. I could see the wheels turning. She thought it might make a good title for her next reality TV show.

"We're living together as friends," I explained. "We're going to raise Adam together, but have separate lives."

Zoe was tough to read. Finally she spoke.

"Didn't they do a piece on this in the *Times*?"

"Apparently so."

"So how's it going?"

"There are ups and downs, like anything else, I guess. I haven't had a real date yet, while he's been the hottest thing on the market since he took off his wedding ring."

As I said the final word, the phone rang. It was like musical accompaniment for the word.

"May I speak with Jack Fenton's next of kin please?" a woman asked.

Next of kin? What will these telemarketers come up with next?

"This is his wife," I said, rolling my eyes to Zoe to apologize for the interruption.

"I'm sorry to disturb you, ma'am, but your husband has been involved in an accident this evening and—"

"Oh my God!" I shouted. "Is he okay?"

With that, Zoe stood and took Adam from my arms while I paced the room getting details. He was at the hospital ten miles from our home, unconscious with possible brain injury and paralysis. Apparently he had a head-on collision with another driver and seconds later was hit by a minivan after his car was knocked into another lane of traffic.

"It was a very serious accident," the woman said. "Five cars were involved, ma'am."

"He's going to be okay, though, right?" I begged urgently. At this point, Zoe was motioning frantically for information.

"I can't say, ma'am," she said. "I'm sorry, but you're welcome to come to the hospital and speak with his doctors when they're available."

"Just tell me this," I began, even then knowing I was

asking for answers that the present did not offer. "He's going to survive this, right?"

"I'm sorry, ma'am," she said with genuine sympathy. "You need to speak with your doctors about your husband's condition."

In less than two minutes, Zoe and I had stocked Adam's diaper bag, grabbed our coats, and loaded into the car. Rushing to the hospital, I realized I had to call Natalie and tell her why Jack would be tragically late for their dinner date. She asked me the same questions I did of the anonymous woman on the phone. Only then did I understand how difficult that woman's job really was. People are at the most stressful moment of their lives and all they want is answers. And the reality is that no one has them.

Doctors brushed by us for the next hour, politely telling me they were doing everything they could. I hated the way that sounded. It was almost like a preemptive apology for his death. *We did everything we could, but the injuries were far, far too serious.*

"What do you need?" Zoe asked.

"Call Jack's parents," I said, jotting their number on a piece of paper from the hospital reception area. "And my mom. Oh, and call Candace and tell her what's going on so the stroller moms don't wait for me at the park in the morning." Zoe gave me a funny look. "They wait like twenty minutes for people. I don't want them to have to wait."

I looked around the sterile reception area and saw five other families that appeared to be just like ours. Some of them were older. Others had several kids. Two families looked different—one Asian, the other black. Another family looked as though they'd been through every struggle life had to offer from economic hardship to bad hair. But as we sat in the hospital waiting room, we were bonded by fear. We all looked absolutely terrified. Shocked. Drama had visited our lives as we were unexpectedly, comfortably coasting through our mundane existences. An accident like this happens in less than the time it takes you to spread jelly on toast, wash your hands, or place the DVD in the player.

"Is he okay, Lucy?" Natalie rushed into the hospital in her casual date clothes—a white cotton oxford, Levi's, and a violet suede jacket that came to her knees.

"No word yet," I clipped. "Natalie, this is my friend, Zoe. Zoe, Natalie." The two nodded politely.

"When are they going to know something?" Natalie rushed. Then she smiled at the sight of Adam. "Hey, you," she cooed. He recognized her and smiled back.

"I don't know," I told her. "It could be a while. The doctors have been coming out every twenty minutes or so to give us an update."

"And what've they said?" Natalie asked as a doctor emerged. "Doctor, how's Jack?" she rushed to him and grabbed his arm. He looked at her, puzzled as to who she was.

"Dr. Friedman, this is Natalie, Jack's sister," I lied.

"We're doing everything we can for your brother," he answered. "If you don't mind, I'd like to ask you a few questions about your family medical history." Natalie shot me a concerned look.

"Natalie is Jack's stepsister," I backpedaled. "Their parents met late in life so she's not going to know any of that," I answered as though she weren't standing three feet from me. "I can tell you what you need to know," I said, fully aware of how horribly timed my feeling of smugness was.

A little after ten that night, Candace came to the hospital and offered to take Adam home to sleep at her house. After four hours of nursing, pacing, and playing, I was ready for the break. Sure, Zoe took him on walks and St. Natalie put in her time, but Adam wanted to stretch out on the floor, roll around, and pursue his dream of sitting up. His attempts reminded me of my own crunches at the gym. I gladly tossed Candace the keys to the house, told her where she could find quarts of frozen breast milk (the freezer), and wondered how I got so lucky to find a friend like her. Not only did she take care of Adam for me that night, she drove Zoe back to the city, then the next morning stocked my fridge with dinners that she and the La Leche League mothers had prepared.

Before I got the pleasant surprise of the Candace cavalry, Little Miss Shared History became history. Ever since she was introduced as Jack's sister, then reduced to his late-life stepsib who had no knowledge of his medical history, Natalie grew quiet. She sat curled on the sofa of the waiting room staring blankly. At first, I thought it was because she was tired. At midnight, this excuse seemed even more reasonable. At 2:00 A.M. both Natalie and I looked like an ad for a do-it-yourself lobotomy kit. When I felt Natalie shaking my arm to wake me, the clock read 4:15 A.M. "Lucy," she whispered. I jarred. "Sorry to wake you, but I need to get out of this."

"Okay, no problem," I said groggily. "What time will you be back?"

She hesitated. "I can't do this anymore, Lucy."

"Of course, of course," I said. "No one expects you to stay all night. Go home, get some rest, and if Jack wakes up while you're gone, I'll let him know when you'll be back."

"Lucy," she said sheepishly. "I'm not coming back."

It was so silent, I could hear that dull buzzing sound that's audible only in the absolute absence of noise. At first, I thought it was Jack flatlining.

"What do you mean?" I asked.

"I mean this whole situation is too much for me," she said, seemingly ashamed at her weakness. "I don't know where I fit into all of this," she gestured at her surroundings. "You're his wife. Adam's his son. I'm a fictitious stepsister."

"Come on, Natalie! I couldn't introduce you as Jack's girlfriend. It would seem weird."

"Because it is weird," she immediately countered.

"And you just realized this tonight?!" I asked. "You didn't notice that things were a little out of the ordinary when you were seeing plays and renting movies and taking our son to the park?!"

"It just hit home tonight."

Part of me thought Natalie was a fair-weather girlfriend who cut and ran when the going got tough. Another part believed that perhaps tonight's incident with Dr. Friedman drove home the reality that our setup was bizarre. She would not be able to marry Jack for eighteen years. They could never have kids. And any time they ran into people we knew, they'd instantly assume she was his mistress.

"What should I tell him?" I asked.

"Tell him I'm sorry, but the situation is too complicated for me." With that, I became angry. Adam and I were being characterized as complications. *Screw you, bitch. You think you simplified my life when you threw your size-small panties in my hamper?!*

"You're sorry? That's what you want me to tell him?" I wasn't going to let her off the hook this easily. "Natalie, I really think you should tell him this yourself."

"You're the writer," she pleaded.

"What?"

"You're good with words," Natalie said. "I'll just screw it up and say something dumb."

Like sorry about the loss of feeling in your body

from the neck down, but this isn't working for me any-more?

"Natalie, I'm not breaking up with Jack for you. When he wakes up, you're going to have to talk to him."

"If he wakes up," she burst into tears. This woman was clearly insane. Or at least overtired.

I grabbed her by the shoulders. "Natalie, don't say that! Jack *will* wake up, and when he does, you need to dump him." A nurse passed us and gave a look as if to say, *what bitches.* "Go home, get rest, and come back and talk to Jack."

Natalie regained composure and started nodding in agreement. "You're right, Lucy. I'm sorry. I'm ex-hausted. And drained. I'll come back this afternoon and see him then." And with those words I knew I'd never see Natalie again.

Chapter 27

Three weeks later, Jack left the hospital with a non-negotiable directive to stay off his feet most of the time and an intensive physical therapy schedule for the next year. The doctors said it was astonishing that he survived the crash. A Puerto Rican nurse nicknamed him *Milagro*, miracle in Spanish. No one could believe how quickly he was healing.

Jack woke up two days after the accident to the sight of his mother and me peering over his hospital bed. He smiled weakly and said, "I've died and gone to hell." You've never heard such an audible sigh of joy from two women. We hugged one another, then gingerly hugged Jack, afraid we might break him.

"Doctor, he's awake!" Susan shouted. "My boy is awake!" I wondered if I'd still call Adam my boy after forty-two years. Susan was on the first flight from Chicago after Zoe called her the night of the crash. My mother-in-law is your standard mashed-potatoes-and-gravy kind of gal, shaped like a pear but would consider the fruit far too exotic to actually eat. Her gray hair is set weekly at a beauty parlor (not a salon) with tight hot rollers, then brushed back to create a wavy helmet. In the summer, she wears sleeveless nylon dresses with bold floral patterns and a Kleenex tucked under her brassiere (not bra) strap. In the winter, she favors dresses with white lacy collars so large, they might easily be mistaken for placemats. Susan wears bulletproof pantyhose and the low heels that were once featured in print ads where women played basketball in them. Much to my delight, Susan is a mother-in-law who's never given me cause to write Dear Abby. She's as hands-off as they come. Much to my disappointment, though, Susan and I never really connected on any more than a very superficial level. When I was a little girl, I'd fantasized about my husband's mother and I sharing secrets as we sliced carrots for the Christmas dinner salad, and hatching delightfully mischievous plans against our spouses. Our mutual rejoicing over Jack's recovery was the closest we'd come to bonding.

The doctors ran into the room, examined Jack, and immediately began a battery of tests. He was lucky to be alive, everyone agreed. With this pronouncement, Susan burst into tears in a rare moment of emotional demonstrativeness. She informed me that she'd be staying in a hotel and coming to the house daily to help me take care of Jack. "You know I'm not pushy about visiting, but I can't take no for an answer this time, dear," she said. "You can't care for the baby and Jack or you'll wear yourself to the bone." Not for a moment did I ever even think of declining the offer.

"I wouldn't dream of it, Susan," I said. "But you'll be much more helpful if you stay with us." She smiled modestly.

The day he woke up, Jack asked about Natalie. I was afraid that any emotional trauma might inhibit his recovery, so I lied and told him that her uncle died and she had to fly to Scotland for his funeral. It was the first thing that popped into my head because Aunt Bernice had just told me about a Scotsman's funeral she'd recently crashed. "I didn't want to mention it while Jack was still in the coma, but now that he's fine, I have to tell you, those Scottish people really have very elaborate funerals. I nevah knew what a gorgeous instrument the windpipe is. When they played 'Amazing Grace,' it really put you in the mood for mourning," Bernice reported.

"I didn't know Natalie had family in Scotland," Jack said. *Yeah, well, so much for your deep history together,* I thought, before remembering that there really was no Scottish uncle. *Yeah, well, bet you didn't know she was the dump-you-through-your-wife-while-you're-in-a-coma kind of girlfriend either,* I revised.

After three days in my home, Susan ran my household better than I ever did. Kitchen timers were ringing to announce the completion of pot roasts. Susan had a chummy (and thankfully completely appropriate) relationship with Jack's physical therapist. Adam was a sparkling clean baby-food ad who heard well more than 3,000 words per hour as Susan read romance novels to him.

My own mother was wonderful about sending things to Jack. Flowers arrived every few days. A cookie bouquet decorated like footballs crossed our familial end zone. Even the long-since-passé singing telegram arrived to entertain Jack into recovery. Day by day, everything showed up but her.

Susan knocked on the door of my bedroom. Thankfully, I was able to convince her that the friends who supplied our fridge full of meals also recently moved Jack's bed into my old office. For his medical needs, of course. She found me weeping tears into my computer keyboard after yet another unsuccessful attempt to bring Desdemona to life. *Why has it taken me so many months to produce fewer than three pages of this novel?* I wondered silently. *Why do I have to be the one to dump Jack for Natalie?* "Oh dear, Lucy," Susan draped an arm over my shoulder. "You're exhausted."

"I am," I declared, looking at her squarely, wondering if she could possibly understand the extent of my fatigue.

"I know," she said. *What did she know?* She continued. "I'm a wife and mother, too."

I burst into tears imagining her doing this whole domestic scene perfectly while my most recent attempt at suburban bliss occurred at a car wash. "Susan, I have to tell you something," I began without thinking.

"All right, dear," she nodded for me to continue.

"Susan, Jack and I, it's not a marriage anymore. We're just friends, living together and raising Adam. It's not like we're really together anymore. That's why his bed is in the den. It's been there for more than a year."

"Oh, I see," she said, blushing at being privy to her son's sleeping arrangements. "All marriages get that way sometimes, dear. Especially after a new baby arrives."

"No, Susan, you don't understand. This isn't a phase we're going through. Jack and I aren't together anymore. We've discussed it. We've split up."

"You both look like you're here to me."

"Physically, but it's only for Adam's sake," I explained.

She leaned in and whispered. "Trust me, it will pass."

"No, it won't!" I said a bit too loud. "We aren't getting back together, Susan. If it weren't for Adam, we'd be divorced."

"Well, thank goodness for Adam then," she said, smiling.

I hate stories where a baby saves a marriage. Kids

shouldn't be cast as the panacea for parental wrong-doings and marital erosion. At this point, a baby's greatest responsibility should be shitting into a diaper.

"I'm sorry, Susan. Jack and I aren't going to have the Hollywood ending here," I said. With a tone of disdain, I began. "It's just so—" I trailed off. *Suburban*, I finished silently. I glanced out of my window and felt I'd betrayed the children riding their bikes past my house. "I'm sorry, what I mean is that Jack and I aren't getting back together. We're not like that."

"Like what?" she asked.

"Like—" I groped for words, still silently apologizing to my lovely neighborhood for my momentary possession by Anjoli.

"Willing to stick with something when it's hard?" Susan said.

"Susan, that's so unfair," I began. "There are a thousand good reasons couples divorce. You can't make it sound as though we're quitters."

Adam's crying pierced through our chat. "Oh, I know, dear. Some of my girlfriends are divorced and Lord knows they tried their darnedest to make a go of it, but there are a thousand good reasons to stay together too. Let me get the baby."

Susan returned to the bedroom with Adam and a piece of advice. "Why don't you take a little time for yourself and take a weekend cruise or something? I can hold down the fort here, and you've certainly earned some time off. Think about it—Bermuda, Jamaica, Antigua." The words "Ann Arbor" escaped from my lips like Citizen Kane muttering "Rosebud."

"What's that, dear?"

"I'm sorry," I said, smiling. "I was just thinking of Ann Arbor. I went to college there. Grad school too. I was thinking of spending a weekend there. Are you sure you'll be okay on your own here?"

"On my own?!" she mock-scolded, then held Adam up and made a baby voice. "I've got my two best guys with me, don't I? Don't I?" she repeated, even more adorably each time.

Before I left for my weekend in Ann Arbor with Zoe, I told Jack that Natalie called to say she was staying in Scotland indefinitely. "I'm sorry, but she said that being with all of her family in their homeland made her yearn for the, the, Scottish things of Scotland."

"Gosh, I always thought she said she was French," he said, resigned.

Chapter 28

As Zoe and I drove to the University of Michigan campus in our rented yellow convertible, I enjoyed the warm breeze rushing through my hair, which I'd just had cut to my shoulders. I wore jeans and a web-thin red t-shirt with the emblem of a hip band I'd never listened to. I knew it was cool, though, because the unmarked, underground shop on St. Mark's Place wouldn't sell it if it wasn't. Zoe wore torn low-riders and a purposefully wrinkled sheer lime button-down top. Neither of us had to mention that we were trying to blend with our environment more than we actually did.

We were now visitors in what was once our home. As the distantly familiar feel of the Michigan spring swept across our bodies, we were free in a way we hadn't felt in a long while. The only reminder of my real life was my swollen breasts in desperate need of relief.

Zoe spotted a group of students walking with their stuffed backpacks. She held her hands in the air as though she were about to drop on a roller coaster and shouted "Wheeew!" They looked at her and smiled. "Savor the moments," she shouted at them. "Savor your freedom, kids, because these moments are fleeting. Drink them in through every pore of your soul, sweet warriors of youth," she shouted, as she let the breeze slip through the fingers of her hand that dangled from the window.

"Wow, Zoe, I thought you had to have kids to have a midlife crisis," I said of her comment.

"What?"

"What, what? *Sweet warriors of youth?*"

"Too much?" she asked.

"A bit."

"I just wanted to give them some advice. You know, enjoy it now."

I remembered bleeding Barney offering a similar refrain and laughed.

"Where to, my little drive-by fortune cookie?" I asked Zoe.

We decided to have a bi-bim-bob at Steve's Lunch even though it was just 11:00 A.M., but when we arrived at our standby Korean restaurant, it was gone. It was still a Korean diner, but they now called it "Rich Jesus Christ." I kid you not. Now, I don't want to disrespect anyone's religious beliefs, but what exactly does Jesus have to do with bi-bim-bobs?

"Wanna try it?" I asked. "Probably the same menu at least." There were many of the same items on the menu, but Rich had redecorated. Once a comfortable hole-in-the-wall, the diner was now a self-conscious attempt at hip modernity. Teacup-sized, brightly colored, smoked-glass-covered light bulbs. The lightboard menu was no longer discolored yellow. And sadly, all of the letters were applied neatly. Not a one missing, or even crooked.

After twenty minutes, Zoe and I left. The waitress was overwhelmed dealing with the seven customers at the counter, and never got around to taking our order.

Two doors down was a new Korean restaurant we'd never seen before. It had a red awning and several full tables that all seemed to have food on them.

"So tell me about this new setup with you and Jack," Zoe asked as her food arrived. "Last time we talked about it, he went into a coma." We laughed, not because his accident was funny, but the way she said it made it sound as though our chat was the cause of it.

"It's pretty much what I told you," I began. "Jack and I wanted two things that seemed incompatible, but we're making it work. We wanted Adam, but we also both wanted out of the marriage," I stretched the truth for ego's sake. "So we're living together as co-parents."

"Wait a second, Lucy," Zoe said before bringing her chopsticks to her mouth. "I never knew you were thinking about divorce. Last I heard you were seeing that marriage therapist."

I savored the taste of my youth, and filled Zoe in on Jack and my years of struggle. The bi-bim-bob at the red awning place was actually better than Steve's, and yet the meal was a letdown. I missed my lower standards. I missed taste buds that had been dulled by a dormitory cafeteria.

At the same time, I missed my youthful dreams. I missed an age where I thought anything was possible because it actually was. I missed believing that I would write a novel, Jack would paint, and the two of us would live in a place of boundless natural beauty and art. It was over Steve's bi-bim-bobs that Jack and I talked endlessly about the artist community we were going to start. In fact, Jack drew the design of the property—our main house and the surrounding bungalows—on a napkin from Steve's.

After lunch, we walked down South State Street, a quaint main street lined with an eclectic blend of people, trees, and shops. On every telephone pole, and posted in every shop window, were fliers for open-mike poetry readings, political demonstrations, comedy performances, and edgy bands. One sign invited students to a free Japanese brush-painting class. Another handwritten sign was a vegetarian looking for a roommate. Several people had posted listings for dirt-cheap summer rentals. For a moment, I considered spending the summer in Ann Arbor with Adam just to be back in this environment. I felt in Ann Arbor the same way I did in the city—like everything was happening and I was missing it all when I wasn't there. I suppose there are several spots on earth where each one of us feels completely at home. For me, they are Ann Arbor, St. Mark's Place, Washington Square Park, and the Westerbeke Ranch in Sonoma County, California, where an overpowering scent of eucalyptus leaves lulls me into a state of believing my world—both inside and out—is at peace. Sitting on the outside patio of Dojo's on St. Mark's Place with a good book is also a Lucy spot. Under the arch at Washington Square Park, where I can still imagine my father playing piano as dogs leap for Frisbees near the fountain in the background. Then there was Ann Arbor, where there was so much to be absorbed, no one person could possibly take it in. But instead of causing me anxiety, it gave me comfort. Jack wouldn't hear of me taking Adam away for so long, but perhaps I could convince him to come to the art festival for a weekend.

Right across the street from the red awning was the fraternity house where Richie lived. I could see the single turret of the Sigma Alpha Epsilon house where we used to smoke pot and watch the sun set during spring semester. In front of his house was a large dirt pit, which was watered down into a mud bowl every homecoming weekend so two rival fraternities could play football. As Zoe and I walked past the frat houses on the expansive Washtenaw Avenue, I noticed that while Richie's house remained in custody of the SAEs, Phi Delta Theta house across the street was replaced by new Greek letters I could no longer read.

Hoping to avoid the subject of whether or not this co-parenting arrangement was torture, I asked Zoe about the status of her and Paul. "Funny you should mention it," she said, laughing softly. "We've broken up, too. But we're staying together for the sake of the apartment."

I laughed. "You are?"

"Honey, we've got a rent-control two-bedroom in the Village. I'm not moving, and Paul's no idiot. He's not going anywhere."

"Really?"

"Yep," Zoe nodded.

"So are either of you dating again?"

"I am. I have no idea if he is or not."

"Will it bother you to see him with other women?" I asked as we turned back toward the main campus. As we window-shopped at our familiar haunts, like Middle Earth and Ulrich's, we took note of a few new stores and their contrast with the old. A latex-and-leather-laden condom boutique faced off with the campus institution, the Village Apothecary, a drug store that would've fit in perfectly in Cape Cod circa 1950. It wasn't until we reached the West Engineering Building Arch, where Jack proposed to me, that I repeated my question to Zoe.

"No, I think it'll be a relief to see him with someone else. I won't feel so guilty about dumping his sorry ass." I wondered if that's how Jack felt about me.

To get to the Diag, the grassy center of campus, we needed to pass under the short tunnel of the West Engineering Building. It made one's entrance that much more dramatic to have the sunlight sparkle through the treetops as the cool stone arch diminished into the foreground. It was almost as if a curtain was lifting for the opening scene of a show.

On center stage was a cluster of scrappy-looking boys sitting on Mexican blankets with backpacks tossed on the grass. Three were playing hacky sack, two were leaning back on their elbows watching foot traffic, and one was reading a beat-up paperback by Milan Kundera. "Let's go see if we can score some pot from those guys, Lucy," Zoe said with a childlike excitement.

"I can't smoke," I reminded her, pointing at my boobs.

"Oh, yeah," Zoe said, clearly disappointed.

"Well, let's go chat 'em up anyway," she coaxed.

"Zoe, they're half our age!" I said pretending to be appalled. Still, I didn't have the energy to flirt with college kids.

"For me?" she pleaded playfully.

As we approached the blanket of boys, my heart sped with fear of rejection. Funny, I had no desire to flirt with these guys, but I would've been devastated if the feeling were mutual.

"Hey, boys!" Zoe said. They sat up and looked a bit startled, as though they might be in trouble.

A guy who looked an awful lot like Ben Affleck caught before his morning coffee tentatively returned Zoe's greeting. His brown hair was molded by a pillow. His broad chest was covered by a thick cotton Michigan t-shirt with an unbuttoned forest-green flannel shirt on top of it.

"How's it going?" She sat down next to them as I was still a few steps from reaching the blanket. "You guys go to school here?" They nodded. "I'm Jenna, and this is Taylor. We're at the law school."

"Oh yeah," another chimed in. "What do you teach?"

There wasn't an ounce of malice or sarcasm. They just honest-to-goodness assumed we were professors, rather than students, as Zoe had hoped to portray. Perhaps this is why she adopted the pseudonyms of the twentysomething set.

"We're students," she said, laughing. A part of me wanted to just lie on my back and watch the sun glitter through the leaves. Another part was drawn into Zoe's tale.

"Law's our second career," I added. *Am I supposed to be Jenna or was I Taylor?*

One of the hacky sack boys teased, "Too rough out there in the real world for you, so you had to come back to school, eh, Jen?" His inadvertently keen observation made me want to cut off his overgrown goatee with a plastic cafeteria knife. But at least I knew that, since he directed his words to Zoe, I was, in fact, Taylor.

They chatted for a while as the hacky sack game resumed and Kundera was once again being read. I rested my head on my purse in the grass and watched the leaves. I used to do this all the time in Ann Arbor. I rolled my head from side to side and watched the sunlight filter in through the various patterns of leaves. I could do this at home. We do have trees in Caldwell. But I never do.

Zoe and the Ben Affleck lookalike were heavy into conversation. When he introduced himself as Adam, I had to refrain from announcing that he shared my son's name. I knew Zoe would kill me for any reference to our already-precarious status as thirtysomethings. I wondered what my Adam was doing and whether he missed me. Of course, I knew he was having a fine time with Susan and Jack, but I hoped he missed me a little. With that thought, I heavily withdrew my wish. I was becoming Anjoli and my child's feelings for me were more important than his well-being. I hated myself for hoping my son would long for me while I was away. But truthfully, I feared he wouldn't notice my absence, and if he didn't even realize I was gone, what good was I when I was there? Candace once said that motherhood amplifies your natural tendencies. For her, this was a good deal since she was kind and nurturing. For neurotic and self-flagellating me, it was less than a bargain.

"So, do you know where we can score some weed?" I heard Zoe ask. I wondered if kids even called it that anymore.

"This isn't, like, a sting or something, is it?" Adam said, half kidding.

"It'd be entrapment," I said, still on my back.

"No, it'd be entrapment if she asked me to sell her some, not if she's just asking where," he returned.

"So, you do have some?" Zoe said eagerly. "It's been sooooooo long, Adam." She paused. "I am not a cop, okay?!"

"Okay, it's back at my apartment."

"Great!" Zoe said.

"Not great," I said.

Zoe crawled on her knees over to me and whispered, "Why not?"

"Because I came to Ann Arbor to see the town, not sit around some dirty college apartment watching you get stoned. And before you say anything, you're not going alone. You have no idea who these people are. You're being completely reckless just because you and Paul broke up and you need a little thrill."

"Um, Lucy. You're, um, well, you're wet," she whispered.

"Pul-ease!" I whispered, laughing. "I am not even slightly—"

"I mean you're leaking," she interrupted.

Looking down at my red shirt, I saw two wet stains the size of cantaloupes. "This'd be a deal breaker, wouldn't it?" I laughed.

She turned her head toward the cluster of guys who were now completely reimmersed in their pre-Jenna-and-Taylor lives. I think Zoe realized that chasing rainbows never leads to a pot of gold. It just leaves you feeling tired and stupid. "Hey, guys, nice chatting with you, but we gotta run."

Adam tried to be polite by asking where we were going, but clearly he didn't care. "Taylor's implants are leaking," Zoe said, as every head within ear range turned to look.

For the rest of the weekend, we quietly walked around Ann Arbor taking inventory of what was old and what was new. What had changed and what had remained the same. Very few things were in just one column, least of all us.

Chapter 29

Susan returned to Chicago just after Independence Day weekend. Her presence made my house seem like a home, and it terrified me that once she left, the peaceful sense of domesticity she created might dissolve. There was something about having an older person—an older woman who'd raised children—around the house that took some of the pressure off me. I didn't have to feel as though I had all of the answers because not only was Susan a wealth of knowledge about childcare, she was readily willing to admit that she felt just as lost as I did when she was my age. As she left, she took me aside and assured me that everything would work out for the best. I've always been a bit skeptical when people made this overly general prediction, but when Susan said it I believed it. I asked her what *was* for the best, and she shrugged. "I don't know, but whatever happens, I believe it will be the best thing for everyone," she said, smiling slightly.

Susan's modest demeanor puzzled me. She could spew out these Yoda-like philosophies effortlessly, then smile shyly like a little girl embarrassed to admit she needed to pee. My mother's entire body was a mood ring. Her face, her body, her hats would all reflect her feeling du jour.

I wondered if Susan had talked to Jack about our relationship during her four weeks with us. How was she so sure that everything would work out for the best? Does everyone get the gift of centeredness in their senior years? Or is it a perk of being gentile?

When I returned from Ann Arbor, I found Jack out in the backyard, painting. Flowers—in watercolor, of all things! Adam tried to pull himself up with the netted walls of his playpen and look at his father's creations. Soon, he'd plop down, pick up a toy, then quickly become distracted by a bird resting on a branch overhead. I thought the forced time off would drive Jack crazy with boredom, but instead, he looked more alive than I'd seen him in years. When he told me about what Adam had done that day, his whole being was animated and filled with an uncomplicated joy.

Soon, he grew tired of suburban landscapes and started painting in oils again. He was starting to venture out of the house on his own and took a camera with him everywhere he went. He wasn't quite sure what he was looking for, but said he wanted to have a camera with him because he knew it was out there to be captured by him.

A combination of two things made me disrobe entirely. It was 102 degrees outside and, in an effort to economize, Jack and I resolved to not turn on the air conditioning. And second, every time I bathed Adam recently, he splashed so much water, I ended up more drenched than Desdemona on the cobblestone road. As I took off my clothing, I tried not to glance in the mirror. I stepped on the scale at the gym the week before and saw that I was five pounds heavier than before I got pregnant. This was the thinnest I'd been in nearly a year and a half (I refuse to speak in months!), but still wasn't the body I'd dreamt of. Every time I flipped through magazines, I'd try to negotiate deals with the gods of beauty. When they refused to come to the bargaining table, I contemplated which surgeries I'd need to look like Angelina Jolie. After realizing that would be the full Angelina Jolie transplant, I settled for her face and figured I could work on the body. My lactating breasts were fabulous, but the stomach they rested on was down right global. I was thankful that Adam was in the bathtub, needing my full attention, or I would've been tempted to play that awful game where I pull my extra thigh flesh and hold it in fists behind me so I could see what I'd look like after liposuction.

As I sat down on the edge of the bathtub, I felt the cool porcelain press against my thighs. The pressure of the tub against my legs accentuated the presence of cellulite on my thighs and butt. I placed my thick ankles on each side of Adam's bathtub chair and suddenly saw only his face. He looked at me and cooed, revealing the slightest hint of a first tooth. The smooth bottom row of gum line was pierced by what looked like a grain of rice lying flat. I noticed the smallest pieces of him and he overlooked the biggest of me. Adam never saw cellulite. He didn't notice that his old room had barely snapped back into shape. He just saw his mommy. As I took comfort in this small space where my appearance did not matter, Jack opened the door and asked if I knew where to find the phone number for the piano tuner. Startled, I shouted for him to leave.

"Don't be ridiculous, Lucy," Jack scoffed. "It's not like I haven't seen you naked before."

My body angst is not ridiculous to me, I seethed. "I am not being ridiculous and even if I was, Jack, I have every right to be if I want!" I shouted. "Do you have any idea how sick I am of you telling me that my feelings don't matter? It's so presumptuous and it completely shuts down any chance of intimacy we might have." *Ooops*. I tried to wipe up my verbal spill. "As co-parents, I think we need to be able to have a platonic intimacy, an open dialogue so Adam can see how healthy relationships function."

"All I meant was—"

"I know you meant well. You always do. I know that. But it has the opposite effect," I said. As soon as the words were out, I knew that whether or not Jack understood what I meant, I would never be bothered again by his directives. He could've looked at me right then and there and told me not to be dramatic, and it would've rolled right off me because for the first time I realized that he alone did not have the power to dismiss me. Every time he made a dismissive comment, I had the choice whether or not I would accept that dismissal. I braced myself for his thick retort, but instead he just said, "Okay."

"Okay?" I repeated.

"Yeah, okay."

"Okay . . ." I asked, extending the word to provide a blank for Jack to fill in.

"Okay," he said. "I won't do it anymore."

"Oh," I replied. "Okay."

"Can you stay like that for a sec?" Jack asked, reminding me that I was naked with my thighs spreading across the bathtub rim like batter hitting the skillet and expanding to a pancake.

"Get out of here!" I closed the door on him.

"No, seriously, Lucy, I want to grab my sketch pad."

"You want to do what?"

"Sketch you. Sitting there at the tub."

"No way!" I shrieked. "I look like a cow. Why do you need the piano tuner's number, by the way?" I asked, remembering the original reason for his entrance.

"I'm going to take up the piano again," he said.

"Again? You never played."

"I quit when I was nine. I've always regretted it."

Yeah, well you quit our marriage when I was pregnant. Any regrets about that?

"Oh, well it's in my Rolodex."

"Seriously, Lucy. Can you stay there for a few minutes so I can sketch you?"

"You're out of your mind! What, are you having a fat girls exhibit at the gallery?"

"I'm going to start painting Renaissance women in contemporary environments. You know, like a Rubenesque nude with a laptop? The two worlds intersecting on my canvas."

"You hate the Renaissance!" I reminded him. "You always said the Renaissance was bullshit. What happened to the tar-and-bone sculpting Jack I knew?"

"What's wrong with expanding my artistic tastes a bit?"

"Jack, three weeks ago you were painting flowers—live flowers, no less—now you're asking me to pin up my tendrils and let you sketch my Rubenesque ass?! This is more than a little expansion of your artistic tastes."

"Lucy, in seven months I've seen the child I thought I'd never have come into the world, and fully recovered from an accident every expert seems to agree should have killed me. Now is the perfect time in my life for a little Renaissance."

Two hours later, Adam was asleep and my naked butt was pressed against the bathtub as Jack sat behind me and sketched my image in pencil. "You're sure no one will recognize this as me?" I asked.

"Depends how many people you've shown your ass to, Lucy," Jack quipped.

I shuddered at the memory of Eddie, the cook. "No one who'd ever be at an art gallery," I turned and winked.

"Still love the jocks, eh, Luce?" Jack said, laughing. He never took his eyes off the page or me. "Seriously, I'm not even going to show the woman's face in this painting. No one will know it's you."

We talked about Adam, Jack's visit with his mother, the exhibits coming to his gallery, and my recent magazine articles. After we'd exhausted news and current events, Jack and I spent the next half hour in comfortable silence. I enjoyed hearing nothing but the pencil tapping against Jack's sketch pad. I could tell when he was doing long, soulful strokes versus furiously quick dashes and dots. I loved that it was all me. With Anjoli as a mother, I never had the chance to grow comfortable as the center of attention, but now as the subject of Jack's undivided focus, I could see why she loved it so much.

To sit still and naked might seem boring to some. In fact, just hours ago I would have said that I didn't have the patience for it, but there was something about the exposed vulnerability that gave the experience the edge I needed to make it exciting. And still, while discovering this quiet comfort, I can always manage to say something stupid to break the mood. Making some sort of preemptive degradation of my body was like a nervous tic. "It's been more than an hour, Jack. I hope you're done with at least one of my ass cheeks by now," I said, laughing.

He said nothing.

"Jack, did you hear me?"

"Yes," he brushed off my comment. "Very funny."

"I was just thinking that you're probably sorry you asked me to pose once you realized how big I am."

"Lucy," he said, not looking up. "Your body is a work of art."

"Oh, it's a piece of work, all right."

He put down his sketch pad in what may have been annoyance or sympathy. Or both. "Why do you always have to do that?!"

"Do what?"

"Make jokes."

"I'm Jewish, that's what we do," I said in an accent like my aunts'.

"There you go again!" Jack said, exasperated. "I know plenty of Jewish people who don't need to make a comedy routine of their lives to hide discomfort."

"When did you become the next Dr. Lee?" I asked, hoping we could drop the topic and go back to my growing enjoyment of being sketched. "What Jews do you know who don't make comedy of their lives? It's part of the religion. I'll bet you think all that Hebrew at bar mitzvahs is prayers, don't you? Fooled you, didn't we? It's stand-up."

"My God!" he shouted. "Do you even know when you're doing it?! You did the same thing when we lost the babies. You kept accusing me of not wanting to talk to you about it, but the truth is I couldn't stand listening to you turn our situation into your own personal tragic comedy about your self-diagnosed inability to maintain a pregnancy."

Who was this man? For the past several years, he was the guy who shrugged and answered my pleas for discussions with one- or two-word responses, mainly consisting of "Dunno." Now, he was accusing me of emotional distancing through humor. Was he reading pop psych books on the side? Did Natalie take him to a relationships workshop? I loved that he was finally opening up to me. It's just that I hated what he was saying. I'd always imagined the day when Jack and I had a heart-to-heart; it would go something like this:

Him: Lucy, I've been such a jerk these past few years. The miscarriages were hard on our marriage. You were strong, but I shut down. I'm sorry I've been such a detached, emotionally withdrawn prick. I'm going to spend the rest of my life making it up to you.

Me: Jack, I've been waiting so long to hear those words. I'm not going to dwell on what an inconsiderate rat fuck you've been all these years. I'm just going to let go of all of the pain you've caused and focus on rebuilding this marriage.

Him: Thank you, Lucy. You won't regret it. Having almost lost you, I now realize how lucky I am to have you as my wife. Oh yes, and I was an idiot to call you "kiddo" all these months.

Then we would kiss and live happily ever after. What was all this crap about me having some culpability for the demise of our intimacy? I hated him for straying so far from the script. I hated him for being so on the mark.

Chapter 30

Real Confessions was once again in the national media, Zoe at the center of it. The show was immediately cancelled when it was discovered that a handful of unscrupulous priests were encouraging parishioners to fictionalize steamy confessions for the sake of good television. These few churches were simply desperate for the money, Zoe explained to Larry King. The vast majority of the show's segments were of honest-to-goodness repentant sinners. Publicly, she was unflappable. But privately, she called to cry, then feared her phone lines were bugged. Before she could ask, I offered her refuge in Caldwell, which she immediately accepted. Candace and her casserole posse once again stocked our fridge. She even sent over a doula to give Zoe a therapeutic massage, which was amazingly generous considering she didn't even know the producer on the sacrificial lam.

I hadn't heard from Anjoli in over a week, which meant a backlog of drama. When people return to work from vacation, they often come to the realization that vacation is just a euphemism for delayed work. There is no vacation from Anjoli; just delayed drama.

"Guess where I'm heading this weekend, darling?" she shrieked excitedly through the phone.

"Just tell me," I said.

"No, guess!" she said, pouting with her voice.

"Brazil," I returned flatly.

"How did you know?"

"Because last time we spoke you said you felt weighed down by the toxicity of your breakup with Dr. Comstock."

"That relationship was wretched for me," she said. *I'm sure you have his wife's utmost sympathy.* "Do you know how unhealthy it is to hang on to anger?"

"Cancer," we said in unison.

"Yes, not to mention wrinkles," she continued. "Louise Hay says—"

"Mother," I interrupted. "Louise Hay didn't say that. I did, and I was kidding."

There it was again. My kidding. Was I pushing away my mother's fear of her own mortality—and wrinkles—by making jokes at her expense?

"Mother, I hope you find what you're looking for in Brazil," I said and meant it.

"Oh yes, darling. Let me not forget my big news." *Uh-oh.* "Are you ready?"

"I'm ready."

"Are you sitting?"

"For Christ's sake, Mother, tell me what's going on!"

"Kimmy is getting married!"

"Married?! Did she and Geoff get back together?"

"Nope," Anjoli said, loving the elongation of the story.

"Someone new?"

"Not at all new," Anjoli said like a carnival gypsy.

"Kimmy's marrying an old guy?"

"I didn't say it was a guy," Anjoli said.

"She's marrying an old *woman*? Wow, how did we miss that one? You'd think with a family like ours, she would've come out of the closet years ago."

Anjoli laughed, amused at her ability to string me along. "Think outside the box, Lucy," she said, which I must say was an especially poorly timed expression to use immediately after discussing elderly lesbians.

"Okay, someone old who's neither a man nor a woman," I pondered, as if it were a riddle.

"I didn't say old, darling," Anjoli said. "I said Kimmy didn't just meet this person."

"This person who's neither male nor female."

"It's a woman."

"So Kimmy is a lesbian?"

"Lucy, hang on to your hat," Anjoli said, forgetting that it is she, not I, who wears hats. "Kimmy is marrying herself."

"Brilliant!" I said without thinking.

"It's an assertion of her independence and self-love that—"

"No, I get it. I get it. It's brilliant. Want to go in on a super deluxe vibrator for the shower gift? Seeing how she loves herself so much," I said. Shit, was I doing it again? Was I using humor to distance myself from my authentic feelings? I paused to consider it. Nah, this was actually funny. Marrying herself?! Only in my family would someone come up with this wacky idea. Only someone in our family would love it. Or would others, I wondered. Would other women think Kimmy's idea of loving herself enough to have a solo wedding ceremony was clever?

A week later, I got my answer.

We received your pitch for the feature about the bride who's marrying herself. It's exactly the type of piece our readers will love. Glamour *caters to smart, savvy, educated, modern young women who know the importance of a healthy relationship with themselves. It's a smart idea that gets across a powerful message in a fun, creative way. And you're right, it doesn't hurt that she's a knockout. Call me as soon as you can so we can discuss the details and set up a photo shoot with Kimmy.*

After reading the e-mail, I screamed with joy and ran downstairs to find Jack spooning applesauce into Adam's now double-toothed mouth. "Good news?" he asked.

"The story I pitched to *Glamour*," I began, struggling for breath. "They like it! They want me to write it."

"That's great, Lucy! Congratulations."

"I'm so excited," I continued. "I'm a little scared, too. This is huge. I mean I've never written for such a major magazine. Wow, I wish I could just enjoy this without immediately getting anxious about it. Just five minutes of celebration would be nice every now and then, you know?"

"That's gotta suck," Jack said, clapping his hands to encourage Adam to do the same with his.

"It does," I said. "Hey, I want a do-over." I ran back upstairs and descended again. "Hey, guess what?!"

"What?" Jack played along.

"I got that gig with *Glamour* I told you about last week. They liked my story idea."

Jack smiled. "Gee, Lucy, that's great. Feel like celebrating?"

"Yes!" I burst into laughter and jumped around my kitchen. "You would not *believe* how much they pay, Jack!"

"Good for you!"

"Wanna get a babysitter and go out to celebrate?" I said without thinking.

"Sure," he said without hesitation. Smiling, he added, "I hope you don't fuck it up, Luce. It's a mighty big magazine."

With far too much adrenaline, I rushed over to him and swatted Jack's head with the first thing I could find, which, unfortunately for him, was a hardcover book. "Oh my God!" I shouted, half laughing, half apologizing. "Your head! Did I hurt your head?!"

He looked at me quizzically. "Who the hell are *you*?"

"Very funny!" I said, still elated. "It'd be nice if you would stop using humor as a wedge."

"Ewww!" he said. "Very good. Touché on that one, Luce."

As it turned out, we couldn't get a babysitter on such short notice. Anjoli said she normally would love to, but with just four days until she left for Brazil, there was simply too much to do. Kimmy was going to hear a band she was considering for her reception. Bernice and Rita were in Florida condo-hunting for a winter home. Zoe left for Paris three days after coming to stay with us. Candace always offered to babysit, but she'd already done so much, I felt too guilty to ask.

"Do you want me to run to Lo Fats for carryout?" Jack offered.

"I've kind of lost my appetite for that place," I said.

"How 'bout sandwiches?" he suggested.

An hour later, I was naked on the coffee table being sketched as I ate my sandwich. If this was a pickup routine, I was totally buying it. He said he saw some kind of irony in my pose. Whatever.

We never had simultaneous orgasms. Jack finishing his sketch at the exact moment I finished my sandwich was the closest we'd come to synchronicity. "Perfect timing!" I giggled.

"Yeah, how often does that happen?" Jack added.

"With us? How 'bout never, Mr. Let's Get Divorced in the Second Trimester," I said, laughing. *Did I just say that aloud?*

"Did I just say that aloud?" I asked. He nodded. "I suppose you're angry at me for making a joke."

"No, I'm sorry that it worked out that way," Jack said, heavily. Why couldn't I sustain a moment of levity between us? "Lay back," he commanded. He moved our floor lamp next to my body sprawled on the couch. *Oy, I am so not ready for my close-up, Mr. DeMille.* I refrained from saying a word until I resumed breathing and relaxed into the heat of the lamp.

"Jack?" I said, almost asking permission to continue.

"Yes?"

"Remember when our whole life was going to be like this? Remember how you were going to paint and I was going to write, and we were going to build that arts community?"

He smiled, remembering. "That was a great dream."

"What happened to it?"

"We didn't have a clue how much it would really cost to buy that much land, not to mention construction of our house and the cabins," he said.

"How much would it cost?" I asked.

"I don't know."

"So we still don't have a clue," I said, smiling. "Does that mean I can still believe it could happen?"

"Lucy, you *are* writing. I *am* painting. Sometimes you have to compromise in life."

"Jack, I'm living in New Jersey. I know all about compromise."

"Do you hate it here that much?"

"I don't hate it at all," I said. "I just don't fit here. It's not home."

"Where is, Lucy? Anjoli's apartment?'

"I don't know, Jack," I said, accompanying the sound of his pencil charting me.

"Don't take this the wrong way, Lucy, but when you figure out where you want to live—not just where you don't want to be—let's talk. Until then, I really don't know what I can do to make you happy."

God, it had been so long since Jack had talked about making me happy as if it were his responsibility. I thought of Kimmy's wedding, and corrected myself. It had been so long since Jack had talked about making me happy as if it was something he wanted to be part of.

He was silent for another ten minutes as he captured me on paper. "Jack?" I said tentatively. "Are you mad at me?"

He stopped sketching. "No, I was just thinking."

"About what?"

"About how I wish I had my camera with me yesterday when I took Adam on the Staten Island Ferry."

"Oh," I said, somewhat disappointed.

"I always have it with me, but yesterday I left it at home and I missed a great shot."

"What was it?"

"There was this group of Orthodox Jewish girls on the deck of the ferry and the wind lifted one of their skirts. Her knees were still covered because she held her skirt down like Marilyn Monroe in that famous shot from *The Seven Year Itch*. Her covered head was tossed back and she was laughing, but she still had the faintest hint of embarrassment. It would've made a great shot."

Great. Just what every woman wants to hear. The man she loves is drifting off into thought about Orthodox adolescents whose skirts have been blown up by the river breeze.

"And I was thinking that I miss you," Jack said. I

tried to remain calm, knowing that peeing on the couch was a definite mood killer. A *Glamour* Don't for sure.

"How can you miss me when I'm right here?" I said innocently.

"I miss the way it used to be between us. I miss the Lucy I fell in love with in Ann Arbor." *This isn't good.*

"What made you think of that?"

"Because I've seen that side of you again recently. And it's made me want it back."

I sighed, and held back tears of joy. "Come here," I coaxed with my finger. I wrapped my naked arms around his shoulders and kissed him with the single-mindedness I hadn't had in years. I felt the warmth and fullness of his lips pressed against mine, and thought if ever there was a night I might be able to give Tantra Yoga a real shot, this was it. "I'm still here, Jack," I whispered, kissing him lightly, teasingly. "And so are you."

Adam let out a wail from his room. "And so is he," Jack said, smiling. "Lemme get this one. You stay right there, and hold that thought."

Chapter 31

Hours later I was awakened by the alarm of Adam's needs. I squinted in the dark, startled to see Jack's arm draped across a pillow. The sight brought an immediate smile to my face. I brought Adam back to my bed and nursed him as I watched his father sleep. I didn't know what the future held for our family. Jack very well may have woken up and announced that our brief reconciliation was a mistake, a fleeting moment of passion between two old friends. Or, it could've begun our journey back together. Whatever it was, I wasn't naïve enough to think that one night together would be the panacea for years of resentment between us. But this was a very nice start.

I never got the chance to debrief with Jack. That sounds terribly unromantic, but I didn't want to get my hopes up and characterize it as morning-after pillow talk. The phone rang a few minutes before six the next morning. It was Cousin Ralph, Aunt Rita's son-in-law. He was a Chanukah card relative—one sent by his wife nonetheless—so I knew he was calling with news of death or illness. I wasn't prepared for it to be the fatal heart attack of Aunt Rita. She was an elderly woman with a heart condition in the Florida summer heat, but still, it was completely unexpected. After getting the details of the funeral, which would be in New York later in the week, I called Bernice at her cousin Sylvia's in Miami.

"We had such a gorgeous day yesterday," Bernice began. "We should all die like this." I glanced at Adam and Jack still sleeping in the bed together. I walked down to the kitchen and opened the fridge to pour a glass of tomato juice, a drink Rita always had well stocked. "In the morning we found the perfect condo for ourselves. In Hollywood. Right across the street from the beach, which we'd nevah go to, but the breeze helps keep things coolah. And the apartment has a balcony with a view of the Intracoastal."

"The what?" I asked, wondering why she wasn't wailing with grief.

"It's a wartah-way. I could sit there for hours wondering where the boats were heading. Rita loved it too, which, as you know, dawling, is no small achievement. So we signed the paypahs, then went to Sylvia's for the matinee of *Goys and Dahrls*, which is Rita's favorite musical evah." She sang a few notes. "Luck for my lady tonight." She sighed and sniffed. "I will miss her. So aftah the show is ovah, a group of ladies decided to go to the Red Lobstah for dinnah. Now, I don't know if you know this, but Rita adored lobstah, but was always too frugal to spend like that. But you know how it is when you go out with a big group. The bill comes and some big shot says we should split it, nevah mind if she had the lobstah and you had nothing but a bowl of chowdah," she said. "So Rita figures she's going all out and ordered lobstah *and* rock shrimp. Have you ever had rock shrimp?"

"Huh? Oh sorry, no," I said.

"Next time you come to Florida, you *must* try rock shrimp. It will be our tribute to her! I don't know what got into Rita last night, but you know how we're always dieting? Not last night! Aftah she ate her lobstah and rock shrimp, with buttah—they're so succulent, they taste exactly like lobstah—my sistah decides to ordah key lime pie. Lucy, I can't tell you what comfort it gives me to know that she ate every last crumb of that pie before she died."

What is it with older women and pie?

Bernice continued. "It was like that story about the Buddha who ate the grape before he was eaten by tigahs."

"Do you mean the Zen Buddhist?" I asked.

"Exactly! My sistah Rita, the Buddha of Red Lobstah. Oy, she'd die if she heard me say she was like that tubby Chinaman."

"So Rita just died right there in the restaurant?!"

"As soon as the waitah gave her the check, she started clutching her chest. We all thought she was joking, saying the bill was so high, but she fell ovah onto the floor and we all started screaming. The manager thought she was choking and started giving her the Heimlich maneuvah, but some other man came over and checked her out and said she was having a heart attack. By the time the ambulance arrived, she was gone," she said, sniffing again. "I'm heartbroken, of course, but it was such a Rita way to go. She ruined everyone else's dinnah at the Red Lobstah. Can you imagine watching someone die at the next table while you're trying to enjoy dinnah? Anyway, the manager was absolutely lovely. Our meal was one hundred percent on the house. You know how she could always get our restaurant bills reduced by complaining that this wasn't right, or that didn't please her? She wasn't even trying to get a discount this time. I only wish she were here to laugh about it."

"Wow," was all I could say. "You sound like you're taking this very well."

"I'm devastated," Bernice said, her voice growing heavy. "We were together every day. We were going to live together like we did when we were girls in Brooklyn. She perked up. "I've made a decision, though, and before I tell you I want you to know that I'm not crazy. I had a lot of time to think about this last night, so promise me that even if you don't agree with it, you'll help me."

"Okay."

"I've decided that if I make it to ninety, I want to check out the way Rita did."

"Auntie! You can't plan a heart attack at Red Lobster."

"Listen to me, big shot! What I want is to have a gorgeous day with the people I love most, have a delicious dinner—rock shrimp—then I'm out."

"What do you mean?"

"I don't want to be caught by surprise. Irv died on the bathroom floor. Rita left a mess on the table with all those lobstah shells."

"You want to tidy up before you die?"

"I'll be ninety! I'll have a girl take care of that. My point is that I'm not going to let death catch me off guard. After my perfect day, I'm going to jump off my balcony into the Intracoastal."

"What?!"

"I'm going to jump off the balcony and into the Intracoastal," she repeated as though I was a dullard for not absorbing it the first time. "And I need you to help me climb up onto the rail. I couldn't pull that off now, much less in eight yeahs."

"Auntie, I think you may be in shock," I said. "It's been a stressful twenty-four hours. Why don't we talk about this in a few weeks?"

"Okay," she said sweetly. "So what's new with you?"

"Auntie, I think you need some sleep," I suggested.

Aunt Rita was not the expert on funerals that her sister was, but she had definite ideas about how hers would be conducted. She left behind a twenty-four-page typed manual on handling her burial and memorial service. She even wrote the eulogy for her son.

Whenever someone dies, some moron always says, "This is the way she would have wanted it." And chances are the deceased is rolling over in her grave wanting the exact opposite. To clarify what it is that I do want, I am leaving behind a few notes. Think of it as Death's Little Instruction Book.

Rita was right. No one would have ever guessed that she would have wanted such a lavish memorial service. Not once in her life did she entertain in the manner that she would for her death.

As directed, after Rita was buried next to her husband at a Jewish cemetery in Queens, her friends and family gathered at Tavern on the Green for lunch. I sat in this same room for my high school prom—the large room that looks like a greenhouse with windows covering most of the ceiling and wall space. We overlooked a quiet patch of lawn with thick-trunked trees and chipper squirrels. Each table had a clear glass vase with large white stargazer lilies. Black rocks sat at the vase bottoms, holding the stems in place. A string quartet played Mozart. Unobtrusive waiters laid decorative plates of food before us. Filet mignon with tiny sprigs of asparagus resting over a Rorschach design of hollandaise sauce. I was impressed by their ability to lay more than one hundred plates before us in just a few minutes.

"How are you doing?" Jack whispered, as he placed his hand on my knee.

"Sad," I answered, patting back. Adam was at Candace's for the day as Rita unapologetically specified that no one under the age of thirteen could attend her funeral or memorial. When I heard this, I half expected there to be some juicy content in the eulogy. Rita always hinted that she was a hot number during World War II. I imagined Rita and Bernice with their hair rolled neatly, brown skirts to their calves, and fabulously wide-heeled shoes one can only find in retro shops. I saw Rita with red lipstick and a cigarette walking the boardwalk in Coney Island, turning her limp into a sexy swagger. But at the memorial, there were no tales that required a PG-13 rating. Rather, Rita didn't want any children's chatter to detract from her memorial. Especially after she'd worked so hard on the eulogy.

Jack patted my hand again, but this time left it there. "It's gotta be tough," he said.

"It is," I returned. "Plus, she was right there near my dad's plot, so I feel a double whammy of grief. *And* I feel guilty about it. I keep hearing Rita's voice saying, 'This is *my* day. Mourn your fathah on your own time!'" Jack laughed. "Don't laugh," I whispered. "We're going to get in trouble."

"Bernice is holding up remarkably well," Jack said.

"She's out of her mind," I whispered. "She's working the room like a bride. I overheard her say that she was sorry that Rita wasn't here to enjoy the party, but she was sure glad *she* was."

"Give her a break," Jack said. "She's been through a lot."

"I just wish she'd act normal."

Jack smiled. "What's normal?"

I glanced at my cousins seated around the table and leaned in toward Jack. "Obviously, this isn't the time, but I think we need to talk about the other night."

"You think it was a mistake?" Jack asked.

"No!" I whispered, then shot my eyes around to look at my cousins. "Let's talk about this later." After a moment, I tapped his knee under the table. He leaned in and I whispered, "Do you?"

"Do I what?"

"Do you think it was a mistake?"

Jack shook his head emphatically. "I'm glad it happened."

Our smiles broke when we heard a fork tapping a glass. Bernice in her green sequined gown called for the group's attention. "Excuse me, everyone," she said as the guests began to settle. "On behalf of my family, I'd like to thank you all for coming to Rita's farewell luncheon." She blew into the microphone and asked if it was on. "I wanted to share a little story with you about grieving Rita." Finally some admission that this was, in fact, a memorial reception. "The rabbi asked me this morning how I planned to grieve the death of my sistah. We saw each othah every day. We tawked on the phone. We knew every secret the othah had. I was there when she was born and she's been my best friend evah since. I'm an old woman, and life is getting a little more rocky than it's evah been. Friends are dying. A few years ago, I went to my sixty-year high school reunion, and seven people were there—two in wheelchairs, one with a walkah. I don't hear at all in my left ear anymore, so when I go to the movies, I have to sit with my right ear pointed toward the screen, which means I get a crick in my neck from trying to see what's going on. I don't complain, but that doesn't mean I don't have troubles. So, at eighty-two years old, I'm not going to make myself any more uncomfortable than need be. When I remember that Rita has passed away, I'm going to simply pretend it nevah happened."

A hundred faces glanced sideways at each other, wondering if we should interrupt her or let her continue with her toast to denial. "When I think to call her, I'll just pretend she's on vacation. Or, I'll just close my eyes and pretend she's there. I know what she would say. After eighty yeahs with her, it's not like she could shock me with some new revelation anyway. So, if you feel a hole in your heart today, where Rita used to be, fill it by pretending she nevah died. Raise your glasses with me and toast her. To Rita. Pretend she nevah left us. Pretend she's still here. Just pretend."

Again, the guests looked around at each other for guidance. Should they toast to insanity concocted during Aunt Bernice's obvious breakdown? Could they raise their glasses and say "Pretend" in unison?

"To Rita," Jack said, filling in the awkward silence. "To Rita and her beautiful life!"

"To Rita!" the crowd repeated, relieved.

Chapter 32

When Jack's cell phone rang during dessert, half of the room glanced at their own, then looked annoyed at him for forgetting to turn his off. He knit his brows with concern when he saw who the call was from, so I gave him a look as if to say it was okay, that he should answer. He stepped outside, then returned twenty minutes later.

Still standing, Jack asked, "What would you think if I sold the gallery and we ran off together and joined the circus?" He kissed my forehead then sat beside me.

"Look around, hon," I said, gesturing to my family, and Aunt Bernice in particular, who'd just recently suggested we all go out for karaoke after the luncheon. "Marrying into this family was joining the circus."

"Seriously, Luce," Jack persisted. "What would you think if I sold the gallery and spent more time on my own painting?"

"Wow, this is out of left field," I said, wondering how long Jack had been unhappy with the gallery.

"So was the car that nearly killed me," he said.

"Everything's changed, Luce. And here we are," he gestured to our empty table with half-filled water glasses and chocolate crumbs. "Rita was an old woman, but still. One day she's on heart medication, thinking everything's under control, and the next week we're at her funeral." He sighed and reached for my hand. He turned his body squarely toward mine and leaned in to speak more softly. His eyes gazed up at mine and I knew that whatever he asked of me, I was already halfway there. "I'm not happy running the gallery. I was once, but now I want to paint again. What do you say we take a drive out to The Berkshires and look at some land? With what I could sell the gallery for, we could buy a house on a couple acres, then build the artist community little by little. I've been looking at the real estate ads, and I think we might be able to swing it. In ten, fifteen years, we could be living our dream."

Anjoli always says that anxiety is two equal portions of excitement and fear, and to work through it, a person should separate them and address each individually. Excitement: Jack is talking about us being together ten years down the road. He is referring to "our" dreams. The artist community would be heaven. At the very least, it wouldn't be Caldwell. Fear: Jack is talking about us ten years down the road. One more good whack to the head and he could go the other way again. Or, more likely, the sunny optimism of survival will eventually become a dim realism, and life with me might not look so appealing anymore. Okay, real confession here. The artist community always sounded like a splendid idea, but I sort of always knew it was never going to happen. The fact that it might was thrilling and terrifying. I could finally write my novel. In fact, I'd be expected to. And God knows, Desdemona is barely on speaking terms with me anymore.

"What do you think?" Jack asked again, looking expectant.

"I don't think we should make any rash decisions," I said, pleased with my levelheadedness.

"What's so rash about it? We've been talking about this for years."

"Is this really a good time to sell the gallery?" I asked.

"I'd say so," Jack said, smiling. He knew he was making headway with me. "I'd make a shitload on the real estate alone, and the business is profitable. It'd be a great investment for someone. Plus, I'm done with it. I want to paint, Lucy. I don't want to spend my time running back and forth from home to work, hustling to make other artists successful. I want to do my own thing."

Excitement took over and I saw myself at the keyboard of my computer with a large window in front of me that overlooked lush green trees. It is lightly raining and bulbous drops of water glisten on the leaves outside. A diversity of wildlife from boldly colored birds to gray squirrels find refuge in my yard, which always offers a full plate of nuts and seeds. My office is all wood and glass. A framed silk scarf with large pink flowers on it hangs on the main wall. I sip peppermint tea. I am happy.

"Let's talk about it tonight," I offered.

"It'll have to be," Jack said. "That was Wex. I need to go in for a few hours."

"Now?!" I whined.

"Luce, this is what I'm talking about. That gallery owns me."

"Do we really have enough money for this?" I asked.

The smile melted from Jack's face. "Not quite. We'd have to take a loan for some of it. I haven't sorted out all the details, but don't write it off, Luce. We could do this." He told me he'd be home in a few hours and kissed me good-bye, this time on the lips. It was a memorial service, after all, so a peck was all I got. But at least we were moving in the right direction.

I slipped out of the restaurant without saying good-bye to anyone, knowing exactly how my well-intended brood would handle Jack's disappearance. They couldn't conceive that a thirty-nine-year-old woman could find her way home alone, so we'd spend a half hour in a conversation that would have me begging for a noose. It'd go something like this:

ME: I'm going to get going now.

IDA: (Looking around) Where's your husband?

ME: Oh, Jack had to go to the gallery. I'm going to take the train back home.

IDA: You'll do no such thing! Izzy, tell her she'll do no such thing.

IZZY: Listen to your Aunt Ida. (It's always been commonly accepted that Ida and Izzy are my aunt and uncle, though they are really cousins of my Uncle Irving.)

IDA: The trains are dangerous for a young girl. Your cousin Richard will drive you.

ME: That's very sweet, but really not necessary.

IZZY: Don't tell your Aunt Ida what's necessary, big shot. You're a mother now.

BERNICE: What's all the commotion ovah here?

IDA: Richard offered to drive Lucy home, but she refuses to ride with him.

BERNICE: Well, if Richard's going that way, Lucy, why be such a big shot? Richard, *mamaleh*, come here.

RICHARD: (Clueless) Bernice, I'm so sorry.

BERNICE: You don't need to apologize. It's Lucy who's being rude.

RICHARD: Why, what'd she do?

ME: Hello! I'm right here.

RICHARD: What'd you do, Lucy?

IDA: She refuses to drive with you!

IZZY: Says it's not necessary.

IDA: She'd rather take the subway than be in a car with you, I guess.

ME: Richard, this has gotten out of hand. All I said was that it wasn't necessary for you to drive me home. I can take the train. It's not even a subway. It's a nice, clean train.

IDA: You think my Richard's car isn't clean?!

IZZY: My boy is as clean as they come!

IDA: Mr. Big Shot had to leave in the middle of a funeral to do his music deals, and leaves his wife here to take the subway home alone.

FERN: What's all the *mishegas*?

IZZY: She refuses to ride in a car with Richard. Says he's dirty!

FERN: Dirty?!

ME: I never said he was dirty! I said thank you, but I could find my way home. I don't want to inconvenience anyone.

BERNICE: It's no inconvenience. We're family.

RICHARD: Hey, doesn't she live in Jersey?

ME: Yes, I do!

RICHARD: I live in Queens.

FERN: Close enough!

IZZY: He's angry about being called dirty! Who can blame him?

ME: I didn't say he was dirty.

RICHARD: I'm not mad, but it is kind of way.

IZZY: They are horrors! Ever since we stopped having the cousin's club, they forgot they were family.

RICHARD: She said she can take the train.

IDA: She's just saying that.

ME: No, I'm not.

IZZY: You're a pregnant woman!

ME: No, actually I'm not.

FERN: Don't be a *schmuck*, Richard. Take your cousin home. It's not too far for you.

RICHARD: I don't think she wants the ride!

ME: I don't!

FERN: Don't be a moron. You'll put a little Purell on your hands after you get out of the car, and you'll be fresh as new.

Instead of enduring some variation of this, I slipped out the door and decided to take a walk through Central Park. I don't know why people say New Yorkers are unfriendly. Bikers smiled as they zipped by me. The Sabbrett's vendor jovially tempted passersby with promises of the best hot dog they'd ever eaten. Even the hardest vogue bitch stopped to snap a photo of tourists when she was asked. As I walked past hundreds of people lounging on beach chairs and blankets in Sheep's Meadow, I heard the familiar clopping of horse hooves behind me.

When I w   kid, horseback riding was my sport. I was shu   ry competition in New York state by
                  llow Gremlin. A hold-out from the
                   er probably always imagined I'd
                    ve rock collecting or something
                    inexpensive). Instead, I dragged
                   ian clubs, one more posh than
                  't complain, though looking
                 s and private lessons probably
                oklyn studio.

As I heard the sound of hooves hitting the ground, I felt my youth behind me, which in the height of coincidence, was exactly what it was. When I turned to look at the horse, I immediately recognized the rider. It was none other than Richie Cantor, my apparently not-so-dead college love.

Chapter 33

———————

"Richie?" I said, standing in his path.

"Holy shit, if it isn't Lucy Klein. How the hell are you?" His smile was contagious. I self-consciously attempted to turn down the wattage on my own smile, knowing I was too happy to see him again.

Richie wore jodhpurs and a blue blazer over a white button-down top, which I couldn't help thinking must've been miserably hot. On his head, he wore a black velvet helmet with the strap hanging loose. I imagined someone made him wear the helmet, but he immediately unstrapped it upon leaving her sight. God, he looked good. Like a men's cologne ad. I looked at him carefully, trying to decipher whether he really looked as sexy as I thought, or he just looked good compared to the dead guy I thought he was for the past few months.

"I can't believe it's you!" I said softly as his horse halted. "I thought you were, you were—"

"Dead?" Richie raised his one eyebrow. How did I forget that cute gesture?

"Yes!" I said, too excited.

"Nah, managing a hedge fund," he said, smiling.

"Mom and Dad got a lot of sympathy cards outta that one, though. Never knew I had so many friends at Michigan." He shrugged and exhaled a tiny snort.

"I don't understand," I said, looking up at him. The sunlight poured in through the leaves, creating a halo effect. He looked like a mythological character ready to scoop me up and return me to my past. As if he was reading my mind, that's just what Richie offered.

"Hop on," he said, patting the front of his saddle. "Let's catch up on what's been going on."

Without hesitation, I climbed on. I wanted to ask why his obituary appeared in the alumni magazine, what he'd been doing with his life for the last fifteen years, and whose rules he was breaking by unfastening his safety helmet. But not before I drank in the uninterrupted pleasure of feeling his familiar thick arms wrapped around my waist. My back rose with the tension of attraction, then I leaned into him, hoping my attempt to melt into him wasn't too obvious.

"Last I heard you were working on some sort of novel," Richie said. I immediately regretted sending in the questionnaire to our alumni magazine. Seven years ago, I got this wild idea that I'd write a historical romance set in seventeenth century Italy. I remember the day exactly. I'd just seen a play about—guess what—a tragic love set in war-torn seventeenth century Italy. All morning at work, the only thing I could think about was this novel I was going to write. During our staff meeting, my co-workers brainstormed ideas for roach killer while I quietly jotted notes for my outline of the book. It was going to be one of those books where the lives of eight separate characters are painstakingly dissected. About three-quarters of the way through the story, I would bring them all together for a tragic climactic chapter that centered around some horrible battle where half the characters ended up dead or maimed.

I spent an extra-long lunch hour at the library researching the period, then stayed up all that night developing character outlines. The next day, I received a letter from the University of Michigan alumni magazine asking what I was doing. In a state of overexhausted frenzy, I bragged that after graduating from Michigan, I stayed in Ann Arbor to earn my MFA from the university. I was writing (clear throat and sit erect) a novel. I wrote some other pretentious drivel, hoping to communicate that my novel would be terribly important and incredibly literary. The problem was that about a week after I sent my masturbatory note, I lost all interest in the book. Until Richie mentioned it, I hadn't realized the alumni magazine even printed my pompous update.

"Oh, the book was never for publication," I said. "It was more of a, of a—"

"Thing for yourself?" Richie asked, trying to help me complete the thought.

"So what about you?!" I turned and smiled, hoping that asparagus only affected the smell of pee, not breath. "You're obviously not dead. How did that get printed anyway?"

"Different Richard Cantor," he said, resigned. "Same class and everything. The obituary said the guy was from South Bend, Indiana, but I guess folks didn't get that far into it. My parents got like a hundred cards." He laughed. "Didn't you see where they put a picture of the guy in the next issue? My mom called the alumni office crying that she couldn't write another letter clarifying that her son was not dead, so they printed a follow-up."

"Wow, Richie. You're the only person I've ever met who can actually say that rumors of his death were highly exaggerated."

"I know."

"So, you haven't been decomposing. What *have* you been up to?"

Richie looked at his watch and said he had to be back at the stable in a few minutes but would like to catch up with me more over dinner. Now, there's dinner and there's *dinner*. I've never been one to flatter myself, but I definitely got the impression that he wanted *dinner*. Still, you can't presume. Even if you're absolutely correct, the person can shoot back, "Jeesh! I just wanted to catch up with an old friend over a meal. In case you haven't noticed, you currently weigh slightly more than a side of beef. Sex with you was the last thing on my mind. I just thought it'd be fun to see just how much food you can put down."

"Um, dinner?" I repeated, biding for time.

"Yeah, dinner," he said, not giving me any hint of his real agenda.

"My husband might get kind of jealous," I said, hoping to address the issue without actually bringing it up.

"So don't tell him," Richie shrugged. "I'm sure as hell not going to tell my wife." He winked. Well, at least I knew what I was dealing with now. A definite *dinner*.

"Oh," I said. Timing was a cruel thing. For more than a year, I was free to pursue a relationship with Richie. Admittedly, it would be an affair, but at least I wouldn't have been cheating on my own husband. A year ago I was so angry at my lot in life that I probably would have done it, justifying that I deserved a little fun with someone else's husband. I would have told myself that I didn't even know her, and if she couldn't keep her husband faithful, that was her problem, not mine. I'd imagine that she'd gained weight since she married Richie. I'd say the poor dear became a bore and lost sight of her dreams and her goals. She sat around the house all day in her tattered pajamas wiping baby snot from her son's nose. Then I remembered that this image was, in fact, me. All my life, I had watched Anjoli change married lovers with the seasonal styles. She once even joked that men with wedding bands were "the new black." I remember vowing that I would never have such reckless disregard for other women, and that no matter how great the temptation was, I'd stay away from their husbands. And yet a few months ago, I would have gladly had *dinner* with Richie Cantor because I was famished. It's like those people who have to survive together for a month in the Arctic and wind up cannibalizing each other. If you rewound the clock and visited them in their cozy homes before their excursion, each would swear he'd rather die than eat another human being. A short month later, one of the elders would keel over and the rest would fight over who got the ribs. But I wasn't in the Arctic Circle any longer. I wasn't at Club Med either. But where I was there were snacks, so the insanity of starvation didn't overrun me. Sure, Richie Cantor's familiar body looked great. Okay, it felt like heaven and smelled like chocolate cake too. (Then I remembered it was actually me who smelled like the cake from Rita's luncheon.) I loved riding on Richie's horse, harmlessly flirting and recapturing a small piece of my past. But I honestly didn't want to take it to the next level. *Dinner* was not a real temptation at this point. Timing is a wonderful thing sometimes. It can save us from ourselves.

"What do you say?" Richie said.

I dismounted from the horse and gave my old boyfriend a friendly pat on the thigh. I had a dozen retorts, all branding him a scumbag. The funny thing about having a mother who engages in despicable behavior is that it makes it difficult to judge others too harshly. If I called Richie a scumbag, that would make Anjoli one too. Conflicted as I am about my mother, there is no question that I love her. To think of someone else calling her names—though I'm certain there are dots all over the tristate area map where women gather to do this regularly—brings marbles to my throat.

"I think we've caught up enough," I said.

He looked puzzled, as though women don't often decline his dinner invitations. Especially heavy women.

"You sure?" he said. "Could be fun."

I smiled, not because I was flattered by the persistence, but because I realized that I was quite sure.

"Richie, it was great seeing you," I said, and meant it, though not in the way he probably thought. "I really have to get home now. I have to pick up my son at a friend's house and get dinner on the table for my husband."

Richie shrugged. I was not his first dinner invitation and I wouldn't be his last; my declination was more of a bothersome amusement, than anything else.

"Lucy, Lucy! There you are," my Aunt Ida shouted as Richie waited on his horse in front of Tavern on the Green. "We wondered what happened to you, *mumaleh*."

Richie glanced over at my family, then waved at me. "You ever change your mind, I work downtown at—"

"Ida!" I shouted to interrupt. Today, I was feeling noble and pure. Knowing where Richie worked was information I didn't need. Another day, it might prove too tempting. "Ida!" I ran and hugged her. "Do you think Richard could give me a ride home? Jack had to run to the gallery and I don't want to take the train."

"Of course, *mamaleh*!" She embraced me. "It's been such a hard day for everyone. Give Tanta Ida a hug." I buried my head in her enormous bosom until I heard hooves gallop into the distance. "Richard!" Ida shouted. "Richard!" This time louder. He appeared slowly, battered by a lifetime of her requests. "Richard, you're driving Cousin Lucy home to New Jersey. Clean that filthy car of yours and bring it around in ten minutes. We'll wait out front for you."

Chapter 34

Bernice went on a shiva cruise in August after she was mugged in a supermarket parking lot a week after her sister's funeral. Shiva is the week-long mourning period in the Jewish faith where family and friends sit on wooden boxes, drape black covers over mirrors, and bask in discomfort. It's basically the deceased's way of saying, *You think you're uncomfortable, try death, big shot.* It's the ultimate in one-upsmanship *Legs hurt? I only wish I had pain 'cause it would mean I wasn't dead, you selfish schmuck!* Of course, as in all religions and cultures, there is contradiction, such as the lavish bagel and lox spreads brought in by Sheppy's. We Jews believe in a lovely catered meal for the grieving family—as long as their asses go numb from sitting on crates. Suffer but eat well!

Shiva cruises recently became popular. In a way it makes sense. If you're grieving the loss of a loved one, prepared meals, maid service, and the company of other mourners can be of great comfort. On the other hand, shiva is all about discomfort, not pinochle and shuffleboard.

A week after Rita died, Bernice was still having her happy breakdown, as her kids dubbed it. Sadly, she was the ideal target for a mugging—an elderly woman carrying on a conversation with herself in a parking lot. She was laughing at one of Rita's jokes when a woman approached her and asked directions to the bank. Bernice supplied them in excruciating detail. "You turn left at the light. I'm not sure what the street name is, but there's a Lincoln-Mercury dealer on the corner. Irv and I bought ours there, and he always said, 'Bernice, make sure you come here to get the car serviced because these people know how to fix a Lincoln.' And I always have. So after you pass the dealership, you'll pass a Subway sandwich shop, a 7-Eleven, and a clothing store for ladies' plus sizes." Mind you, these were just shops the woman would have to pass. The woman didn't have to make another turn for six blocks. The woman thanked her, then offered to help load her groceries into her car. "How nice of you, but I can manage," she said. As soon as her back was turned, the woman pushed her to the ground and tried to grab her purse. I say tried because Aunt Bernice landed right on her own pocketbook, so the woman couldn't snatch it. Soon a getaway car came to pick up the thwarted mugger and left my aunt on the ground of the parking lot. "All my life I've been trying to lose weight," Bernice told people who scurried to her aid. "Today I was glad for my fat *tuchus*. It padded my fall nicely."

The people who witnessed the mugging told the police officer that my aunt was punched in the face, but she insisted she wasn't. "Can you describe the woman?" the officer asked.

My aunt thought about it for a moment. "She was a very elegant lady with the most exquisite hat. I thought she was coming from church with a hat like that on. All those feathers. In this heat, you have to be pretty devoted to wear a hat like that."

The officer was puzzled. "Black, white, Hispanic? Hair color? Eye color? Young or old? Any tattoos or birthmarks?"

"Oh, I don't know about any of that," my aunt apologized.

"You don't know if she was black or white?"

"She was a black woman, but don't just run out there willy-nilly and pick up the first black lady you see. Sometimes that happens and I don't want to see any more problems between the blacks and Jews," she said, smiling as though she weren't offending the officers. "Please, I don't need Chaka Khan stirring things up."

"Did you see the driver of the car?" an officer asked.

"*Oy*, is she going to get in trouble with her pimp!" Aunt Bernice lamented. "I heard they get very impatient with their workahs when they don't bring in the money."

When her kids heard about the mugging, and how she was unaware that she was punched in the face, they insisted she take time to feel her grief. They couldn't have their mother complimenting muggers' hats or pretending her sister was alive and well. She needed to spend some time in serious mourning. The shiva cruise was their compromise.

Anjoli went along with her. I've always appreciated how my father's and mother's families continued a relationship long after my parents' divorce. It was a refreshing departure from the world of my friends' parents who exchanged notes and angry glares at family events. The only thing unusual about my mother's offer to join Bernice on the shiva cruise was that she always said she wasn't a "cruise person." She didn't like having a ship in charge of where she was going. I suspected that Anjoli might be scouting for widowers, though she would never admit this to me. A few months ago, I told her I found it vile that she accompanied Bernice to the funeral of a firefighter simply to ogle the men in uniforms. As she put it, men in uniform are hot. Especially police officers and firefighters, who are required to keep themselves in good physical condition. Anjoli didn't let on her true motives for joining Bernice on the shiva cruise. She didn't have to. As soon as she self-consciously said that she needed to "clear up" her "bereavement issues" in time for Kimmy's wedding to herself, I knew she was on a hunt for a new date. This was a step in the right direction. At least the guy wouldn't be married.

After spending the week with us after Adam was born, Anjoli discovered that she wasn't all that necessary around the Drama Queen after all. Alfie and his regular cast of unemployed stage actors and crew kept the shop running more smoothly than when Anjoli was there. Her depth of knowledge of theatre proved extremely helpful when chatting with customers, but with her out of the daily running of the store, there were no more late tax fees from the IRS, no more fines from the City of New York for code violations, and no more letters from Con Ed threatening to turn off the gas and electric.

"Let's get in the car and check this place out!" Jack said, hovering over the newspaper one Sunday morning while still in his pajamas. "Don't say a word, Luce," he insisted. I held Adam to my breast and watched his open eyes looking at me. He seemed to be saying, *Don't say a word, Mom.* "Rustic paradise. Spacious yet cozy four-bedroom treehouse in the splendid woods of the Berkshires. Charmingly quaint while thoroughly modern. Five acres with two guest houses. Peaceful getaway." Jack paused and looked at me hopefully. "Let's just go take a look."

"Just hop in the car and go to the Berkshires?" I asked, stunned. He nodded.

"Gallery's closed tomorrow. Let's make a family weekend of it. We can find a bed and breakfast there and ask locals about the area." I was silent. "We don't have to buy anything today. We're educating ourselves about the market, so we know what's out there."

The last time we "educated" ourselves about the real estate market, I wound up in New Jersey. This time would be different, though, Jack promised. "Think about it, Luce," he pushed. "You don't like it here, so you're refusing to look at ways to leave? How much sense does that make?"

"Plenty," I quipped. "I may not be perfectly suited for Caldwell, but at least I know what I'm getting. It's close to the city and I know my way around. I'm in a walking group and have my La Leche League meetings."

"Lucy!" Jack said, laughing with exasperation. "You go to a La Leche League meeting once a month. I'm sure they have a group out there. How long do you think you're going to be breast-feeding anyway?"

"Listen, I could go another five years, no one there would think a thing of it," I said, waiting for Jack to laugh.

"Seriously, Luce. This is our dream. Let's make it happen. I promise you, we won't buy anything today. We'll look at one place, that's all."

An hour later, we were on the road with a diaper bag packed with wipes, Elmo, diapers, A and D ointment, chew toys, and three changes of clothes. I sat silently as Jack sang along with Adam's *Kid's Songs* CD and tried not to smile too wide. I glanced out the window and watched the landscape transform itself from sprawling green lawns to freeway to mountain woods.

When we arrived at the property, I got out of the car agape. I'm sure I looked like a character in a horror movie staring at the house oozing blood and shouting "Get out!" Only my shock was not fear. I was simply stunned that this property was an exact replica of the one I'd always envisioned when dreaming of the perfect home. It was the Westerbeke Ranch and St. Mark's Place rolled into one, and unlike the *Amityville Horror* house, this one beckoned, "Come in." There's a scribbling of graffiti in the ladies' room at Dojo's I am always haunted by. In Sharpie pen, someone wrote, "Find your home and live there." I suppose it always struck a nerve with me because I hadn't. And I didn't. This house was, without question, my home.

"I want this house," I whispered to Jack as he reached to the car to unstrap Adam from his seat.

He smiled and shifted his eyes as if to tell me I shouldn't give away my enthusiasm to the realtor. "Don't you think we should check out the inside?"

We walked into an entryway of natural wood, stone, and an endless expanse of window. It had the feel of ski lodge meets New Age spa with wool area rugs and stone sculptures where water cascaded from one level to the next. On the hallway wall, a collection of wooden string instruments was mounted, from a sitar to an ornately decorated bass. In the common area were clouds of couches and chairs in delicate blue and white gathered around a stone fireplace. The ceilings reached for the sky in a sharp slope with glass windows set into the wooden roof. I walked straight to my office without having to ask directions. And there it was, just as I'd imagined, complete with the bowl of seeds and nuts outside my window. The only thing that was different was that the painting on the framed silk scarf was blue, not dusty rose as I'd imagined. And you know what? I liked it better in blue. It was the first time in my entire life that my reality looked better than my fantasy. Jack followed me in moments later, holding Adam in his baby sling.

"I want this house," I said, moving toward him urgently. He laughed, delighted, but hushed me for the sake of bargaining power. "Jack, I'm not kidding, I want this house."

"I'm glad you like it," he said, smiling.

"I don't like it, I love it. I don't think you understand, Jack. This is my home and I want to live in it. Get me this house."

The more we toured the main house and the property, the more convinced I was that this was my home. Mentally, I started moving our things in, figuring out which paintings would look best where, and whether or not I could write the blue flower print into the offer. There was a large greenhouse in the back that Jack wanted to use as a painting studio. The guest houses were small, but just attractive enough to entice a starving artist to come and stay in it for free for a year.

"Could we build more guest houses in the future?" Jack asked the realtor.

The middle-aged woman with long gray hair and a wool poncho nodded, knowing she had buyers. What she had, unfortunately, were not buyers, but dreamers. When Jack and I returned to Caldwell that night, we took a long, hard look at our finances to see how we could swing buying the four-million-dollar property. God knows, it seemed like a stretch. We hadn't even furnished our place in Caldwell, but Jack seemed to think that with the sale of his gallery, the appreciation on the house, and a full cash-out of both of our retirement plans, we could do it. We stayed up until one in the morning punching numbers into a calculator like a gambler rolling dice in Las Vegas. I felt as though I should be in a sequined mini-dress, blowing a Bazooka bubble, encouraging, "Come on, baby! You can do it, big guy." Each time Jack would come up with a new idea, he'd frantically press his pencil eraser onto the calculator buttons, then eagerly await the total. The result was always the same. Jack's broad shoulders deflated and he'd sigh. In our best case scenario, we still came up a million dollars short. And, as Jack explained, banks weren't exactly keen on the idea of lending money for a non-revenue-generating arts community.

"How would we pay the loan, Luce?" Jack reminded me. "If I'm painting and you're writing, we can't pay a mortgage."

"Jack!" I shouted, almost waking Adam, still sleeping in his portable car seat. "This has to work. That's my home. I've found my home, now I want to live in it."

Chapter 35

"Have you tried chanting in front of the house?" Anjoli asked when I told her of our million-dollar shortfall. "*Nam-myoho-renge-kyo*," she repeated a few times. "Tina Turner swears by it, darling. Didn't you see her movie, *What's Love Got to Do With It?*" Upon hearing this, Aunt Bernice added that she too enjoyed *Love Doesn't Have Much to Do With Anything*.

"It means, I bow to the God within," Anjoli explained.

"Oh," I said, unimpressed. "What's the chant for 'I want this freakin' house?'"

"How do you think the universe will respond to your calling it a freaking house? Will it think you deserve this home that you curse, darling?"

Bernice and Anjoli had returned from their shiva cruise and came to Caldwell for lunch. I invited Candace to join us, but she was at a weekend class learning how to be a La Leche League leader. She'd started her course work in June, she said. I felt guilty for not keeping in better touch with her over the summer, and promised I'd strive to be as good a friend to her as she'd been to me. Candace was one of the truly pure-hearted people in the world. Over the months, we had witnessed mothers at their lowest. One mother was so exhausted that when she showed up at the July La Leche League meeting, she walked straight into the sliding glass door, despite the fact that it was fully decked out with butterfly stickers. Candace never laughed. She insisted on driving the woman home, saying she would never allow a mother to drive while overtired. Whenever a mother had a new baby, Candace was always the one e-mailing a meal drop-off schedule. Sometimes she'd call just to ask if there was anything I needed. Me, with my one child. Still, I liked Candace. Her generosity made me feel inadequate at first. Now, I just felt lucky to have her as a friend.

Jack brought a large shrimp salad to the table and placed it in the center so we could serve ourselves. Bernice reached her tanned arms toward the serving tongs and placed leaves on one of our new aqua-blue glass plates.

"How was the cruise?" Jack asked them.

"Very refreshing," Bernice said, smiling. "Lots of people crying, of course, but once you get used to it, it was sort of like background noise."

"I found it very disconcerting," Anjoli chimed in after delicately placing a forkful of spring greens into her lacquered mouth. "It was as though the only thing these people were focused on was their own loss, their own grief." Jack shot me a look as if to ask if that wasn't the whole point of a mourning period. "Frankly, I found the whole thing troublingly self-centered. I lost my husband. I lost my brother. Me, me, me. What about the people who made the transition? Do they even bother thinking about *them*?"

"Made the transition?" Jack asked.

"Died," Bernice clarified.

"Oh."

"I think they *are* thinking about their loved one, though, Anjoli," I said. "They're thinking about how much they'll miss that person."

"That's my point entirely, darling! It's all about them and their loss. Why not rejoice that when a human sheds its body and makes the transition to the spirit plane, they are at total peace. Instead of focusing on their loss—which locks a person into lack of consciousness anyway—why not celebrate the fact that their husband or wife is now in euphoria?"

"Maybe because it's not a fact," Jack added.

Anjoli sat straight. "Oh, but it is, though. They say the other side is like having an eternal orgasm."

Oy.

"*Who* says this?" Jack asked. "The people who send postcards back from the other side? 'Wish you were here. It's one big orgasm.'"

"No, no, I've got it," I piped in. "You'll be so happy this is where you're *coming*. You'll understand soon enough. Wink, wink."

Bernice laughed as Adam amused himself jumping in a bouncing duck that hung from a door frame. This hand-me-down from Candace was a lifesaver. He found hours of amusement not just springing about, but looking up and trying to figure out how the crazy contraption worked.

"Laugh if you want, but the completely self-indulgent mind-set of these mourners got me thinking of a way I could help," Anjoli said. Sometimes I am too hard on Anjoli. Sure, she has flaky ideas about life—and death—but deep down she truly cares about people. "I go to enough workshops to know what people go for, and I've got a winner. I'm going to lead a workshop that helps people move beyond the selfishness of grieving and focus on how truly blessed their loved one really is now. I'm going to call it 'Good Mourning.' Don't you love it? I may even write a book. My friend Chris is a literary agent and said it was, and I quote, 'quite a concept.' "

My mother is going to write a book?!

My mother is going to teach a class on how to be less self-centered?!

My mother is going to tell people that they shouldn't grieve? That a ninety-year-old woman should just get over it and be happy that her lifelong husband is now hosing down dead Playboy bunnies with his endless supply of jiggy juice!

And you know what the worst part of this will be? That Anjoli—the maid of honor at my cousin's wedding to herself—will be wildly successful. People will flock to her seminars, and wait hours in a line to speak with her. When they finally get to speak to her, they'll weep with gratitude and tell her how she changed their lives. They will look to her as the Maharishi of Selflessness. Within a year, she'll fly first class around the globe, kissing orphans and spouting pearls of wisdom, like "Don't worry, Mommy and Daddy are having one big orgasm in the sky." Anjoli will even have stalkers, which I'm sure she'll love. She'll claim that she's too selfless to get restraining orders against them, and that they have every right to send her sacrificial samples of their flesh.

"Mother," I said tersely. "What is wrong with people mourning the loss of a person they loved?"

"It's selfish," she said, smugly wiping the corner of her mouth with a napkin.

"So what? Maybe you're right that a person dies and goes to Plato's Retreat. Who knows, maybe you're right," I said, glancing at Jack who was smirking. "Maybe death is the fabulous adventure you say it is. Still, isn't a person entitled to grieve for her own loss?! What would your friend Louise Hay say about suppressing grief? I mean if not expressing anger causes cancer, and possibly wrinkles, wouldn't it stand to reason that suppressing any emotion would carry some dire health consequences?"

"I think Lucy has a point," Bernice said, coming to my aid. Jack continued eating, his head following the conversation like a tennis match. "Who was it that said half the value of theatre was catharsis?"

"I think it was the Germans," Jack offered.

"It wasn't the Germans, you moron!" she snapped, then apologized for name-calling.

"Ever since Rita died, she's been adopting her mannerisms and speech," Anjoli explained.

"Oh my God!" I gasped. "Mother, why haven't you mentioned this before?"

"Don't make such a fuss," Bernice assured. "I told you, I like to pretend Rita's still with us, so I try to think of what she would say if she were here. Most of the time, I keep it to myself and Rita and I have a private little joke, which believe me we had plenty of when she was alive. But every once in a while, I slip. Whenever I feel she would've wanted me to say something, whenever I feel I can bring her into the conversation, I like to. And when I heard Jack say it was the *Germans* who thought up catharsis, I nearly choked. You know it wasn't the Germans, don't you, Jack?"

"I was joking," he said like a schoolboy being reprimanded.

"Well, let me give you a tip, big shot," she said with her Rita edge. "Whenever the punch line is 'the Germans,' it's probably not a very funny joke."

"So, as I was saying before, we found a house in the Berkshires we'd like to buy," I said, trying to resuscitate our lunch conversation.

"Seriously, you should see this place," Jack joined me. "It's five acres out in the middle of—"

"I adore the Berkshires, darling," Anjoli said. "It's a magical spot, isn't it?" She continued. "I danced in the Catskills one summer. It was glorious."

"I nevah heard of ballerina recitals in the Catskills," Bernice said.

"Modern jazz," Anjoli said with self-satisfaction. "We had a little break-off group. Do you remember my friend Kiki? She was in it and—"

"Anyway," I said. "We're in love with this house—in the Berkshires, not the Catskills—so we're trying to come up with some ideas on how to raise a chunk of change fast."

"Invest in my seminars!" Anjoli suggested. "I'm telling you, darlings, we are going to be rolling in it when self-less nonmourning becomes the new Qi Gong."

"They need to make money, not flush it down the toilet, you moron!" Bernice snapped.

"Why, that was uncalled for!" Mother barked back.

"I agree," Bernice said. "I'm sorry. Would you all excuse me please? I'm getting one of Rita's migraines." She stood and began walking toward the couch.

Jack and I looked at each other in shock. Auntie had gone off the deep end.

Anjoli offered, "Try chanting '*Nam-myoho-renge-kyo*.' It's wonderful for clearing the mind."

Chapter 36

Desdemona had been thinking about death a lot lately. She wondered what it felt like to die, and if there was an afterlife. The pneumonia had only grown worse, yet her mother insisted it was just a bad cold and kept giving her echinacea and goldenseal. She wondered why Claude hadn't come to care for her. Desdemona wondered if she was destined to be alone for the rest of her life. At this rate, that wouldn't be too long.

After *Real Confessions* had been cancelled, Zoe went through a bit of a depression. She hid away at our place for a few days, then found a bargain vacation to Paris and took off for three weeks. When she returned, she announced that she was quitting the agency and returning to her true love, purse designing.

"I adore your bags!" Kimmy shrieked when she heard the news at her bridal shower. "I get so many compliments on the bowling ball." She paused for a moment, then burst with a request. "Design my wedding purse?! I beg of you, Zoe. Something as unique as the wedding. Something that says, 'I love me!'" A few of Kimmy's friends laughed, though we knew what she was saying was not about ego. The wedding to herself was therapeutic. It's just that very few of us have *Glamour* featuring our therapy sessions. At Jack's and my marriage counseling session, the therapist didn't even bother to show.

"What should I do, a mirror bag?" Zoe joked, though as soon as she said it I could see everyone's faces light with excitement.

"That's fabulous, darling!" Anjoli chimed in. "Kimmy, you should have tiny mirrors sewn onto your dress like one of those disco balls."

Kimmy shrieked, placing her palms on her cheeks. "Zoe, can you do that?! I want to be a disco ball for my wedding to myself!" There are very few phrases a person can say that have never before been uttered. "I want to be a disco ball for my wedding to myself" is one of them.

"I'm not sure," Zoe said, trying to bring down the excitement level flooding the room like water on the Titanic. "The wedding is two weeks away. I've never designed a dress before." She gently placed a glass of iced tea on a table in Anjoli's living room, then brushed away imaginary lint from her black pants.

"Come on!" Kimmy pouted adorably. Clearly this is a maneuver she'd successfully employed before.

"Kimmy, I'm sorry, but—"

Anjoli interrupted. "I'm sure *Glamour* will mention your name. Especially since Lucy's writing the article."

"Done," Zoe said, smiling.

I tried to offer a caveat. "You guys know that an editor has final discretion on everything that—"

"Readers will want to know who made Kimmy's dress!" Anjoli insisted. "Wait until you see what she's going to design."

The weekend after Labor Day, the wedding finally arrived and Kimmy was sitting in her silver bra and panty set in Anjoli's changing room as a makeup artist from *Glamour* applied layers of perfection onto Kimmy's face. No wonder I always look like crap. I never use under-eye concealer. I didn't even see what Kimmy had to conceal, but once it was on, I had to admit, she looked five years younger and infinitely fresher. The woman with the black Cleopatra bob and translucent skin then meticulously sponged a layer of moisturizer over Kimmy's liquid foundation and finished it with powder. When I saw the six different shades of eyeliner from light gray to charcoal sit beside four blushes (each with its own brush), and three shades of lipstick (again, each with a brush of its own), I thought, for sure, Kimmy would look overdone. Instead, she looked as though she was wearing the slightest shimmer of silver around her eyes and a smidge of lip gloss. I was amazed at the effort it took to look effortless.

"This is absolutely amazing," I said. "I would love to get a makeover like this some day. Kimmy, you look stunning."

The makeup artist said she had extra time and offered to give me a "touch-up." This was a euphemism for washing off everything and starting fresh. "I didn't expect it to go so quickly with the bride," she said. "I've got an extra half hour." So quickly?! Was she kidding? She'd been working on Kimmy's face slightly longer than it took Michelangelo to paint the ceiling of the Sistine Chapel, and yet she thought it might have gone longer. As if on cue, Anjoli appeared right as the words "half hour" were being spoken.

"Let's do it!" I said, snatching the chance. "Do you mind, Kimmy?"

"Why would I mind?" she asked as a woman pulled sections of her blond hair into tight rolls.

"Mind what?" Anjoli asked, slipping into her pumpkin-colored leather shoe.

"Marigold is going to do Lucy's face," Kimmy said. "I didn't take as long to make up as she expected." Kimmy seemed a bit self-satisfied with this fact, but before I could stop to ponder whether or not I was bothered by this fact, I had to defend my territory.

"Oh, Marigold, darling," Anjoli said.

"No!" I snapped.

"What are you carrying on about, Lucy?!"

"Marigold is doing my makeup, not yours!" I said, finally pausing to consider this woman's ridiculous name.

"I know that, darling. Kimmy told me that a moment ago."

"You wanted to see if she would do your makeup instead of mine."

"I wanted to offer her a Diet Coke," Anjoli said. "Calm down. The bride is supposed to be high maintenance, not the magazine reporter."

"I'd love a drink," said Marigold.

"Me too," said the hairdresser, Kendra.

"What?" Anjoli said, turning her head to them.

"The Diet Coke," Marigold reminded. "I'd love one. It's hot in here."

"Oh, of course," Anjoli said, popping her head from the room and shouting to a waiter. "We need a tray of colas. What are you doing up here, anyway? You should be downstairs in the kitchen! Never mind. Just bring the colas." She shut the door.

I sat in a chair as Marigold held my face and turned it in every thinkable direction. I suppose she was trying to find my good side. Into my tape recorder, I said, "We all know we should love ourselves, but one New York bride is taking it one step further—she's marrying herself."

"I can't have you doing that," Marigold said.

"Talking?"

"Talking or moving," she said firmly. "We are focused on making you beautiful and I can't do that if you're talking."

"Beauty and talking don't mix?" I asked. She confirmed. Priceless.

A half hour later, Zoe and my mother helped Kimmy into her full-length, fully mirrored wedding gown that looked as if it was straight from the ceiling of Studio 54. She glistened with the lights in the room, and in a moment of glitz meets Gestalt, I caught the reflection of every face in the room on a separate penny-sized piece of Kimmy's dress. *Oh my God, is that me?!* I thought, remembering I'd been distracted by Kimmy's gown before I could check out Marigold's work.

"Zoe, you truly outdid yourself," Anjoli said, as I turned to the vanity table. I gasped audibly, but no one noticed in the commotion of Kimmy's dress making its debut.

"Marigold, I look amazing," I said. "Thank you so much. I can't stop looking at myself." It was embarrassing to admit, but I really couldn't stop staring at my own reflection. "You're a miracle worker. I can't even believe this is me." I wanted to beg her to leave me step-by-step instructions of exactly what she did, and what brands and shades of makeup she used. But all I could manage to do was stare at my reflection. For the first time in my life, I was absolutely, positively, unapologetically in love with my appearance. I wanted to marry myself.

I did have the good sense to take Marigold's business card so I could call her later and schedule a makeup application lesson. But for the wedding day, I'd be lucky if I remembered to take notes about the wedding and not stare at myself in the reflection of the living room windows. "I'm going to go downstairs now," I whispered to Kimmy and Anjoli. With Zoe by my side, I turned for the door.

"Lucy," Anjoli said. She hugged me. "You look pretty, darling. Daisy did a lovely job."

Zoe and I sat in the back row next to Alfie and his new boyfriend, George. My mother's living room seated seventy-five folding chairs. They were decorated with white ribbon because when they arrived from the party rental place, Alfie said it looked as though we were hosting a bridge tournament at a Floridian retirement condo.

This was exactly where Aunt Bernice was. She had just moved into her new place in Hollywood, and Jack and I were able to convince her cousin Sylvia to stay with her for the first few weeks so she didn't dive into the Intracoastal or scare off any of her new neighbors by channeling Rita.

As Kimmy appeared at the top of the staircase, twenty camcorders whipped out, including Zoe's. "Sorry, hon, it's too bizarre not to capture on video. I could sell it to FOX." When seeing Kimmy, Adam uttered his first word, "pretty." From my mother's CD player, we heard the voice of Whitney Houston claiming that she believes that children are our future. I was confused by her suggestion that we teach them well and let them lead the way. What did child rearing have to do with weddings? As Kimmy descended the staircase, there was an explosion of white light from flashbulbs reflecting off her dress. Although it may have seemed rude to sit during the bride's walk down toward the altar of narcissism, I feared I might become dizzy and fall with Adam. This, as it turned out, was a wise move, for I surely would've fainted when I saw Anjoli handing out silver cigarette lighters and urging everyone to light them as we belted out the chorus. "Learning to love yourself, it is the greatest love of all," the guests sang, swaying back and forth.

"Dearly beloved," a woman named Summer began. Mother said she was the hottest New Thought minister in New York and that she recently started her own church after she and the head honcho at the Unity Church in Lincoln Center had irreconcilable spiritual differences. She was the "It" minister in the gay community.

"Dearly, dearly beloved," she said again with the charisma of a Baptist preacher. "Today a woman is marrying herself. How many of you here got your invitation to this little shindig and thought, 'Well, now I've seen everything'? Even in New York?" This got a laugh revealing that more than a few guests had a similar reaction. How could they not? "But wouldn't it be wonderful if everyone loved themselves enough to actually want to spend the rest of their lives with themselves? Now, some of you may be thinking, 'I already am spending my life with myself' but what I'm talking about is *wanting* to spend the rest of our lives with ourselves. I am not pointing fingers at anyone, but I can tell you from my own experience in life and counseling others that at some point most of us would divorce ourselves if we could. Now breathe, 'cause I'm not talking to you. I'm talking to the guy next to you. I've met a lot of people who wouldn't even want to go out on a date with themselves, much less tie the knot. I think a lot of people popping the question to themselves would sound something like this: 'Self, how the heck did we wind up in this mess?' That's why we turn to drugs, alcohol, gambling, compulsive shopping, promiscuity, abusive partners, and voting Republican." Another laugh. "Kidding aside, I think Kimmy has done something wonderful here today. She's said that she's looking within herself for happiness. Now some of you are asking yourselves, 'Isn't it okay to look to other people and things for happiness?' Certainly it is. And as soon as we learn to love ourselves, really love ourselves unconditionally, faults and all, we'll be amazed at how much deeper our love for others and for life becomes. Breathe with me again. I feel like I'm going to lose a few of you here today."

Summer paused, never looking down at notes. "No one has to do something as radical as marry themselves in a public ceremony like this, but here's what I ask of you all today. Not as a gift to Kimmy, but as a gift to yourselves. Find some small way of showing yourself love and do it." This prompted a hoot from the back row of Alfie and his friends. "Ah yes, someone's mind is in his boxer shorts," Summer said, smiling. "My friend Jennifer loves macadamia nuts. Whenever she eats them, she feels that someone is taking care of her. When she was a little girl in camp, her mother sent her packages of games, candy, and macadamia nuts. For some reason, it's the nuts that make her feel loved." She paused. "What are your macadamia nuts? Is it ice skating in Rockefeller Center when the Christmas tree is out? Is it a frozen hot chocolate at Serendipity? Is it taking time to read a magazine while you're in a bubble bath? What is it that makes you feel loved? Then do it!"

She smiled, then turned to Kimmy. Summer asked her if she promised to love and cherish herself for all her days. Kimmy did. The minister asked if she promised to obey her inner wisdom and always do what she knew was best for herself. Again, Kimmy said she did.

"For those of you who promised yourselves that you'd enjoy more sunsets, look out there." She motioned her hand toward Anjoli's expansive window at the most glorious pink and purple cotton candy stretching across the city skyline. "God is great," she said with energy.

"All of you are here to witness this magnificent affirmation of self-love. Congratulations, Kimmy. As your aunt's friends on Broadway say, you are your own wife."

Amid cheers and applause, and a random *mazel tov*, Alfie turned on the CD player at full blast to the Divinyls singing, "When I think about you, I touch myself . . ." Kimmy scrunched her mouth to one side and shook a fist playfully. Then the blushing bride gave Alfie the finger.

"And the first dance will be Kimmy alone," announced the DJ as he popped in Billy Idol's "Dancing With Myself." She twirled around the center of the living room like a silly child as people watched and began chatting again.

"Remind you of our wedding?" Jack asked, elbowing me.

I laughed. "Not in the least."

"Same venue," he returned. "May she have a smoother road than we did."

"Jack," I said. "We really need to talk."

"You're not dumping me, are you?" he joked. He wasn't being cocky. It was just so clear that we were happier these last few months than we had been in years. Maybe ever. We were joining each other in the mundane things the way we used to back when we dated. We took trips to the supermarket together so we wouldn't have to interrupt our riveting conversation about nothing. I washed; he dried. I changed diapers while Jack took out filled trash bags. We had our time together, after Adam went to sleep, where Jack used me as a model for his paintings. We drove by a garage sale and picked up a couch that seated us perfectly as we both reclined on opposite ends to read. It was like a flesh puzzle where my leg would drape on the back of the couch while his would fit right underneath. We met in the middle without getting in each other's way.

Our new favorite activity was "visiting" the house in the Berkshires via Internet. It still hadn't sold and the price had been reduced by $150,000, but we were still far from being in a position to make an offer.

"Of course I'm not dumping you, Jack," I assured him as I stopped a waiter for another canapé. "I just think we need to talk about where our relationship is going."

"We're still married, Luce. What else is there?"

"But we almost got divorced, Jack. If I wasn't pregnant, we would be divorced right now," I reminded him.

"See, it was meant to be," Jack dismissed with a laugh. "Adam saved our marriage."

"Jack, I don't want our baby to save the marriage. I want us to," I said when suddenly Jack realized I was serious. "I think we should go to a couple's counselor."

"Again?!" he protested. "It didn't work for us last time."

"Because Dr. Lee blew us off. We can get another one. Jack, I really want to do this. Everything's great right now, but I want to figure out what went wrong last time and not let it happen again."

"It's different this time," Jack said. He was right. It was more comfortable between us. I was able to tell him how I felt without him immediately suggesting I flip a switch and feel something else. I tried to use humor as an escape hatch less often, but it was tough. I seemed to have a reflexive instinct to try to inject humor when, frankly, some things were no laughing matter. Still, I wanted an expert to inspect our new marriage and stamp it kosher.

"Can you humor me and just go to counseling for a few months?" I asked.

He nodded. "Can you humor me and dance with me to this cheesy song?" Jack held his hand out, then wrapped it around mine and led me to the dance floor. The lights were dimmed and Kimmy's wedding dress sparkled in the center of the room. The crowd joined in for the chorus: "I've been to paradise, but I've never been to me." Jack rolled his eyes as we danced with our sleeping son in a sling sandwiched between us.

Chapter 37

The following week, we started seeing Dr. Etta Rosenblatt, who came highly recommended by Mary, the La Leche League leader. Without a moment of hesitation, she said that when she and her husband were having "adjustment issues," Etta worked wonders for them. I appreciated her candor and wasn't sure if I'd be as willing to share with a group of casual acquaintances that my husband and I needed a therapist. I took some comfort in seeing several mothers casually jot down the therapist's name between recommendations for fenugreek herb and lanolin.

Dr. Rosenblatt's reception area was decorated with framed Chinese paintings and olive and orange satin pillows strewn across a comfortable black couch. She had three small fountains where water drizzled down a pyramid of rocks, which patients were probably supposed to find relaxing. They reminded me of the ones in the house we couldn't afford. Hanging from a clear fishing wire in front of the window was a crystal, refracting sunlight and getting Rosenblatt's feng shui all in place. Feng shui has always had the opposite effect on me than what it was intended to do. Instead of opening my energy channels to peace and prosperity, it annoyed me. Something about a person—or in this case a room—telling me to relax and turn on my heart light or unblock my chi always made me want to break things.

The dark wood door opened as Jack and I looked at each other with anticipation. A short senior with milky-white skin and red hair pulled into a disheveled bun emerged with another couple. We could only see their backs because they scurried out so quickly. Didn't they realize we were there for the same reason? "Hello," she said, taking a full two seconds to deliver the word.

I'm not going to be able to stand this calm, nurturing routine.

Jack was right. We don't need therapy. We're fine.

That other couple didn't look like they were half as happy as Jack and I are.

I wanted to make a run for it, but went inside her office anyway. Jack and I sat on a small blue love seat while Dr. Rosenblatt turned her desk chair to face us. Surely her removing the barrier between us was some sort of feng-shui-meets-psychotherapy way of telling us how very *with* us she was. Behind her sat a white dry-erase board and a bookshelf filled with small plastic toys, keys, action figures, and a hand mirror.

She folded her hands onto her lap and leaned forward to show that she was listening. "So, Lucy and Jack. What are you here for?"

Good fucking question! I didn't say aloud. How I hoped she would not make us play with the action figures or have me look at my vagina with the hand mirror. The image of a circle of women in my mother's living room saying loving affirmations to their vulvas is still burned in my memory like a POW remembers his internment. Surprisingly, Jack showed no resistance.

"Lucy and I almost got divorced a while back," he started. "We're happy now, but she thinks we need to come here to keep it that way."

"Well, I wouldn't put it that way," I shot back.

Dr. Rosenblatt held her hand up at me. "Jack, are you finished?" He nodded. "Now, Lucy, tell me why you think you and Jack could benefit from counseling."

"I want to figure out what went wrong the first time around so we don't make the same mistakes again," I said, trying to showcase my sensible responsibility. "We have a child now."

"Are *you* finished?" she asked.

"Oy," I slipped.

"Oy?" Dr. Rosenblatt asked.

"It means—"

"Oh, I know what it means," she said. "I was wondering what you meant by 'oy.'"

Hey, that time I wasn't finished!

"Well, you know, doc, sometimes an oy is just an oy," I said, laughing. Jack laughed too, tapping my thigh as if to say *good one*. The doctor smiled ever so slightly. She reached into her desk drawer and pulled out two printouts for Jack and me. The heading read, "XYZ statements." It advised couples to focus on specific behavior rather than make general complaints. I was supposed to tell Jack not that he was being a big, fat fucker, but rather that *I* felt hurt by his big, fat fuckerness. Or something like that. The main point was that I was supposed to make "I" statements instead of ones that went something like, "You are such a slob!" Instead, I should calmly inform Jack, "I feel disrespected when you leave your socks on the floor."

The follow-up conversation was supposed to go something like this:

JACK: What I hear you saying is that you feel disrespected when I leave my socks on the floor. Is that correct?

ME: Yes, Jack, you heard me correctly.

JACK: Is there anything else?

ME: No, not for now.

JACK: So you are finished.

ME: Yes, I am.

Then I guess we're supposed to kiss or something because I feel acknowledged and heard—and God bless him, he let me finish.

"But does this get him to pick up his socks?" I ask.

"I don't know," Dr. Rosenblatt said, looking to Jack.

"I work hard all day and when I get home I just want to kick off my shoes and socks and be comfortable," Jack defended. "I don't want to worry about throwing my socks in the hamper."

"You know, with all due respect, doctor, I can live with the socks on the floor. Jack and I have bigger fish to fry."

"It's not about the socks!" Dr. Rosenblatt said with her index finger pointing in the air. Then she got up and started drawing diagrams on her white board. She drew a blue dot on one end of the board, which was Jack, and a red dot at the other end, which was me. Then she frantically dotted a black line between the two of us. "The message we intend to send is often not the same message that is received," she said. "To Jack, socks on the floor are a way of relaxing. Jack is saying to you, 'I feel comfortable in my home.' But what Lucy is hearing is 'Jack doesn't care about my need for a clean, orderly house.' What we need to do is teach you to translate each other's messages. Does that make sense?"

"Yes!" Jack said emphatically.

It does?!

For the next twenty minutes, I listened to Jack talk about his childhood role in the family and his thoughts about what it means to be a father. It was all stuff I'd heard before, but it had been a while. Plus, I'd always heard bits and pieces. Memories scattered before me over years without any real cohesiveness or context. I settled into my half of the love seat and reluctantly admitted that perhaps the forced time listening to each other might be good for us.

"Is there anything you'd like to tell Jack about how you've been feeling about the relationship, Lucy?"

"Recently, I've been very happy," I said.

"Is there anything that's hurt you over the past few months?" she asked. "And please call me Etta."

"Well . . ."

"Go on," Etta encouraged. "And remember, 'I' statements. Now face Jack and share."

"Okay," I began. "That time when you—"

"*I* statements!" Etta corrected. "*I* felt such and such when you did such and such."

I raised my eyebrows at Jack, wondering if I should just let this one pass. After all, he and Natalie had broken up. We had been so happy over the last few weeks. We spent hours joyously shopping on the Internet for furniture we weren't going to buy for the house we couldn't afford. We turned his former bedroom into a makeshift studio and filled it with paintings and sketches of my plump body. Why was I about to rock the boat with memories of Natalie?

"G'head, Luce," Jack said. "I can take it. I know we've had a rough year. I think it'll be good to get it out in the open."

"That's the spirit!" Etta said, clapping her hands.

"Okay, Jack. *I* feel angry when you bring women

into our home, have sex with them, then take them to the playground with our baby the next day."

"Oy!" Etta slipped.

We saw Etta twice a week for the next six weeks and somewhere around October I started hearing about parts of Jack's life I didn't know about. There were no dramatic revelations of beatings or abuse by the evil cousin, just little things that helped me make better sense of Jack. Of course, Etta always quieted me when I tried to make an observation, saying that I should be focusing on my response to what Jack was saying—not analyzing him. I hadn't known that Jack's mother never allowed him to mention his father's name after he remarried and stopped visiting. "Upward and onward," she repeated like a mantra in the months after he left. As the visits became less frequent, Susan advised Jack not to think about such unpleasantness. When his father evaporated, she grew impatient with her son's constant inquiries about his father. She had no answers for him. One day, she snapped that he should never speak his father's name again. Jack persisted a few times, but Susan smiled placidly and said, "I'm sorry, but I do not know anyone by that name."

Finally, the week before Thanksgiving, the topic of the miscarriages came up. "Lucy has always said that I blame her for the miscarriages," Jack began.

"Do you?" Etta asked.

"Of course not!" he cried.

"Are you sure?" she challenged.

"Of course I'm sure. What kind of husband would blame his wife for a miscarriage?!"

"Jack, no one's blaming you for blaming her," Etta said with her trademark calmness. "Blame is an emotion, not a rational thought. Blaming Lucy would not make you a bad person. It would make you human."

"You think I'm to blame?" I snapped.

"What does it matter what I think, Lucy?" Etta asked.

"I cannot believe this! You *do* think I'm to blame. I didn't do anything to cause those miscarriages! Don't you think it killed me to lose those pregnancies?! And now you're saying I was to blame. What kind of therapist are you anyway?"

"You have a lot of anger around this issue," Etta said. She stood to write on her white board.

"No! I don't need any diagrams. You know I'm not at fault for this, don't you?"

"Do you?" she shot back.

"What the hell are you saying?" Jack came to my defense.

"I'm saying that Lucy has never forgiven herself for losing the pregnancies. Intellectually, she knows that she didn't cause them, but emotionally, she blames herself. Since the two are incongruous, she puts it on you, Jack. She says *you* must be the one who blames her. She feels blame coming from somewhere so she assumes it must be from you. She accuses you of blaming. And although you're furious at her for a variety of other reasons, and probably blame her for a dozen other things, you deny it. She gets mad because she knows you're angry about something. You get mad because now you have to assure her you're not mad at her about this, and you don't get to express what you really are upset about."

"This is all very confusing," I said.

"I agree," Jack said.

I smiled. "I think I may actually blame *you* now, Dr. Rosenblatt. We were happy a few weeks ago." She knew I was kidding, and the truth was that our marriage felt like sand bags were being tossed from a hot-air balloon.

We began scheduling double sessions at 10:00 A.M., then ran to Pizza Hut starved for food and a continuation of our discussion. I was amazed at how the past ten years of our marriage had been consumed by mundane details like buying paper towels, paying bills, and filling the gas tank. Jack and I had stopped getting to know each other. As we ate pizza together, I listened to Jack's stories from his early life and was rapt by his observations about how they related to our present. It occurred to me for the first time that Jack is an insightful guy. I don't know if this was a new thing, or if he always was insightful and I was just noticing it. But as I listened to him between chomps of his deep-dish pepperoni pizza, I realized that I was pretty lucky to have a man like this.

Chapter 38

Anjoli's Thanksgiving dinner was an intimate gathering of friends, including Anjoli's new boyfriend, Miguel, a former defender for the Mexican soccer team and now a high school coach. He was a mere six years her junior—and single! On her honeymoon, Kimmy met Steve, an attorney for Planned Parenthood, who she'd been dating for six weeks. I had to refrain from making jokes about Kimmy's need for Planned Parenthood services now that she was married to herself. The usual suspects, Alfie and Kiki, were there, along with their friends George and Chris.

As Alfie brought the carved turkey to the table, he suggested we go around the table and say what we were thankful for this year. I knew Jack cringed at these forced "go 'rounds," but he looked surprisingly unfettered by the suggestion.

"What a splendid idea, darling!" Anjoli claimed. "It will put us in gratitude consciousness."

"A good place to be on Thanksgiving," George teased. Anjoli dismissed him with a wave of her hand.

"I should start since I'm the hostess," she said, then

held her hands out for her flankers to hold. This was our cue that the circle of gratitude would serve as our evening grace. "After I ran away from home, I was fortunate enough to find myself adopted by the beautiful and elegant Miss Dorothy at the Joffrey Ballet Company, who spotted my gift on the very first day of class." A few incredulous looks were exchanged by newcomers, wondering if my mother was kidding or not.

"Anjoli, love," Alfie interrupted. "Your life has been so charmed. Let's keep the gratitude about this year, shall we?"

"I was doing that!" she protested. "I was about to say that without that experience, I would never have had the opportunity to work with the wonderful people at the Drama Queen, like you, Alfie!" It was going to be a long night. "I am blessed with an abundance of beautiful, creative people like my daughter, Lucy, and her family." *Huh?* "The new bride, Kimmy. Miguel." She did not elaborate on him anymore, but the tone of her voice suggested it was a torrid romance. "My oldest and dearest friends, Kiki and Alfie, and now our new friends, George and Chris. Oh yes, and I'm thrilled to be off to Findhorn in Scotland in the spring to teach Selfless Nongrieving. I know it's going to be the next big thing!"

She glanced at Miguel beside her, who with a smoldering simplicity said, "I am grateful for the love." George said he was grateful for being among new friends—and that he landed a part in Anjoli's latest production, *The Queen and I.*

Jack said that this year he got two second chances at life. "Car accident," I explained to the newcomers.

"We had our first child, and I remarried my first wife," he added with an openness he'd never before possessed. Jack made me blush. Pardon me, *I* felt flushed when Jack made this comment.

"Figuratively," I explained. "We never got divorced, in the legal sense, at least." Who was this man who was open to couples counseling, sharing with strangers, and painting upbeat, almost pop-art-style paintings these days?

Then it was my turn. "Well, to be perfectly honest, it was a tough year and I'm grateful to have it behind me," I began. Anjoli dropped her hands from the clasps of others and urged me not to bring down the group with sad stories. "I'm not going to tell sad stories, Anjoli. I was just being honest. It's been a difficult year with Jack's accident, and well, changes in the family."

"Oh, but there have been some real hoots too, Lucy!" Anjoli reminded me. "Tell about how the news crew showed up right after you gave birth to Adam. Or how 'bout when drunk Barney showed up at that breast-feeding party?" I could practically see the thought bubbles over people's heads, wondering what a breast-feeding party was.

I flashed back to a dozen afternoons on Etta's couch, where she asked me what my role in the family was. I told her I didn't know. I told her my family was too small for us to have roles. I told her I was Kimmy's understudy. Until that moment at the Thanksgiving dinner table, I hadn't realized that I had forever been the court jester in Anjoli's queendom, amusing her with anecdotes about our lives. I remembered sitting at this very table, hearing her ask me to tell her and Kimmy one more story. To do one more imitation of her friends or an actor we saw in a show. It was my job to keep everyone happy. And in my home, happy meant laughing.

"Half the people here weren't at Kimmy's wedding to herself!" Anjoli suggested, glancing around the table for support. "You should hear Lucy's dead-on impression of the minister. She's got a piece about the wedding coming out in January *Glamour*," she said, this time specifically to Chris. "She's a writer, but she could've been an actress."

"Mother! You said I was too chubby to be an actress."

"A comedienne, then," she said, annoyed. I'd just broken the unwritten rule. I was never to portray her in anything less than a mega-bright pink spotlight of flattery—even if it was the truth. No one wanted to think of the fabulous Anjoli contributing to her daughter's body issues.

I had always told my friends about how spectacularly adventurous my mother was when she disappeared to Monaco for ten days while I was in high school. I knew she was safe because she left a note and a few hundred dollars on the dining room table. I never mentioned that it was the weekend of my junior prom and that the limo driver took pictures of my date and me in front of the house. The story about my mother trotting off to the Cannes Film Festival is weighted down by the pesky reality that she left while I had a dangerously high fever. She left Kimmy in charge with the telephone number of her Reiki master, herbalist, and naturopath. When she had an audience, she characterized my father's death as "the tragic demise of an enormously talented musician," seemingly disconnected to the fact that my dead father was attached to that catchphrase. Often, she asked me to sing a few bars of his song that went platinum immediately after she mentioned his ever-so-hip heroin overdose. That night at Thanksgiving, Anjoli bragged to Chris that I was a writer. What she failed to mention was that I was also the family editor.

"Mother, there was nothing funny about my year," I said. "Okay, the bleeding drunk Barney and film crew were funny. And Kimmy's wedding to herself was too, but poor Aunt Rita dropped dead at Red Lobster in Florida where Aunt Bernice is now channeling her sister's spirit and threatening to jump off her balcony and into the Intracoastal. Meanwhile, my best friend, Zoe, will probably be there to video the whole thing for a new reality suicide show since *Real Confessions* went down in flames. None of this is the least bit amusing!" I paused. "I am so unbelievably grateful that my son survived gestation and my husband survived a car accident that should've killed him. That's not funny, Mother, but that's what I'm grateful for. That and the fact that we reconciled our marriage after a virtual divorce, where we lived under the same roof while Jack dated a worthless twit who'd dump a guy the second he went into a coma, and I screwed retards in car washes. Well, just one car wash. One retard."

"You had sex with a retarded person?" Jack asked, more concerned than jealous.

"No," I snapped back. "He was just very, um, slow." *And yet quick in all the worst ways.*

"I'm grateful that we actually started acting as if we might someday move in the direction of leaving Caldwell and start the arts community we've talked about since we met," I said. "Sorry if this isn't funny, Mother, but it's my life and it's what I'm grateful for."

"Kids!" Anjoli said to Miguel. "Tell them they're talented enough to be a comedienne and they flip out. Some people don't know how to be happy. The mother is to blame for everything, darling," she said as she smiled at her guests, trying to lighten the moment. I laughed. My mother was not perfect by anyone's measure, but she was not the cause of all that held me back in life. Just knowing that doubled my love for her, and myself.

"Have you ever thought about writing a book?" Chris asked me.

"I've been working on a novel for a year and a half," I said with a defeated tone. "I have fifteen pages of trite, cliché bullshit about some French woman named Desdemona who gets pneumonia after standing out in the rain too long."

"Why are you writing about that?" Chris asked, focusing her pale blue eyes on me.

"I don't know what else I'd write about," I said, shrugging.

"Why not this?" she offered.

"Thanksgiving dinner?" I asked densely.

"No, what you just told everyone here. About your marriage nearly breaking up while you had a baby, and all that other stuff."

"Are you a writer?" I asked.

"An agent. Currently with two authors on the bestseller list, for which I'm extremely grateful, thank you very much." She turned to the others, who politely clapped. "It's your call, but if you ever do decide to write it, I'd like to take a look."

Jack placed his hand on my thigh and squeezed, remembering the days in grad school when I sent out twenty proposals to literary agents and promptly received twenty rejection form letters.

"I don't think so," I said.

"Chris is going to represent me when I write my selfless nongrieving book," Anjoli said.

Chris furrowed her brow and reminded my mother that she mainly represented authors of fiction.

"Oh believe me, Chris, my mother writing about selflessness is fiction."

"Such a smart-ass," Anjoli teased.

"I hope I don't sound too shallow," Kiki chimed in. "I had an exceptional year with my investments and I'm very, very grateful for that because things were a little tight for the past few years."

Why didn't I invest in the stock market anymore? Why wasn't I willing to move past page fifteen of a novel? Ten years ago, if a literary agent offered to look at a manuscript I hadn't written, I would have been jotting my chapter outline on cocktail napkins right there at the table.

"You should invest in my workshops, Kiki!" Anjoli said. "Get in on the ground floor. You'll have your best year ever," she lilted.

"I used to invest," I said aloud to no one in particular.

"What?" Jack asked.

"Oh, excuse me," I said to the other guests.

"Go ahead, say what you were about to say," Chris encouraged.

"I said that I used to invest," I said. "I don't know why I gave it up. It's how I paid for grad school."

"Really?!" said Kimmy.

"No, not really, darling," Anjoli corrected. "If you recall, the market crashed in 1987. Your portfolio was worthless. When I spoke to your broker, he told me the whole thing was worth something like nineteen thousand dollars, so I paid for your grad school."

"You did?" I asked, incredulously. "Why didn't you ever tell me?"

"Haven't you ever heard of quiet generosity?" she said smugly.

"Wow, I'm shocked. Thank you. I'm really touched, Mother." Jack leaned in to whisper to me. "What?" I asked him.

"What happened to the stocks?" he asked. "Did she ever sell them?"

"Mother, did you sell the stocks?"

She looked at Miguel as if to say *she's only half of my gene pool.* "I just told you, they were worthless."

"So you didn't sell them?" Jack asked excitedly.

"Jack, they were worthless," Anjoli reminded him.

"*Were* doesn't mean still are, Anjoli!" he shouted. "What do your annual statements say they're worth now?"

"Annual statements?" Anjoli asked.

"For taxes," Jack explained.

Anjoli shook her head. "Never received a single one, darling."

Jack pondered for a moment. "Have you ever received solicitations from brokerage houses?"

"Constantly," she said.

"And let me guess, you throw them away without opening them?"

Anjoli confirmed. "Who has time for junk mail?"

"Where is Lucy's portfolio?" Jack said, hurried.

"Oh, I don't know, in the filing cabinet somewhere in her room," she dismissed.

"Jack, it was all a bunch of worthless junk," I reminded him.

Adam began to rustle, waking before I'd expected. "Luce, keep an eye on the baby. I want to check this out. What's the password to get onto your computer?"

"It's *Jack*," I said. "I never did change it."

An hour later, as we were eating organic pumpkin pie, Jack shouted my name from my bedroom. My first thought was that the file cabinet toppled on him because he never closes one drawer before opening another. When he ran to the wooden rail and started shouting my name again, I was relieved he was all right. "Get up here, Lucy!" he called.

"What is he carrying on about?" Anjoli asked, as though I had any more information than she. All heads were turned upward to Jack, wondering what his excitement was about, but I already knew he'd discovered gold up in them there hills.

"Find some good ones?" I shouted back up to him. I

looked at the group and reminded them that he'd gone upstairs to scour my old portfolio. They all nodded and mumbled that they recalled.

"Lucy, you'd better get up here!" he shouted. This time, we all got up from the table and raced upstairs, Anjoli at the head of the pack with Miguel behind her. I could have sworn he bodychecked me as I tried to pass them, but I could have been mistaken. It all happened very quickly. For some reason, we all stopped at the doorway and peeked in the bedroom. Instinctively we formed a pyramid of heads so we could all see. Jack turned impatiently. "Lucy, get in here!" We all scurried around the desk where Jack was sitting and looked at the computer screen he was reading. It told us nothing.

"Are some of my stocks actually worth something, honey?" I asked.

"Uh, yeah," he said, laughing.

I'd never heard so much silence in my mother's home.

"Great!" I said. "Enough to make a difference in our lives?"

Jack laughed, enjoying his last moment of being the only one in on the joke. "Lucy, you better sit down. I don't want you to hurt the baby if you faint."

"And they call Anjoli the drama queen?" Alfie quipped.

"Don't be ridiculous, Jack. Tell me how much we have!"

The group echoed my request. "Tell, tell!"

"Guess," Jack urged.

"Fifty thousand?" I asked. Jack shook his head and shook his thumbs up emphatically.

"Two fifty?!" cried Chris, as excited as if the money were hers. Again, he gestured higher.

Imitating Dr. Evil in the first Austin Powers movie, George guessed, "One million dollars?"

"How 'bout one point four?" Jack asked.

"One point four what?" I asked.

"One point four million dollars?!" Anjoli shrieked.

Before I could correct her, Jack confirmed.

"What do you mean?" I asked. "You mean my stocks are worth one point four million dollars?"

He nodded, knowing he needed to keep it very simple, for I was in a state of stupefied shock. "Anjoli was right that most of these stocks are worthless, but four of them aren't. One in particular. Remember investing in a little software company called Microsoft?"

I recalled a phase I went through in college where I was fascinated by computers. A boy in my class had handed in a flawless term paper, and when I commented that I was impressed by his lack of Liquid Paper marks, he told me he'd done it on his PC. He assured me that within ten years everyone would have one in their homes. I doubted that *everyone* would have one, but even if one out of a hundred families bought a computer, then this software stuff might do pretty well. When I was a sophomore, I put money into four software companies. The others had crashed and burned, but Microsoft, well, you know the rest.

"Mother, are you sure you didn't sell these stocks?" I said, grabbing her arm. I begged my heart not to race before I knew for sure.

Jack spoke. "Lucy, I checked it out. Look at me." I did. "I checked it out. I couldn't believe it either at first, which is why I checked your account online eight times before I called you up here."

A celebratory shout erupted in the room, which was like New Year's Eve on a roller coaster. Amid the shouting of "Oh my God!" there was double-cheeked kissing and hugging as Jack, Adam, and I were passed around the roomful of embraces.

I was caught between panic that this was all a huge

mistake and confetti-throwing joy. I felt frenzied and rushed with excitement, like I'd better get out there and start spending my money right away to make up for years of austerity. Even as the group was done kissing me, I kept fluttering to each person for a few seconds, squeezing their hands and moving to the next. As my skin moistened with intensity, it occurred to me that I was now sweating rich woman's perspiration. My mother suggested that we pop a few bottles of champagne. "And some sparkling cider for you, Lucy," Anjoli offered. She turned to Miguel and explained, "She's still nursing."

After an hour of celebrating, a tipsy Jack turned to me and suggested we call the realtor of the house in the Berkshires. As of last week, it was still available, even reduced another 50 K.

"We can't call her on a holiday!" I said, still euphoric. "It's nearly ten."

"Let's call!" he urged.

I scanned the room for feedback.

"Darling, she'll make six percent of the sale of a multi-million dollar property," Anjoli said. "Call and make her Thanksgiving one to remember. Trust me, she won't mind."

Chapter 39

After a thirty-day escrow, Jack, Adam, and I moved into our new home. We opted to leave behind the new couch and seven La-Z-Boy chairs and start fresh, decorating our home to reflect our new phase of life together.

Perhaps it wasn't prudent of me to plan Adam's first birthday party just four days after we moved in, but I wanted it to be somewhat near the actual birth date, since this was his first. I looked at the ruins of boxes spread across the living room floor beside a dozen of Jack's covered canvases and wooden cases of paints. We had a lot of unpacking to do. And yet, I didn't worry too much about appearances, as the only ones who would schlep all the way out to the Berkshires for Adam's birthday party were the ones who had seen our life in far worse condition than this.

Anjoli was already at the house. As a housewarming gift, she chanted away any evil spirits that may have been lurking in the house. A few weeks before, she'd taken a "ghost busters" class and was overjoyed with the chance to finally put her de-spooking skills to work. Everyone was now giving us gifts of their time and talents, playfully reminding Jack and me that if there's something we want, we can afford it. She also helped us by supervising the movers, which in her world meant flirting with them as they delivered boxes of books and dishes to the correct rooms. The day of Adam's party, she held a "first steps" workshop with him while Jack did something with the cable wire and I drove to pick up the cake. When I arrived home, the table was set and we were as ready for a party as we were going to be that day.

"Did you do all of this?" I asked Anjoli, pointing at the paper plates and napkins on the table.

"Yes, darling. I did suggest to Jack that he pick up some Chinese for your guests. You can't ask people to come all the way up to the godforsaken Berkshire Mountains, then hand them a slice of cake and fruit juice."

"Oh, okay, good idea, Mom."

Anjoli smiled. "Poor thing had to drive to place the order. Didn't have a menu. But in other exciting news," she paused, "my grandson is now walking four steps on his own!"

"Really?!" I shouted. "That's fantastic," I said, a bit less enthused. *I missed it. I missed my son's first steps.*

"Why so pouty, darling?" she asked.

"Oh, it's nothing."

"Tell me, darling. You know secrets are toxic. Express it, release it, and be free of it." *Oy.*

"It's just that I would've liked to have seen his first steps," I explained.

She smiled, not dismissively, but sympathetically. "He'll be taking steps for the rest of your life. You'll see them." She perked. "I think I have a natural way with children. He really responded to me." I imagined her encouraging Adam to "let go, let God" and repeating positive affirmations as he fell on his diapered tush. "You are walking boldly, step by step, and so it is."

"Mom, are we done setting up for Adam's party?" I asked.

"On time and under budget," she chirped. This was her favorite new saying to gleefully follow with, "How silly of me to forget. There is no budget, darling!"

"Cake, drinks, food on the way, plates and cups out on the table? Music in the CD player?" I glanced at the dining room table and boom box on the floor, and was amazed at how much faster these things went with someone actually helping. "We have two hours till people get here," I said in astonishment. I remembered the sign I saw as we drove past the last snow-dusted main road approaching our home. "Mother, do you mind watching Adam for another hour or so?"

"Of course not, darling. Where are you going?"

"To get some macadamia nuts," I told her.

"Call Jack's cell phone and have him pick some up on his way home," she suggested.

"Not that kind of macadamia nuts," I said. "The ones I have to go get."

"Thank goodness Mommy has millions, darling," Anjoli said to Adam as they sat together on the floor. "Now we can call her eccentric instead of plain crazy." Turning to me, "Go get your nuts. What time shall I tell Jack you'll be back?"

"No later than two."

As I drove up to the wooded property, I realized I should have called to make an appointment. My car snaked into the driveway, and I saw a woman rustling about in the stable in the distance. "Hello!" I shouted to get her attention. Her brown ponytail whipped around and landed on the other side of her well-worn leather bomber jacket. She lifted a leather-gloved hand to wave at me, clearly mistaking me for someone else.

"I hope I'm not bothering you," I said. "I just moved to the area and I saw your sign for trail rides. What a beautiful horse you have there." The muscular brown stallion seemed to know we were talking about him and nodded his head cockily.

"I'm Gwen," she reached out her hand.

"Nice to meet you. I'm Lucy. Lucy Klein. My husband, son, and I just moved into the old Adler place on Wednesday."

"Welcome," she said, as she went back to adjusting the bit on her horse. "So you want to go on a trail ride?" I nodded, but said I'd understand if I needed to call ahead of time. "Nah, your timing's good. I'm just about to take Chester out, isn't that right?" she asked the horse. "Have you ridden before?"

"Many times," I said. "But I haven't since I was thirteen."

Gwen laughed. "So, today's the day you want to take it up again, eh?"

She reminded me of my first riding teacher, Marie Costello from Jamaica Bay Riding Academy. Like Marie, Gwen was short as a shoe box with skin that transcended leathery and was the texture of a raisin. Her eyes were cloudy, her teeth yellow. As I helped Gwen check the girth of the saddle, the scent of horses and leather took me back to my youth when I rode in shows, with my father as my fan club of one.

When I was ten years old, I won first place in my division of the Manhattan Classic. The deal was that all first and second place winners between the ages of thirteen and sixteen competed for the children's division championship. There was no category for children under thirteen. "Pin your number back on," my father implored as I walked out of the ring with the blue ribbon. "You're going for the trophy."

"Daddy, I'm too young," I reminded him.

"Let me have a word with the judges," he said, narrowing his focus to the female with the wavy hair and big smile. As I saw my father talking to her, I started pinning my number back onto my blazer because it was clear I was going back in.

"I'm not going to win," I told him.

"Not today," he said. "You'll be the crowd favorite, though. Everyone loves a little scrapper." He was right. The moment my horse and I walked into the ring, the crowd let out a collective "Ah." Even one of my competitors winked at me. If there were a people's choice award, I would've taken it easily. Since it was a contest of riding skills, I placed last. However, three years later I was the youngest girl in the history of the show to win the championship. That was the last time I saw my father.

This seemed like far too much information to give Gwen upon meeting, so I simply said that my riding coach moved when I was in eighth grade, and I became interested in soccer instead. She shrugged and hopped on Chester. My horse, Madison, was a snow-white copy of hers, wearing a chocolate brown English saddle. The feel of my foot pressing into the metal stirrup was both thrilling and terrifying. I leaned in toward Madison and whispered, "Okay, here's the deal. It's been a while since I've ridden. You go easy on me and I'll go easy on you." With that promise, I loosened the rein and stroked his neck.

"Ready?" Gwen asked, then made a clicking noise to signal the horses to go. "You can lead. These guys know the trail." After a few minutes of walking in the crisp mountain woods, the horses began to trot, exhaling fumes of cold from their mouths. Pine and maple trees were dusted with snow, which carpeted the ground. In some spots I could see the dirt and rocks along the side of the trail that would reveal itself fully in the spring.

In a moment, Madison stepped up to canter and I felt the familiar rhythm under my body. My fears of falling dissipated as soon as Madison broke and I heard Gwen hoot behind me. "You can ride, girl!" she shouted.

As hair whipped behind me and wind gushed around the form of my body, I tucked the reins between the saddle and my pants. I held onto the reins as I turned back to Gwen and shouted, "Can I let go?"

"I don't know, can you?" she shouted back, teasing. With that, I dropped my hands and held them straight out to the sides and gripped my legs around Madison's body. I'd never used these muscles harder. My nose turned red with cold and tears painted my temples. The top of my body was pushed back by the wind, which rushed through my splayed fingers with the force of an ocean current. Madison and I galloped this way for a few minutes before he slowed back down to a trot, quickly forcing me to pick the reins back up.

"Have fun there?" Gwen asked as we walked back to her stable.

"You have no idea."

When I returned home, Jack was hanging soft blue streamers from the ceiling. The entire house smelled like Chinese food. Though we hadn't furnished it, and most everything was still boxed, I looked out our ice-framed window and knew for sure this was home. "I figured I'd just get the food while I was there and just keep it warm till everyone got here," Jack explained.

Kimmy was the first to arrive and brought ten copies of *Glamour*, featuring her wedding. The magazine had sent me a copy several weeks ago, and it had been on the newsstands for nearly as long, but we all rushed to it as though we hadn't seen it before. "Page one-sixty-four!" she gleamed.

"You look stunning!" Anjoli said. And she was right. "Look Lucy, there's your byline! It's gorgeous."

"Do you think it makes me look fat?" I asked.

I'm writing another piece for the May issue of *Glamour* about celebrity mother-daughter relationships. I'm not starstruck by any means, but I am more than a tad excited about my upcoming interview with Goldie and Kate. (I get to use their first names now, since I know their publicist personally.) The editor I worked with recommended me to write a piece in the *Condé Nast Traveler*. Zoe, Candace, Anjoli, and I are doing a four-spa tour of Florida next month. The four of us sample the menu of treatments, they give me the low-down, and I write a five thousand-word comparative, ranking each with one to four hearts. One heart means they yanked out someone's pubes too briskly. Four hearts means we all came away feeling like goddesses of tranquility.

In the month between Thanksgiving and New Year's, there were two deaths in the family. Not Aunt Bernice, thankfully. She's doing fine in Hollywood where she's abandoned the idea of jumping into the Intracoastal and taken up bridge instead. She's back to funeral crashing and says the selection is much better in Florida. Bernice still keeps Rita alive in small ways, but two therapists and her podiatrist all agree that there's nothing too wrong with keeping oneself happy at her age. When I asked her to join us for the spa tour, I heard her spit into the phone. "What do I need with spas? There's a beauty parlor in the lobby and I'm making the Valentine's Day party for the building. I'm needed here." Anjoli and I will spend a weekend with her at her new place before spa wars begins. Rumor has it that her kids had maintenance extend the metal railing on her balcony so it reaches the ceiling, making it more a cage than a patio. I doubt it, though. My family has never been one to put accuracy before entertainment. Three generations are laughing at the image of Auntie in her condo cage. They're happy with this version of the story and that's all that matters.

The first death was that Findhorn killed Anjoli's Selfless Nongrieving workshop. No one signed up, and upon further review, they decided it wasn't in line with their mission. My mother bounced back from this within minutes, saying that every time she sat down to write her course outline, she wondered why she'd committed herself to this "pain-in-the-ass project." Suffice it to say, there will be no book deal.

Which leads me to the second death. Desdemona's pneumonia finally got the best of her and she died peacefully in her sleep with her mother and husband by her side. These two characters will remain frozen by Desdemona's bedside for eternity, as I have no idea what they would do after their beloved made the transition. Instead, I decided to take Chris's advice and take a stab at writing the story of our first year with Adam. My New Year's resolution was to write every day, and for the last five days I've been doing it faithfully. I'm on page fifty of the draft, the part where Henri the harp player comes to Anjoli's apartment and doesn't have sex with me. Jack bought me a laptop computer for Chrismukka, our blended-faith holiday, so I can write wherever I go, no excuses.

"Please tell me that's Chinese food I smell," said Zoe as she shook snow off her hat outside the doorway.

"When did it start snowing?" asked Candace, who arrived ten minutes earlier with Manny and their parcel of children.

"I'm starving," Zoe said, ignoring the question.

"Let's do the cake first," Kimmy suggested.

"Please give me a potato chip," Zoe whimpered at me. We walked into the kitchen where Kimmy was nestling a candle shaped like the number one into a white-frosted sheet cake with "Happy Birthday, Adam!" written in blue gel icing. I handed Zoe some Cheetos. She snapped the bag, and apologized. "Believe me, you want me fed. I tried to get back on the Blubber Flush wagon, and would kill for food."

"Will kill for food. That'd make a good cardboard sign for panhandling," I suggested.

"Jack!" I shouted. "Is Adam in his chair?" He confirmed. Where's Anjoli?" I saw that she was outside and asked Jack to call her in. "Turn down the lights," I said in that kid-show-host sing-song way that I hate. I struck the match and lit the wick of Adam's birthday candle. As I emerged from the kitchen with Kimmy and Zoe by my sides, the others began singing "Happy Birthday."

Happy birthday, dear Adam. Happy birthday to you.

We all clapped as I tried to explain the concept of blowing out the candle. "Don't touch," I said, rescuing his hand from the flame. "Make a wish, and blow," I said, filling my cheeks with air and demonstrating what he should do. He reached his hand out toward my face and touched my mouth. "Now blow," I tried to redirect his attention back to the cake.

"I can't believe you started without me, darling!" Anjoli said, entering from outside through the kitchen door. "I was just giving thanks for the first snowfall of the new—"

Before she could finish, a light breeze from outside rushed in and extinguished his candle.

"Owww!" our disappointed guests exclaimed.

"It's okay, sweetie," I said to Adam, who was the

only person not distraught about the candle being extinguished. I took the box of matches from our new neighborhood Chinese take-out place and lit another. As I connected the flame and the wick, I suggested we try again. With a second flame burning before him, Adam smiled at his cake. "Come on, sweetie," I urged. "Make a wish. It's not too late."